ELLE GRAY | K.S. GRAY

OLIVIA KNIGHT
FBI MYSTERY THRILLER

THE
GRAND
HEIST

CHAPTER ONE

T HE STEEL DOOR CLANGED SHUT WITH A RESOUNDING thud that echoed in the vault. Special Agent Olivia Knight's heart pounded. Sweat beaded on her brow, trickling down her temple in a ticklish trail of stress. The room around her was cold, sterile, lifeless. The only things that existed other than her in the room appeared to be a Vanguard Core security system panel near the vault door and a briefcase from which came a low muffled beeping sound.

"You've got ninety seconds..."

The words she'd heard before echoed in her ears.

Olivia took one of those ninety seconds to breathe and survey the area. A dim light illuminated her surroundings, which weren't much. The hum of the security panel reminded her just how alone she was. She was trapped, with no way out unless she could override the security system on the door. Either that or the bomb in the briefcase over there exploded.

Don't panic.

Olivia dropped to her knees beside the steel door. Fingers slick with sweat, she pulled out her phone, her only lifeline. She tapped an access code she'd managed to get from the inside. The screen flickered, connecting her to the terminal's encryption. *Good. No immediate alarms. Seventy-five seconds.*

Her fingers shook as she pressed the wrong key on her phone. A low, warning buzz hummed as a result. She grimaced. Each second she wasted was time she didn't have.

Olivia tapped through the commands on her phone harder, trying to bypass the system's protocols. The phone screen showed a complex digital map of the security system, but with no field kit, her options were limited. The app she used was designed for emergencies, but it only gave her a rudimentary version of the real interface. She could see where the circuits ran, but nothing specific to disengage the lock.

A flash of light from the terminal. She'd triggered the system's anti-hack alert.

Seventy seconds…

She needed to stop counting in her head and focus on the task at hand. The alarm would go off at any second. But it was hard not to focus on how much time was left. Seventy seconds wasn't long to manually override the latest in security systems before she was blown to bits. She had to act. There were no tools to bypass it directly. No jumper cables. No circuit analyzer.

Frantically, her eyes darted around the room. There had to be something she could use. A few tools lay scattered around. Now that her eyes had adjusted to the dim light, she could see them. An old screwdriver, a chair, a few loose bolts. Far from ideal.

She lunged for the screwdriver and shot back to her place at the terminal. She twisted the back panel, hoping it wasn't attached too tightly. Sparks flew, startling her already high senses. But the back panel cracked open and the innards of the Vanguard Core panel flashed at her.

Fancy.

She reached in with trembling hands, yanking the wires free. Her anxiety spiked upon realizing that they were high-security encrypted cables, meant to be off-limits without the proper code.

She found a loose wire, just enough to short-circuit the system temporarily. She bit her lip, praying it would work. Sweat beaded on her brow, and she found herself guessing the time it had taken. *Is it thirty seconds, yet?*

A faint spark of light glimmered as the system powered down for a second. But it wasn't enough. The digital terminal flashed a red *denied* message.

Her stomach churned and panic began to creep in. The timer in the briefcase kicked up, with a more high-pitched beep. She now had less than thirty seconds to manually override this door.

She glanced frantically at her phone as another error message flashed. She hit the screen, trying to bypass the message, but the screen froze.

"No!" Blasted technology, she was out of time! Was it down to twenty seconds now? Had to be. There were no more shortcuts. No more tricks she could play.

Think, Olivia, think!

Olivia's heartbeat was deafening. Her breath, short and uneven. She looked back at the panel. Then, she saw it. The manual lock override. If she could get this open, she may have a shot at surviving.

She pried the mechanism open and let out a grunt realizing it was jammed. The timer behind her increased in pitch. *Ten seconds.*

She jammed her fingers into the small slot, but it wouldn't budge. She tried to twist it, but no amount of force would make it move.

Five seconds...

Brock's voice echoed in her head. *You've got this, Olivia. I believe in you.* But reality had set in.

Three...

She gave it one last desperate push. She was not going down without a fight.

Two...

If only Brock were here.

One.

A high-pitched alarm blared a repetitive pattern and a red light flashed, illuminating just Olivia and the briefcase. She slumped against the wall, defeated. The blaring alarm made her eardrums cower, but not as much as the defeat kicked her.

Failed. She had failed.

A hiss sounded overhead and the door slid open. There, standing beside Brock with a half-finished cup of coffee in his hands was her instructor, Dane. With a stopwatch in his hand and a displeased look on his face he said, "Congratulations. You're dead."

She didn't need him to reprimand her. Olivia sighed and hung her head. "I couldn't get it. The system was too advanced and I don't have the right equipment." She fed him excuses even though she knew he didn't need them. The truth was evident. She had screwed up.

"You won't always have the right equipment in a real-life situation." Dane rolled out his words, leaving no room for argument. "Next time it won't be an alarm."

Brock stood next to Dane, slowly looking down at his cup as he swirled the contents inside. He couldn't speak up or speak out on her behalf, because Dane was right. If this wasn't a mandatory training session, she'd be in pieces all over the floor.

"I'm sorry." Olivia got to her feet to accept her fate. "I will do better next time."

"Let's get this room situated for the next candidate." Dane barked the orders as other agents started filing in to clean up the mess Olivia had made. Olivia sighed and looked down at her phone. Maybe she would have made it if that stupid app hadn't frozen up. Then again ... would she have? She'd run into problems before even opening her phone.

She clicked her phone off and stepped out of the vault. Sweat still clung to her body. Why had she gotten so worked up? It wasn't like it was a real bomb.

Brock approached her, compassion in his eyes. "Hey. You'll get it next time, Olivia. That's what the training's for, right?"

The chances of her manually overriding anything like this in the near future were slim to none, so it wasn't that. It was an overwhelming sense of failure that split her gut. She looked up at Brock, defeat in her eyes as she nodded. "Yeah. Sure."

Brock studied her for a few moments before nodding. She knew they'd talk later. "Okay."

Brock drove on the way back to Belle Grove while Olivia yelled her frustrations against the windshield.

"Why can't I get this?" She threw her hand up, curling her fingers as she gestured her frustration into the air. "It's not like I don't know the material!"

Brock nodded as he let her rant. Olivia appreciated that he didn't try to coddle her, but that he just let her say whatever she needed to say. She didn't hold back. She was so angry at herself that she could boil water simply by touching it. "What kind of an agent am I if I can't do a basic override?"

"It's not a basic override," Brock gently corrected. "It's a new and more advanced security system that a lot of places are using right now. Government buildings, banks. They're designed to keep hackers and thieves out. You're doing well, Olivia. Do you know how many agents pass the test on the first try?"

"Well...."

"Exactly," he cut her off. "Less than half. Most of them don't make it past the second try. The system is designed to be higher tech, so of course it's going to take you some time to get used to it."

Olivia let her hand sink through her hair. A sigh clouded the window, obscuring the trees from view. "I feel like such a failure."

Brock looked over at her. "Hey." He reached for her free hand, threading his fingers through hers. His touch felt so warm, a direct contrast to the cold shoulder she was giving herself. "You're not a failure. You're the smartest person I know, but you can't know everything. That's why we learn and that's why we have training. So, come on. This isn't something we do every day. Next time, you'll remember what happened during this training session and not make the same mistake twice."

"You know what ticks me off the most?" Olivia closed her eyes, tears gathering. She hated this. Hated admitting it to herself, let alone Brock. "I hesitated. I doubted myself. Why did I doubt myself?"

Brock sighed through his nose. His thumb stroked the peaks of her knuckles, bumping along the ridges of her fingers. "Because you want to be perfect. You always feel like you gotta be perfect, Olivia. But hey, guess what?" Affection doused his tone. "You don't have to be."

He said that, and Olivia knew that perfection was a far-off fantasy. But still, she hated her failure.

"Okay? You know that I love you, right?"

Olivia finally dragged her gaze from the window to Brock. "Yeah, I know. I love you, too."

"Don't sound so happy, there." Brock chuckled. "Just remember. I've seen you work your way through cases that anyone else would cower at. You've gotten to the heart of so many matters, you've put away the worst of the worst, so they can never hurt people again. Isn't that worth focusing on more than some stupid electronics test?"

Olivia found a smile. She laid her head on his shoulder. "I guess. I still feel like crap, though."

"Hmm…" Brock removed his hand from hers and laid it on her head, instead. As he stroked her hair, Olivia couldn't help but think how much better his touch felt on her head than her own aggressive fingers had been.

"How about we grab some dinner at the diner tonight?" Brock suggested.

"That's your solution to everything."

"And it works every time, doesn't it?"

Despite herself, Olivia breathed out a soft laugh. "I guess so."

"Then it's settled. Their Philly cheesesteak will cure whatever's ailing you."

"I'd like that," Olivia murmured against his shoulder. If anyone could make her feel better after the lousy day this had been, it was Brock.

CHAPTER
TWO

B RAZEN AUTUMN COLORS MET OLIVIA'S GAZE WHEN SHE
opened her curtains a few days later. Burnt oranges and
dull browns mixed with classic reds set the view on fire
with stunning hues. Olivia hooked the curtains in place to let
in some natural light and made her way to the kitchen. The
morning gave her a chance to regroup and try to forget about
her failure at the training facility in the field office.

Brock sat in front of the TV, watching a weather report.
"They're saying it's going to be a colder winter this year."

"Yeah?" Olivia grabbed an apple and plopped down next
to him.

Brock nodded. "When was the last time we took a vacation?"

"When you proposed to me," Olivia told him as she bit into her apple.

"Hmm." Brock nodded as he studied the TV. Olivia could tell that something else was on his mind.

"Why do you ask?"

"I was thinking about planning to go to a warmer climate for a while during the winter months." Brock turned to face her on the couch. "Last time we went on vacation, we'd just been through the wringer."

Olivia nodded, sobering for a few moments as she reflected on where they'd been. Brock had just recovered emotionally from the mental strain of losing his old friend Yara Montague and the horrific games that Adeline Clark had put them through. The vacation was wonderful – Olivia had left Spain a fiancée – but there was still that shadow hanging over them. Now that some time had passed, she agreed. They needed a vacation where they could unwind and relax without using it to seek healing after all they'd been through. "You can say that again. Where are you thinking?"

"Maybe somewhere like the Bahamas or Cancun." Brock threw out the suggestion with a shrug of his shoulder. "We've got some time to look into it. What do you think?"

"I like the idea of staying close." Olivia smiled. "But just far enough to get away."

Brock's cell phone rang just as Olivia bit into her apple. He held it up, reading the caller ID. "Looks like we might have our next assignment." He answered the call. "Agent Tanner."

"Tanner, it's Calvin." The man hardly had to identify himself. "How you doing? How's Olivia?"

"We're fine. And she's on speaker," he added as he clicked the button.

"Sorry about your test, Olivia. But you know, most agents don't make it the first time. I'm confident that you'll get it done next time."

Olivia was glad it wasn't a video call, so her boss couldn't see the world-class eye roll she made at that statement. "Yeah, I've been brushing up on things and studying hard for next time."

"Well, that's good to hear. Now, you're probably wondering why I called…"

"Oh, I figured you just wanted to chat," Brock cracked, with a sly wink to Olivia. Hugh Calvin was perhaps the polar opposite of their last SAC, the recently deceased Jonathan James. Where Jonathan had been all business, all professional, straight to the point, Calvin preferred to vaguely saunter around on his way to the point. And his chipper, friendly attitude was inexhaustible, even when dealing with horrific crimes. Olivia didn't know how he kept his spirits up.

"Don't I wish! Remind me sometime to tell you about my last fishing trip down in the Outer Banks. Caught enough drum to start a marching band! Anyway, I've got another undercover investigation, and wouldn't you know it, it's got your name all over it."

Oh, boy. Here they were just talking about vacation. Was it going to be like the last one where they had gone to South Carolina to investigate some missing teens? Olivia leaned forward on the couch, intently listening as she chewed her apple with mindful quietness.

"Okay." Brock grabbed a notepad. "Whatcha got for us?"

"This one is local, that's why I picked you two for the task."

Well, local wasn't bad, either. Less travel, less tired.

"The Virginia Museum of Art History had a pink diamond on loan from India. It was called the Ratnashree diamond. They were featuring an exhibit on it. The original diamond was stolen and replaced with a replica. Curator's assistant is the one who discovered it was a fake, and the curator reached out to us for help. Since this involves international matters, this is above local police. You and Knight are to go undercover as guards who were called in for an extra measure of security due to the breach, and we need you to track down where the diamond may have gone—as well as keep an eye on any of the other priceless exhibits."

"We can do that."

"All right, great. I'll be in touch shortly with the details and such. The museum curator's name is Selena Vance. She is fully aware of the situation and is willing to cooperate with the Bureau. That's all for now. I'll email you the information."

"Thanks." Brock hung up and turned to Olivia. "Well, looks like we aren't going anywhere for a while."

"A museum, huh?" Olivia's eyebrows lifted as she finished off her apple. "Who knows? You might learn a thing or two while you're there." She hid her smile behind the core.

Brock matched her humor and lifted his own eyebrows. "Are you saying I don't know anything?"

"Can you tell me the difference between Degas and Monet?"

"Sure. That was on 'Jeopardy' last night." Brock played with her, set his fingers to his chin and tapped his jawline in pretend thought. "Hmm. Oh, yeah. Monet is the gangster word for *money,* am I right? 'Moe-nay!'" He rubbed his fingertips together, emphasizing the point.

Olivia promptly stopped eating her apple. Her head shook from side to side. "This assignment is going to be good for both of us."

Brock chuckled. "But don't forget. This is a museum of art history, so we're basically learning the history of art while we're there, trying to find a jewel that came up missing with a name no one can pronounce."

"So it's a win-win for everyone involved." Olivia grinned. "All right, I'll start packing." She rose from the couch.

CHAPTER THREE

OLIVIA ENJOYED THE TWO-HOUR DRIVE IT TOOK TO GET
to the museum in downtown Richmond. The fall
colors only deepened, adding a fresh, crisp feel to the
air. She may as well be sipping cider and reading a book for
how contented it made her feel. The excitement of having a
new case to focus on, along with the concentration of driving
there, gave her pause to forget about her training failure and
prepare for next time.

Brock sat in the seat next to her, thumbing through a file he'd
taken the time to print out. He filled her in as she drove along the
highway, relishing in the colors as she crossed over a bridge. "The
Museum of Art History was built in 1898 and has continued to

be a pillar of the community since," Brock read from the file to her. "Selena Vance took it over in 2003, and has been the curator ever since."

"Why does that name sound familiar to me?" Olivia asked.

"You've probably heard it before. She is listed here as one of the best curators in the world. She has a great reputation and is revered all over the world for her care in historical artifacts, along with the relationship she shares with clients who help her with exhibits."

"So this sounds like the first issue she's had," Olivia pointed out. "It doesn't sound like she has a lot of enemies, looking at it on the surface."

"We'll know more after we talk to her about that side of it." Brock flipped the file closed. Olivia pondered the sort of questions she'd ask as she continued the rest of the drive. When she pulled up, her breath was stolen at the sight of the picturesque historical building. The gabled roof was held up by several tall, stately columns, and the red brick shone brightly against the orange and yellow trees all around it.

"How quaint!" Olivia could hardly believe that such a case was handed to her. "Boy, is this a step up from back streets and serial killers and trafficking rings!"

"We got lucky the last few undercover assignments." Brock grinned. "I'll admit. I'm enjoying the break, myself."

"I am, too." Olivia pulled into the parking garage and found a spot near the top. She and Brock got out at the same time and headed around to the front. They found themselves in front of the museum, towering above them in its two-story splendor. A flock of birds took off from the high peak, fluttering wings carrying them far away.

Side by side, Olivia and Brock took the flight of stone stairs to the top where he held the door for her.

The greeting area was built like a small rotunda. Famous paintings lined the inside, looking down on the visitors below. Olivia slowly craned her neck to look upward. Underneath the windows that spilled golden light onto the floor, replicas of famous paintings lined the underside of the rotunda. Olivia recognized van Gogh's *Starry Night*, a portrait of George Washington kneeling, and in the middle, Rembrandt's *Storm on the Sea of Galilee*. She didn't recognize the others, but she was sure given some time here, she'd learn.

The mahogany reception desk sat between two doors that led to the inner museum. To the left was a gift shop, with wind catchers hanging in the window to draw the eye. Behind the reception desk, a girl with pink highlights in her hair sat next to a young man in a dress shirt and buzz-cut brown hair. Both looked to be about the same age.

The girl smiled as Olivia approached the desk. "Welcome to the Museum of Art History! How can we help you today?"

"My name is Olivia," Olivia gestured to Brock. "This is Brock. We are here for an interview with Ms. Vance?"

"Ah, the new security she wanted to hire." The young man grabbed the phone, plastering it to his ear. "Ms. Vance? The new security guards are here." After a brief pause, he nodded and put down the phone. "She'll see you now. Right this way, please. By the way," he stood, extending his hand for them both to shake, "I'm Toby. This is Tessa."

Tessa opted for an open-palmed wave over a handshake.

"Nice to meet you." Olivia shook the young man's hand.

Toby stepped out from behind the reception desk toward a hallway across the room from the gift shop. "Right this way, please."

Toby led Olivia and Brock at a brisk pace down a hallway that stopped at a door. He gave a single knock.

"Come in."

Toby pushed the door open and held it for them. Olivia stepped into the office ahead of Brock, taking a moment to look around. It was just what she was expecting in a museum curator's office. A large oak desk sat in the middle of a room lined with bookshelves, all filled with old artifacts Olivia didn't care to differentiate. Her eyes went to the woman sitting behind her desk and the young man standing beside her. The young man was silhouetted against the light from the open window behind him.

"You must be Olivia and Brock." The woman got to her feet. Salt and pepper gray hair framed her smiling blue eyes as she reached across the desk. She didn't need the white suit to make her look professional. The way she carried herself was already like a queen of a small country. She grasped Olivia's hand with warmth and strength as she made direct eye contact with her. "I'm Selena Vance, curator here at the museum. This is my assistant, Levi Whitaker."

She nodded to a man probably in his early thirties, who stepped toward her. His dark eyes and dark hair with a beard to match directly contrasted Selena's pale features. He shook her hand, then Brock's, with no less confidence and respect than Selena did. He radiated a quiet attitude and eyes that seemed raw with honesty. Olivia would know more after talking to him.

"Thank you, Toby, that'll be all. Can you tell Tessa to have the tour ready by eleven?"

"Right away." Toby ducked from the room. Once he was gone, Selena turned back to Olivia and Brock. It was like a mask had been untied, falling from her face as soon as they were alone. Concern replaced professionalism as she gestured to the chairs. "Please. Have a seat."

Olivia settled in beside Brock, who took the lead on asking questions. "Thanks for meeting with us, Ms. Vance. I realize this is a vulnerable matter for you."

Selena and Levi took their seats across from him. Selena gracefully folded her hands on the desktop. "It has been. I appreciate the Bureau looking into this for me."

"It's our job." Brock cut her a small smile. "So, tell us what happened and we'll go from there."

Selena looked at Levi, giving him permission with just a blink. He started out, holding nothing back.

"We were all running late one morning. It was a Saturday morning, you know. Day after payday." Levi spoke with a quiet voice and didn't try to hide anything as he made eye contact with Brock, swinging it over to Olivia on occasion. "I was helping move the more important displays out of the archive room when I noticed something. This may seem stupid to you guys, but being in the museum business, I'd taken a course a while back on how to spot counterfeits, so it caught me off guard. So I looked closer and I noticed the diamond was reflecting rainbows inside, not just outside. Real diamonds reflect grays and whites inside the stone. They also have a certain type of brilliance. They don't reflect rainbows inside the stone, though. Anyway, I took it into the back room and ran a few tests on it. It's a fake. So I brought it to Selena's attention immediately."

"When was this?" Brock asked.

"I noticed it on the morning of October 6th," Levi replied.

"I was in my office that day. Levi showed me the tests…" Selena's head shook, bewilderment in her voice. "I've been taking care of this museum for over twenty years. I've never had anything like this happen before."

"What about your security personnel?" Brock asked. "Do they have any leads?"

"Our chief of security, Darren Steele, has been monitoring his staff, but hasn't turned up anything yet. You'll liaise with him tomorrow, but crucially—he's on the outside of the investigation. He doesn't know you're FBI."

That shot up Olivia's eyebrows. "Your chief of security isn't in on this?"

"We thought it best to maintain as narrow a circle as possible for this investigation," Levi said.

"Darren is great, but he's not a detective, so to speak," Selena added. "He's more for the protection of our guests and to help in emergency matters. For the protections of the exhibits, we have high-security measures. We even installed the Vanguard

Core Security System, implemented on the vault where unused artifacts are kept."

Olivia fought the urge to cringe. She and that system were enemies, only proven a couple of days ago. She nodded as she listened.

"I understand this is a difficult time for you," Brock said.

"This is more than just a missing exhibit, Agent Tanner," Selena stated, leveling her chin with the desk. "This exhibit was on loan from India. I lose this diamond, we get in trouble with India. And not just the museum. Our reputation as Americans is at stake here."

Olivia gently cleared her throat as she sat forward. "What exactly is this diamond, Ms. Vance? Can you tell us more about it?"

A look of admiration came into Selena's eye as she looked beyond Olivia and Brock as if envisioning the diamond herself. "The Ratnashree diamond was rumored to have belonged to a wealthy merchant during the time of the Gupta Empire. It was given to Chandragupta II by a wealthy merchant as a blessing, an omen if you will, for a prosperous reign. Yes, even the name means 'Jewel of Glory' or 'Diamond of Prosperity,' depending. It has been passed down since 380 CE, when it was gifted to Chandragupta the II and later passed into other hands as the Gupta Empire declined. It disappeared for a while but was excavated in the 19th century and donated to museums. Considering what it meant back in 380 CE, it is held in very high regard. It has been through so much ..." Her gaze dropped to the desk. "Only to wind up missing."

Olivia wasn't expecting an entire history lesson, but she felt the weight of Selena's burden. She didn't know much about the Gupta Empire, other than that it was contemporaneous with the Roman Empire and had a lasting influence on the development of Hinduism and Indian culture. "We're going to help you track it down, Ms. Vance." She knew she couldn't promise anything, but she couldn't stand telling her that.

"Has there been any unusual activity around the museum lately?" Brock asked. "Or at least since the diamond came in as an exhibit? Maybe a patron who was too interested in the diamond or an employee who took too long a look?"

"Not that I've noticed." Selena shook her head, slanting a gaze up at Levi. "You?"

"I haven't noticed, either," Levi replied, defeated.

"I have no idea who could've done something like this." Selena's voice rose a bit, despair leaking into her tone. "I trust all my employees, but this puts me in a predicament. What am I supposed to do with this?"

"We'll handle it," Brock assured her. "That's why we're here."

"In the meantime…" Olivia cut to the chase, getting straight to the legal stuff. "In order to conduct the best investigation possible, we're going to need access to things like employee lockers, personal rooms, personal belongings, even. We don't need a warrant if you permit us, so do we have your permission to conduct a search while we're here?"

"Please, please do! Anything I can do to be of help, please just inform me. All the resources of the museum are at your disposal." Selena nodded, keeping her regal posture and letting gratefulness flood her gaze. "I still can't believe this happened."

"We can start you tomorrow as undercover security guards," Levi said. "If you can be here by seven forty-five, we've told the staff you're transferring from a different security company."

"Are the staff aware of the missing diamond?" Olivia asked.

Selena's eyelids drooped, the despair back in her expression visible even through closed eyes. "Yes. Someone leaked it. I don't know who, but I got flooded with questions overnight. I told them that because of the security breach, I was bringing in extra security. That's why you guys are here."

Brock took a moment to ponder this before he nodded. "Okay. Well, at least we don't have to come up with a convincing story about why two new security guards are hanging around."

Selena laughed a bit, for the first time since Olivia had met her. "I guess you're right."

"We're going to ask a few more questions, and then we'll be here tomorrow." Brock flipped his notebook open. "Maybe you haven't seen any unusual activity, but what about the museum itself? Have you received anything in the form of a threat or something that can be perceived as such?"

"No." Selena shook her head.

"Who all has direct access to the diamond?" Olivia pulled out her own notebook.

Selena's eyes searched the ceiling. "The exhibit designer and her assistant, the conservator, the collections manager, at least when things first come in. Levi and myself. And a partridge in a pear tree."

She wasn't kidding about that last part. Olivia realized that they couldn't just look for opportunity here. She hadn't had a good case like this in a while. The last time she'd taken on something this big was to discover who had killed Abby Fisher, the generous, big-hearted next door neighbor, who had been the victim of a narcissistic two-timer. It wasn't something she could say she really got into. She did it for Abby, and for the grief over what had happened to her. This one sounded like something interesting.

She could hardly wait to get started.

CHAPTER FOUR

"**S**O, WHAT DO YOU THINK OF SELENA?"

Olivia unfolded her business suit and hung it up in the hotel closet. She and Brock would be trading their usual garb for a uniform black shirt with black pants, and of course, all the fun little gadgets that security guards carried around. Flashlight, whistle… how were they supposed to guard anything when they were armed like a toddler with toys?

"I felt like I had to wipe my nose." Brock unplugged the iron he'd used earlier and coiled the cord around the base. "I forgot we were in Virginia for a moment and thought we were in England or something."

"She didn't have an accent," Olivia laughed.

"No, but she has a certain grace and poise of nobility."

"I suppose that's true," Olivia admitted. She plopped down on the bed with a sigh and glanced around the hotel room. "It's going to be an interesting case one way or another. Do you have any thoughts on it?"

"My thinking is either someone outside the museum snagged it, or one of the employees." Brock shot Olivia a teasing grin she couldn't resist.

She snorted a laugh. "Wow, I never would have thought of that myself. The answer is so obvious."

"See? That's why you need me around," Brock teased back.

Olivia studied him for a few moments as he set to work putting things away around what would probably be their room for a while. She tilted her head, letting her hair fall over her shoulder. She needed him for more than just his silly input and they both knew that. Her mind flashed back to the car ride back to Belle Grove after she failed the test and how he'd been a pillar of strength for her, redirecting her wayward thinking. She still beat herself up about it. But at least she wasn't letting it control her like she usually did. She had confidence in solving the case and she knew she owed a lot of that confidence to Brock.

"It's not just that, you know." She decided to be sappy rather than keep up their usual banter.

Brock turned, looking over at her, silently urging her to finish her thought. Olivia got to her feet and strode over to where he stood. She looped her arm under his shoulder and pressed herself against him. She laid her face against his chest and let him return her embrace. "I love this," she whispered. "Doing anything with you makes it less tedious."

"I love doing this with you." He combed his hands through her hair, threading his fingers through. His touch was so soothing, as was feeling the rise and fall of his chest as he breathed. "I couldn't have asked for a better partner. In the Bureau or in life."

"You stole my line." Olivia shot a teasing glance up at him, her eyes shining.

"It's not copyrighted." Brock shrugged, aiming a smile down at her. "What do you want to do for the rest of the evening? Want to grab room service and catch a movie?"

Olivia felt like a little girl again, overly excited about doing even the simplest thing with him. Eating three-star hotel food and watching whatever was available on their limited TV was more appealing to her at that moment than the finest date at a Michelin-star restaurant. "I would love that."

"Great." Brock smiled down at her. He lowered his lips to hers and savored their kiss for a few lasting moments, bringing Olivia into a state of calm delight. When he pulled away, she felt as if she could gaze into those loving eyes forever. "I'll call it in."

CHAPTER FIVE

OLIVIA FELT LIKE A ROOKIE WHEN SHE AND BROCK arrived at the museum the next day. The black pants and black shirt made her feel like she actually was a security guard, demoted from the FBI agent she'd worked so hard to become. But the thrill of digging into a new case kept the pep in her step, especially as she and Brock would be working side by side on it as they did everything else.

She and Brock strode through the museum door with purpose. Tessa and Toby were behind the reception desk firing up the computers and putting some things away. When they came in, Tessa looked up and let a smile brighten her face. "Morning, guys!"

ELLE GRAY | K.S. GRAY

"Hey, morning!" Brock greeted her. Levi chose that moment to come down the hall of Selena's office and glance around. "Great, you're here. Let me call Darren, and have him show you the ropes." He got on the radio hidden away in his pocket and spoke softly into the speaker. While he was busy, another young girl strode out of the gift shop, her dark blonde hair piled atop her head in a bun. Olivia estimated her to be nearing 5'9", but she didn't look any older than twenty-one.

"Hey, Skylar, these are our new security guards, Olivia Knight and Brock Tanner." Tessa pointed each one out to them.

Skylar turned, giving them a smile just as bright as Tessa's welcoming grin. "Welcome to the museum. You ready to guard a bunch of old artifacts no one has any interest in stealing?"

Olivia forced a laugh. *Interesting way of putting that. Someone was interested in one of them, at least.* "We're here to help in any way we can."

The doors to the museum opened. A man, shorter than Olivia by at least an inch, came through the door. Levi clapped a hand on his shoulder and introduced him to Olivia and Brock. "This is Darren Steele, our chief of security. He's going on, what, seventeen years with us now?"

"That's right." If Darren felt threatened by the two new arrivals, he didn't show it. He wasn't overly friendly like the front-of-house staff, but his smile wasn't lacking warmth either. "So you're the fresh meat they tell me I gotta break in, eh?"

Brock laughed. "Oh, I'm not too sure I like the sound of that!"

"There's nothing to it." Darren opened the door. "Come on back. I'll give you a tour and explain what we do here."

"Thank you," Olivia thanked him and sent a nod in Levi's direction. He was good at hiding the fact that he knew Olivia and Brock were far more than security guards. Olivia did, however, catch a knowing twinkle in his eye before she departed out the door.

The doors opened into another rotunda room, grander than the front of house. "The museum's pretty easy to get around,"

24

Darren explained as he pointed everything out. Natural light spilled in through the windows that made up the ceiling of the rotunda. *That must be scary during a hailstorm,* Olivia thought.

"This is our main exhibit room," Darren spoke as he walked. "It's where we showcase our exhibit of the month and our most popular items. We had some artifacts from Egypt here last month. Too bad you couldn't have come out before then. It was very fascinating."

"I can imagine," Olivia followed Darren into the spacious room, keeping space between her and Brock. They had decided that it was better to not showcase the fact that they were engaged to limit as much drama as they could. Her eyes went directly to a large glass display case in the middle of the room. "What are the exhibits of the month this time?"

"The Ratnashree diamond of India." To Olivia's relief, Darren drifted over to the display case. She wanted to see what they were dealing with before they took another step further. What did the diamond look like? She'd seen pictures and an advertisement hanging in front of the museum, but she hadn't seen it with her own eyes. She gazed into the glass box, taking rapid-fire mental notes.

Well, Levi had a good eye. This counterfeit looked real. If it were the real thing, it would be stunning. It was several times the size of Olivia's engagement ring, she figured. Its outline was about the size of a votive candle, but instead of being round, it was cut into a square with softly rounded corners. A pale, purplish-pink color radiated rainbows and prisms upward. Olivia reminded herself about what Levi had said about real diamonds and wondered if he was the only one who would notice as he walked by. Reflexively, she checked the display case for signs of damage, but in the short amount of time Darren lingered there, she couldn't see anything of worth. They'd have to wait until after hours to explore the case.

Darren moved toward the curve of the room. The outer wall faced the street outside, but the inner wall was lined with doorways, each leading somewhere. Near the far left, one door led to a ramp with a sign above the door that read *Employees Only.*

"Right in here are the vases and architecture from each Chinese Dynasty we could get our hands on." Darren started toward the inner wall, choosing the first door. Over the next hour, he took Olivia and Brock on a tour of the museum. He started with the hall of Chinese art history, then went to more contemporary pop artists and their famous paintings. One room led to another, filled with famous paintings, sculptures, vases, and even some abstract art in some rooms.

"How many of these are the original artifacts?" Brock asked.

"Many of the Chinese vases are," Darren explained. "And some things in the music room, along with a few lesser-known paintings. But most of the paintings are all replicas. It's not all about viewing the originals, more like learning their history. Selena wants to teach kids and adults alike how to appreciate art by illustrating its history."

"Sounds like fun," Olivia said. Her eyes drifted upward to the wall above the paintings. Painted above the rows of paintings was a quote by Selena Vance. *Every artist has a vision, and that vision is the fingerprint that showcases in their art.*

"Now the exhibits in the main hall, they're all the real thing," Darren went on. "Well. For the most part." As he entered what looked like a music room – the dead giveaway being a bust of Beethoven's oh-so-happy face near the front – he turned and gave Brock and Olivia a stare. "I probably shouldn't be asking you this. But do you know what happened?"

"About what?" Brock asked, leaning closer as if interested in whatever juicy gossip was floating around.

"About the jewel?" Darren asked, unashamedly.

Olivia let Brock answer the questions. She cast him a look as he nodded. "We heard something about it, but we don't know much. From what I understand, that's why we're here."

"Such a tragedy," Olivia followed with a shake of her head.

"Yeah, it was. The whole museum is up in arms about it. But don't tell anyone I told you. The guests don't know, just us here on the staff."

"Not a word," Brock promised with a pantomime of a zipper across his lips.

Darren turned and strode into the music room. He started talking again as if he hadn't just breached museum security by confessing one of its secrets to them. "We do rounds throughout the day; we don't stay in one spot."

Good. Olivia hated the thought of being stationed near a bust of Beethoven's head all day while the real thief could be figuring out how to steal a replica of a Degas painting.

"Selena has asked that as we're doing rounds, we keep an eye out for any suspicious behavior, regardless if it's sticking a piece of gum on the side of a vending machine or someone eyeing a painting too closely. She's really shaken up about this whole thing."

And it was probably best not to talk about it in the open like this, Olivia thought. But no one was out touring, yet.

Darren took them through the music room before exiting back into the rotunda. "When you're off duty or on break, the employees-only area is down here." He removed his ID tag and scanned it. The door clacked open. "You'll need your ID cards to get in; no one can get in or out of this room without it."

Olivia nodded. "Got it."

"We have those for you in the lounge," Darren explained.

The ramp led downward, where it turned into another hall. "Over here, we have the vault." He pointed left to where two sliding doors opened into a gaping room that took up most of the area. "During storms and emergencies, this door is locked down and you can only access it from the control room upstairs. We implemented the Vanguard Core Security System last year."

Olivia suppressed a sigh. She supposed that she really would be studying up on it.

Darren pointed to the other side of the vault. Compared to the massive room, the door beside it appeared tiny. "Back in that corner's the maintenance closet and the janitor's area. And down here," he started down the other side of the hall, is the employee lounge.

He strode into an area crammed with lockers and a break room across the hall. He went to the break room first where several people were gathered. "Here is where you clock in and out. And these are the rest of our amazing museum staff members. Guys!"

He called attention to them and all the faces in the room turned to greet them.

"This is Olivia Knight and Brock Tanner, they are the new security guards Selena hired to help out."

A nerdy-looking young man with red hair and glasses shot to his feet. His eyes were so wide that they nearly bulged past the rim of his glasses. He eagerly thrust a hand out at them. "Olivia *Knight*? Like the Knights of the Round Table?" he asked, more excited than Olivia had seen a grown man act in years.

Olivia forced a laugh and shook his hand. "Sure, I guess."

"You guess? I'd be honored to be named after a knight!" The young man drew back his hand, looking at Olivia like she was some kind of celebrity. "You know, the code of chivalry," he made jazz hands and rocked back and forth, enunciating every word. "*Largesse, pité, courtousie, franchise?*"

Was he speaking French? Very, very poorly? Olivia slowly nodded up and down. "Well, I wouldn't say that I'm as familiar with the laws of chivalry as you are, Mr. ...." *Let him fill in the blanks.*

"Oh." He straightened, as if proud. "I'm Nickolas Erikson-Stark. Norwegian heritage. My grandfather came over here in the early 1800s, but he brought a strong Viking strain with him. You can call me Nick, though."

"Nick." Olivia nodded. *Good, because no way am I remembering all of the above.*

Nick turned to Brock, his excitement clouding over. "Knight's pretty cool. But, Tanner?" He sucked in the air through his teeth and winced. "Ooh, that's not nearly as cool, man. You know that tanners were the lowest of the low during the Middle Ages! The tannery always smelled so horrible that they were outcasts in the towns where they lived."

Olivia nearly burst out laughing but she had to see Brock's reaction. He didn't disappoint. He blinked, clearly trying to compose himself. "Uh," he stuttered and Olivia nearly guffawed. "Yeah, that's... that's not cool."

"Don't mind Nick." Thank goodness, one of the older gentlemen sitting around the table stood to his feet. "He's a history buff and he loves giving out historical facts."

"Sorry," Nick laughed as he backed down. "Sometimes I get a little carried away."

"That's fine," Olivia smirked. "Any time you want to talk about knights and chivalry, or the Middle Ages, I'm down for that." She side-eyed Brock a stare. He glared back at her with a look that said, *really? How come you get the cool name?*

"Simon Westbrook." The white-haired man in his sixties extended a hand far more slowly than Nick had dared to. "I'm the collections manager here."

"Nice to meet you." Olivia smiled.

"This," Simon pointed to the dark-haired man who stood behind him. "Is Graham Holt, the conservator. You probably won't see him much as you're doing your rounds; he likes to work in his area restoring old pieces."

"How do you do?" Graham greeted them.

"I suppose you'll see me around." The only woman in the room stepped forward. Her pale face was framed by wavy black hair that made her shining blue eyes stand out. She probably weighed less than what Olivia ate for breakfast and extended her hand. Olivia wasn't surprised that it was cold to the touch. "Ivy Landon. I'm the exhibit designer and manager. This is my assistant, Elliot." She nodded to the twenty-something kid beside her.

"Pleased to meet all of you," Brock said. Olivia wondered if Brock's polite greeting included Nick and his quirkiness.

"Come on, let's get your badges and I'll show you the ropes." Darren turned to leave, nearly running over a man in the hallway.

"Oh, sorry Dorian." He touched his shoulder as he brushed aside. The man walked with a hunched-over posture, burdensome eyes looking up at the employees as he pushed a mop bucket past the door.

"Olivia, Brock, this is Dorian Hale, our janitor. He's on channel two if you see something that needs fixing or cleaning," Darren said flippantly as he walked into the locker room.

Olivia wasn't one to push past anyone, no matter how low-end their job seemed. "Hi, Dorian," she greeted him with a wave.

His lips lifted in a smile before he pushed the mop bucket further down the hall.

After Olivia and Brock received their badges, Darren shadowed them for most of the day around the museum. It wasn't too busy, so a perfect day for training—if it could be called that. They took their lunch around the off hour at 1:00 p.m. in the lunch room where they could talk privately with one another.

"Seems to me like everyone in the museum is a suspect." Olivia leaned into Brock, keeping her voice tone low.

Brock tore open the to-go box containing a sandwich that he'd brought with him. "I know it. This is going to be trickier than I thought."

"We'll sort it out," Olivia promised as she worked on her own lunch. "We can't rule out that it might have come from outside the museum, too. Everyone seems nice enough in here, but you and I both know that could be a facade."

"A lot of people have access to it." Brock shoved a bite of the sandwich in his mouth.

Olivia grinned as she looked up at him. "You and Nick sure hit it off well."

Brock nearly choked on his food and put a hand to his mouth to hide his delight. "I could not believe that!"

"What? That I'm named after some famous role models dressed in shining armor that everyone looks up to, and you're named after, well." She grinned, taking a bite. "The nastiest job of the Middle Ages. You'd be the one stuck with all that rotten flesh, the smell, and the constant worry about who'd go home with the worst rash."

Brock looked down at his sandwich. "Thanks for enhancing my lunch."

"Oh, any time." Olivia waved him off and took a bite of her own. "Hmm. Maybe I'll keep my maiden name when we get married." Olivia shrugged, casually.

"Maybe I'll take yours, and leave this legacy behind," Brock countered.

As the day drew to a close, Selena found them in the music room halfway through their rounds. "How's the first day on the job been?" She glided into the room, regal as ever.

Olivia and Brock turned to face her. Olivia cast a glance around the room to ensure no one was well within earshot. Not that she was going to be talking about anything important out here in the open. "We're slowly starting to get the hang of it." She sent Selena a wink to let her know the true meaning behind the words. "You have a great staff here, Selena."

"Yes, that I do." Her eyes drifted out onto the floor and she sighed. "I hope. I just... I couldn't bear it if one of them betrayed me. We're all like a family, here, you know."

"I know." Olivia nodded, eager to get off the subject just in case anyone was listening. "Listen, Brock and I are going to have to stay late to check a couple of things out. Is that cool with you?"

"Perfectly fine." Selena dipped her chin in a nod. "I'll let the staff know we're working on paperwork for you or something. I think I'll also put you in for a few of the late shifts and let Darren leave at five. Tell him he needs a break or something."

"That works perfectly for us, thank you," Brock said.

"Thank you," Olivia nodded to her. "You really do have a fine museum, Selena."

"Thank you," Selena answered. Her eyes drifted around the room with a flicker of sadness before she turned, gliding back out of the room through the open doorway.

CHAPTER SIX

OLIVIA AND BROCK WAITED UNTIL EVERYONE HAD GONE home for the night. As the museum hushed to a lull and emptied space, Olivia and Brock made their way to the back room on the first level where the exhibits were kept overnight in a secure storage room behind the exhibit hall. It was a straight push through the locked door near the employee ramp and into a secure area sealed by another steel door.

Olivia used her ID card to get into the room. "Do they keep track of who goes in and out?" she asked.

"I think so. But I'll make sure to take care of that tomorrow. We can come up with some story about how Selena asked us to check on an artifact or something. If Darren even notices," Brock replied.

Leaving the doors open behind them, Olivia listened to the hum of the electricity, their only companion in the empty museum. Her sandwich from lunch was starting to fall short, but she continued to focus on the task at hand. She was hungrier for some real evidence than food at this point.

Tucked farthest away from the door was the glass display case for the diamond. Olivia donned a pair of gloves from the field kit she set down beside it. "You got the pictures?"

"Yeah." Brock pulled out a camera. He snapped pictures of the top and all four sides of the glass case, then some close-ups. When he was done, Olivia leaned closer. "No sign of a break-in," she narrated out loud to him. She traced her fingers down the edge where the hinges were, seeing nothing but smooth glass. "The door wasn't jimmied at all unless this is a different display case."

"Selena said it was the same one," Brock reminded her. "She knew better than to mess with it, knowing that law enforcement needed the evidence from the original. Levi only removed the diamond to perform the test on it."

"Smart." She grabbed the key Selena had let them borrow and unlocked the case. "Maybe someone with a key could've done this. There's no sign of the door being tampered with at all, so that's my guess."

She opened the door and carefully reached in, grasping the jewel. When it was secure in her hands, she handed it to Brock. "I'll let you swab it. I've got the case."

Brock set the fake diamond on a pile of archive boxes and started the work on it. Meanwhile, Olivia noticed a few fingerprints around the bottom half of the container. "Did you take a pic of these fingerprints?"

"I zoomed in on every angle, so yes."

Olivia removed some tape from her kit and carefully laid it over the prints. When she'd lifted them, she folded the tape over on itself and slid it into her kit. When she was done, she looked inside the display case. Her eyes went to the pedestal where the diamond sat. Olivia dusted it, seeing no fingerprints left behind. "Someone knew what they were doing," she mentioned to Brock. "Makes our job harder. Those other fingerprints could've belonged to anyone, and they were outside the case."

"Tells me we're not working with an amateur," Brock said. "So probably not a crime of passion. Someone who saw it and wanted it when it came in. This person knew exactly what they were doing."

"My thoughts exactly." Olivia looked down at the pink silk lining the bottom of the display case. Near the back of the case's door, she noticed a few drops of discolored pink on the silk. She frowned, looking closer. Sure enough, some stains resembling teardrops or eye drops bleached the silk.

"Hey, Brock?"

"Yeah."

"Take a look at this."

Brock set the fake diamond down and came up beside her. Olivia pointed out the stains on the bottom of the case. His lip creased in confusion. "You think it's water?"

"No. Water darkens this kind of material." Olivia reached into the case and took hold of the pedestal. When she had set it aside, she gathered the silk and drew it out of the case. "I'm going to bring this in, find out what those stains are. Maybe our thief left something behind?"

"Maybe he *was* sloppy, after all," Brock mused. "Or maybe it was something left over from cleaning the diamond? Maybe something like hydrogen peroxide or something that stains delicate material?"

"Maybe. A fancy museum like this would notice if anything was off, even if it was a tiny stain on the display." Olivia folded the silk and put it into her field kit. "Find anything?"

"No." Brock held the fake diamond up for display. "Pretty much the same story. The person switched it with an exact replica. So either they knew exactly what they were looking for, or they work here and have intimate knowledge of how the diamond is supposed to look. If Levi hadn't tested it, who knows how long it would have gone undiscovered?"

"He mentioned that it was around the 6th when he noticed it missing." Olivia resorted to thinking out loud. "The diamond's first day on display was October 1st. That means that the thief had six days to come up with a good plan on how to replace it and steal it."

"Maybe," Brock pointed out. "But just because Levi noticed it on the 6th doesn't mean it was stolen that night. He could've not noticed it before, or someone else could have moved the diamond in and out and he just happened to do it that day. We have a six-day window of possibilities when it was stolen."

"That's comforting."

Brock gently set the pedestal back inside. "Let's go talk to Selena. I think she's still in her office."

CHAPTER
SEVEN

O LIVIA FINISHED EXAMINING THE DISPLAY CASE. OTHER than the strange stains on the silk display, nothing out of the ordinary caught her eye. She'd run the fingerprints, but like Brock said, they could belong to anyone for any reason. She and Brock made their way up front to Selena's office where she sat hunched over some paperwork. "We're all done for tonight, Ms. Vance."

Selena looked up at the sound of Brock's voice. "Have you found anything?" She set her pen aside and folded her hands on the desk. "Anything you need to discuss with me?"

"We found a few things that we're going to take back to the lab," Olivia offered. "Do you have any silk to replace the one in the display case? We're following a lead and taking the silk back with us."

"We have some extra silk, yes." Selena nodded. "I'll replace it tonight before I leave so that no one notices it's missing. Did Darren show you how to set the security system?"

"He didn't." Brock shook his head. "I think he may have forgotten we were staying late and figured you would do it."

"I'll set that before I leave." Selena nodded. "I'll have him show you how to do that tomorrow since I'm putting you both on late shift for a while."

"Thank you," Brock said. "On that note, Olivia and I plan to search the employees' lockers tomorrow night. Is that still all right with you?"

"Search anywhere you need. I just want this diamond found." Selena breathed a humorless laugh. "If only you would find it in one of the employee lockers. That would make my life so much easier."

"It would." Olivia doubted it would ever be that easy, but it would be nice.

Selena glanced over at her calendar. "That reminds me. The day after tomorrow, in the evening, we're hosting a staff meeting. I'd like you both to be there if you can." She looked up at them. "It's nothing much. It's just some things about the upcoming events at the museum with the events coordinator, but the security guards usually sit in on those types of meetings."

"We'll be there," Brock assured her.

"Thank you." Selena smiled, wearily. "Well, I'll let you get back to your night. Let me know if you find anything of worth."

"Will do," Olivia promised knowing she couldn't exactly tell Selena what they might find step by step. She was being cooperative—understandable considering the weighty burden this was—but that didn't mean that they could be completely open with her. This was still an investigation. Nevertheless,

Olivia could show her as much grace as possible. It was refreshing to have someone be so willing to let them do what they needed.

Olivia picked up her field kit and followed Brock out the door.

CHAPTER EIGHT

"DO YOU WANT TO STOP AND GRAB SOME DINNER?"
Brock asked as he drove out of the parking lot.

Olivia glanced back at the field kit sitting in the back seat and nodded. "I think so. I'd like to run by the field office and get this stuff to the lab as soon as possible."

"We have a little time to sleep in tomorrow," Brock pointed out. "We don't go in until ten. Gotta love the late shift."

"Actually, I do. It's quieter." A smile lifted the corner of Olivia's mouth.

Brock pulled into a fast-food stop. Olivia ordered some chicken strips and he grabbed a double-stack burger. Apparently, the lunch sandwich wasn't enough for him either. As Brock drove toward the field office, he guided the car with one hand and stuffed his face with the other.

The field office was always busy, no matter what time of night it was. With full stomachs and enough energy to get her through the rest of her investigation, Olivia strode behind Brock into the building. Finding their way around the maze of rooms, they were relieved that the lab only had a few people inside. They could get to work right away.

"Do you want to run the fingerprints through IAFIS or the test on the stain?" Olivia asked.

"I'll take fingerprints. The stain is your thing." Brock smiled at her and sat down behind the computer.

Olivia slipped on a pair of gloves to avoid contaminating her evidence. She took out the piece of silk and flattened it under the fluorescent lights. With better lighting than what she worked with at the museum, she slid the fabric under her microscope. Slanting her gaze down through the lens, she pushed the stain into view. Under the strong magnification, the fibers of the silk looked brittle, losing their vibrant shine to a dull color. They looked like hair that was too dry to be smooth, resembling something like straw. The lack of crystals caught her attention. If it was salt or something else, there might be crystals present, but this was just a barren wasteland of rough, dry, burned weave.

Maybe it was some kind of acid burn? It did have a rather odd bleaching effect. Olivia looked up and reached for a cotton swab, drenching it in distilled water. She dabbed it onto the surface to moisten it as much as she could.

"Bingo." Brock sat back and looked over at her. "Fingerprints came back. We have a match. They belong to Darren Steele."

"Security guard." Olivia nodded in thought. "Not that that's entirely surprising."

"There was another set on the tape you took, so I ran those, too. They belong to Simon Westbrook."

"Why are his prints on record?" Olivia moved closer, weary eyes searching the screen.

"Looks like the museum requires it for all employees. Security protocol." Brock scrolled through the information. "That also appears to be why Darren's are on record, too."

"I wonder what they were both doing with the display." Olivia reached for a pH probe to aim at the cotton ball she'd dabbed onto the stain. "Darren may have been helping someone move it back into the back room."

"Or he could have been helping himself to the diamond." Brock glanced at her. "Look at these pictures. They're down below, near where the door to the display case opens."

Olivia eyed the beeping probe in her hands. "Hold on," she told him, as she read the number. *2? So it is acidic.* She grabbed another cotton swab, drenched it in distilled water, and swiped the rest of the silk cloth. When she aimed the pH probe at that, she glanced over at what Brock was pointing out. She studied the position of the fingerprints. "What are you saying?" The probe beeped again, with a higher number. So it was just the stains that were acidic. What were they?

Olivia took the swab that came back as acidic and worked as Brock talked.

"Think about this." Brock stood up and motioned with his hands as if he were moving something. "If you're moving a display case on lockers and wheels, where are you going to grab it?" He put out his hands flat. "You either push it, chest level, or hold it from the bottom," he carried the invisible item from underneath. "His were along the *side* of the bottom. I don't see how that would've made it any easier to push it into the back room. You'd have to angle your wrist," he demonstrated his wrist at an odd angle, "to get it back there. It isn't like they have to push it into a corner; it's against the wall. Why would he do that?"

"Good point," Olivia mused. "Darren seems like a nice guy and all, but I'm not sure he's the best at his job. To just bring it up like that with us?"

"That he did," Brock acquiesced. "Maybe he wanted to see what we knew. What about you? What have you come up with?"

"The stain came back as something acidic. I'm just figuring out what it is, now."

She played the chemist for a few moments, dissolving the stain in some distilled water solution and dropping some barium chloride into the mix. She watched as the water turned cloudy with a white texture.

"It's sulfur-based," she pointed out.

"Sulfur?" Brock's eyebrow creased.

Entirely curious now, Olivia got up and moved toward the ion chromatograph. "I can't wait for results. I need to know exactly what this is." Her fingers moved swiftly over the controls. After what felt like forever, the screen blinked with her answer. The printer printed off the same. She snatched it, reading the results.

"Sulfuric acid," she read aloud to Brock.

"Not what I was expecting." Brock got to his feet and read the results over her shoulder.

"Sulfuric acid…" Olivia's voice trailed off. "Isn't that what happens when sulfur dioxide mixes with water vapor or something?"

"Yes," Brock agreed. "Basically acid rain."

Olivia studied the paper. "Now why the heck would acid rain be present inside a museum exhibit? A diamond, of all things?"

"It's beyond me." Brock shook his head. "Maybe left over from a previous exhibit?"

"I can see any other cleaning material being used but sulfuric acid is detrimental. It's not something you mess around with just because." Olivia shook her head in bewilderment. "It'll be interesting to see what we find in the employee lockers tomorrow. Maybe we should take some swabs, just in case, and see if there are any chemicals that aren't supposed to be there."

"To see if we can find out if anyone's personal belongings have traces of sulfuric acid in them?" Brock asked. "My question, is, why?"

Olivia nodded. "Exactly." It would certainly narrow down who to look for, but it didn't answer the question. Why were there traces of sulfuric acid on a piece of silk, showcased at a museum?

CHAPTER NINE

OLIVIA PRACTICALLY HAD TO DRAG HERSELF BESIDE Brock into the museum the next morning. Turning the evidence trail over and over in her head seemed like a good idea last night, until she woke up groggy the next morning. She'd have to sail through the day, living on caffeine and adrenaline.

Levi was the first to greet them that morning, looking like he'd been there since the crack of dawn. Olivia hoped that after her sleepless night, she looked the same even if she didn't feel it.

"Great to have you back." Levi nodded to each as he greeted them. "If you have any questions, I'll be working on some paperwork in the office upstairs. Selena's going to be in later."

"Thank you," Brock said.

Levi disappeared down the hall to his office. Olivia didn't say much as she followed Brock into the main exhibit room. The museum came alive with morning light shining in through the overhead windows, causing Olivia's fatigue to lift a little bit.

"Are you going to be okay today?" Brock started down the stairs. "You look a little draggy."

"I'll be fine," she assured him with a smile. "Nothing I haven't had to work through before."

"You and me both." Brock rounded the corner, striding with intention toward the employee break room. The only three who occupied the room were Nick, Darren, and Toby. It appeared everyone else was hard at work already.

"Hello, Knight and Tanner!" Nick called out with much enthusiasm.

"Morning." Darren raised a Styrofoam cup of coffee, as enthusiastic as Olivia felt, which wasn't much.

"How is everyone?" Brock strolled over to the coffee pot, taking his time. Olivia stood back and watched him, admiring how much he looked the part. For being the highly esteemed agent he was, Brock could certainly pull off the slow gait of a security guard who was letting the dead-end job get to him.

"Fantastic!" Nick exclaimed. "Do you know what came in this morning?"

Olivia hid a smile. She loved how Nick immediately jumped into whatever he was talking about. Pleasantries be gone, let's talk about the job at hand. "What's that?"

"A new Norse tapestry, freshly excavated on the Oseberg ship. They're calling it the Tunglskin Tapestry. Well, it's not the whole thing. Just the fragments the excavators pieced together."

Olivia could tell by the way Brock chugged his cup that he hadn't had enough coffee for this yet. "I see." She tried to contain her amusement.

"Did you know that our English phrase 'going berserk' actually came from the Vikings?" Nick went on.

Olivia didn't have to wonder why he chose the word *berserk*. "I did not know that." She accommodated him with a smile. Brock turned around, setting bewildered eyes on Nick, who spoke at the speed of light.

"It's true. During the Viking age, there was a group called the *Berserkers* that fought so out of control that it was believed the gods took them over and that no man could overcome them! That's why *going berserk* means to go crazy!"

"Fascinating," Olivia remarked.

"And I suppose you'd know all about that." Graham side-eyed Nick.

"Of course I do! This tapestry is part of my heritage!" Nick exclaimed, throwing his hands out in an overly exaggerated gesture. "You know I'm Norwegian, right?"

"You've only reminded us twice this week, so no, I'd forgotten." Graham's dull voice countered.

Olivia grinned and sidled up next to Brock, squeezing in beside him to grab some coffee. "Looks like you're gonna need the whole pot today," she murmured off to the side.

Brock hid a smile behind his upturned coffee cup. "Maybe two."

"Well, I guess I better get going!" Nick announced.

It occurred to Olivia that she knew everyone's roles but Nick's. He hadn't bothered to explain what he did when they first met. There wasn't time between that and butchering Brock's name within seconds. "By the way, what did you say you do here, Nick?" She knew he hadn't said, but she didn't want it to sound like she was prying.

"I'm the archivist." He grinned. "Keeps me close to all the historical facts, you know!"

"Oh, of course." Olivia nodded slowly. "Sounds like the dream job for a history buff like you."

"You better believe it! I could so do this for the rest of my life!" Nick quipped and tossed a look around the room. "Well, later folks! If you need me, you know where to find me!"

Nick skipped from the room, and Graham chuckled as he rose. "I hope he doesn't pester you too much."

Brock spoke up this time, a grin creasing his lip. "Nah, not too much. It's not every day you see a kid get excited over history. Or over his job, at that." He paused for a moment. "I say 'kid.' He's probably not fresh out of high school, is he?"

"Believe it or not, he's nearing his thirties," Graham replied. "But young at heart."

"Nothing wrong with that." Olivia sipped her coffee. It tasted like dirt, but at least it would give her a caffeine jolt for the day. "So do you get the pleasure of working on this tapestry, or does Nick have a monopoly on it?"

Graham laughed. "No, it's all mine. It was in tatters when it was excavated, so I have to work to carefully restore what I can. It'll take a while."

"In the meantime," Darren set his coffee cup down. "Are you ready for day two? I hope we didn't overwhelm you too much yesterday."

He had no idea what it took to overwhelm them. Brock chuckled. "Not a chance."

As the day drew to a close, Olivia was glad that it was a lighter day. Darren expressed that it was common for the crowds to be lighter toward the beginning of the week, that most people showed up on the weekends. Olivia and Brock waited until everyone left for the day before finding Levi in his office.

"Selena said she was fine with everything." Levi handed them the keys that led to everyone's locker, kept just in case of an incident like this.

"Thank you." Brock thanked him. He gently touched Olivia's shoulder. "I'm going to run out and grab our kits, I'll be back."

"Okay." She nodded to him.

She leaned against the desk as she waited for Brock to return. "So how long have you been working here?"

"About three years," Levi answered. "I wanted something different. I love learning, so this was the perfect job for me."

His openness with her didn't unnerve her. It was refreshing, rather. Levi's dark eyes stared at her with a rare purity Olivia didn't see often. If he was lying—which Olivia had her doubts he was—he hid it very well. But Levi seemed too honest. He'd been the one to bring to Selena's attention that the jewel was a fake. Something he wouldn't have done if he'd stolen it in the first place, unless he suspected she was onto him or if he thought he'd been caught. But then, nobody would have known anything about it if he hadn't spoken up. The fake diamond could sit there for weeks, months, maybe years before being discovered.

Olivia could think this thing to death, but so far, no evidence pointed toward Levi. The genuineness in his eyes, earned him a few points as well. Olivia's instinct told her that they weren't looking at Levi, but at one of the other employees. But regardless of her personal feelings, she still kept an open mind. Trust no one, she'd been taught. It had kept her alive.

Brock returned with the field kits a few minutes later. "Are we all set?"

"Take as long as you need." Levi gestured to a stack of paperwork sitting on his desk. "I've got this mess to work out."

"Oof, I don't envy you!" Olivia eyed the stack of paperwork, knowing how much she hated it.

Levi breathed a laugh. "Thanks. I'd love to switch, but I guess every job has the one task that no one likes. Might as well be me who does it."

"Great outlook!" Olivia thanked him, then took her field kit from Brock. They made their way downstairs once more to the locker room, this time to do some investigating. The click of the lights as Brock flipped them on shattered the stillness of the early night when barely any traffic was heard outside.

"I'll take the ones to the left," Olivia said. "You start on the right, and we'll work our way toward the middle."

"You got it." Brock gathered the keys and popped open the locker on the far right. "Oh, great. I get to search Nickolas Know-It-All first."

"You two get along so well," Olivia teased. "I've got Simon's."

Even though it was part of her job, Olivia occasionally felt a sense that she was invading someone's privacy when going through their personal space. Unless this was a case of everyone being in on it, most of these guys were innocent and had nothing to do with the disappearance of a rare jewel. Olivia wasn't entirely sure she'd want someone going through her private things. But it was all part of the job, she thought. What they didn't know wouldn't bother them.

Simon's locker creaked as she opened it. It didn't surprise her, considering that he had been here the longest. She read the name scribbled in marker on the front plate, elegant handwriting, maybe indicating that Simon took his work seriously. Olivia creaked it open, her eyes going to the side panel lined with pictures that covered every square inch. Not a single portion of the gray locker appeared through the pictures of family that overlapped one another. They weren't all just family, either. Olivia scanned each one, seeing a few of Simon receiving some type of prestigious award related to his work at the museum.

While poking around in his locker, Olivia wondered if Selena knew about all the artifacts he had stored in there. It made sense for them to be there, Simon being the collections manager and all. But how much of it was his work? Was he open about the items he kept in his locker? Olivia took down a small inventory; a small clay pot and a few stone tablets lined the upper shelf, while uniforms crowded the lower portion. Under the uniforms, more items littered the floor, along with a massive logbook that had the wear and tear of being used a thousand times.

Olivia carefully removed each uniform, checking the pockets, but only finding random phone numbers, business cards, or scribbled notes. None of them had any hidden pockets. "The trouble with Simon's locker is that I don't know how much of this is business and how much might be something out of the ordinary." She lined up a few notes and phone numbers, taking pictures of them so that she could refer to them later after her investigation.

Brock was in the process of examining a hole in one of Nick's uniforms. "We can always track down the phone numbers and ask Selena if she knows about the items in his locker. When I talked to Levi around three this afternoon, he mentioned she'd be back this evening."

"That's true." Olivia snapped a few pictures of Simon's locker. She swabbed a few of the items on the floor before carefully returning Simon's uniforms to their original place. With a twist of the key, she was finished with Simon's locker and onto the next one. Graham Holt's.

Graham's locker wasn't quite as full as Simon's, but it definitely wasn't empty, either. Rather than the familiar pictures lining Simon's door, Graham chose to tape a list on the inside of his locker door. The paper was yellowed with age, evidence of being as well used as the logbook Olivia found in Simon's locker. Olivia scanned the list. "Got some chemical compositions here." She pointed out as she traced her gloved finger over the words. "Nothing with sulfuric acid, though."

"He probably uses them to restore old artifacts," Brock pointed out. "But it's something to keep an eye on for sure."

"Yeah." Olivia snapped a picture of the list. "Especially considering that we found some chemicals in the display case." She glanced over. "Who are you working on now?"

"Still Nick's." Annoyance tinted Brock's tone. "The guy's got enough random stuff in this locker to start a museum of his own."

Olivia breathed a laugh. "Maybe that's his goal. He certainly loves the job he has now." She took out Graham's uniforms, giving the same care and precision she did for Simon and finding much of the same in his pockets. When she returned to his locker, she searched behind a pair of rubber boots. She slipped her fingers inside one of them, her hands brushing against something cold and metal.

"What's this?"

She grabbed hold of the item and withdrew it, surprised to find that the cold metal item was a molding lifter. "Well, this would be uncomfortable to slide your foot into."

"What is it?" Brock closed and locked Nick's locker. He glanced over at the item Olivia held up.

"It's a molding lifter. Flat crowbar, whatever you wanna call it." She handed it up to Brock. "I found it in Graham's boot of all places."

"Ouch." Brock took it and examined it. "Hmm. Funny. This is used for prying off crown molding, or maybe a crate lid. What would he need this for? He restores, he doesn't destroy."

"I mean, maybe he receives shipments in crates and keeps it handy there." Olivia grabbed her notebook. "I'm documenting it. Could be nothing. Could be everything." She'd learned not to dismiss anything, no matter how small. After snapping a picture of it, she put it right back where she found it: in his boot. "If he isn't hiding something and he genuinely doesn't know it's in here, I wish I could warn him so he doesn't break a toe or something."

"Of course you would blow our cover to save someone's toe from getting broken." Brock cracked a small smile.

"Hey, now." Olivia laughed. "I didn't say I *would*. Just that I'd *like* to."

She returned Graham's things to his locker and moved on to Skylar's. She didn't need to read the name on the locker to realize whose it was. The pink floral and '90s Flower-Power stickers dotting the surface told her that it was either her or Tessa. Ivy seemed far too sophisticated for anything like this, and for Selena, it was out of the question. Rather than the historical artifacts found in the other two, Skylar's locker only yielded a small raincoat and a denim jacket. Perfume overpowered any other smell, and the inner walls were speckled with even more pink flowers.

Olivia searched the top shelf and slid a book out of its hiding place. The title caught her attention right away.

Precious stones and gemstones.

"Someone's reading about current artifacts." Olivia flipped through it, the pages falling to where Skylar's bookmark marked the page. Olivia tilted it sideways to read the faded print of the receipt. "Hello."

"Why do you keep finding things?" Brock held up an old Funyuns bag. "And I keep finding trash? This is Toby's locker."

"This is Skylar's." Olivia held up the receipt. "Skylar is using this receipt as a bookmark. You'll never guess where it's from."

"Where?"

"Miller's Pawn Shop."

Brock stopped and looked up at her. "You're kidding." He let the silence settle in the room for a minute before frowning and looking up at her. "Surely Skylar wouldn't go through all that trouble to steal a priceless jewel... only to pawn it at a local pawn shop, right?"

"You'd think the risk of them recognizing it from the museum's advertisement would tell her that's a bad idea." Olivia reasoned. She laid the book and the receipt on the table and snapped several pictures of both. "I'm going to look into this pawn shop next. I think we need to pay it a random visit."

"We can do that," Brock assured her.

Olivia swabbed a few items in each locker. As she and Brock worked their way toward the middle, they both ended up at Ivy's locker. "You wanna take this one?" Brock grinned at her.

"I'd love to." Olivia took the keys from him. She swung it open, blinking in surprise. "Huh. Empty."

"What?" Brock peered around the door to the inside.

"Yep. Empty. Except for this." Olivia reached inside and pulled out a planner notebook. Unzipping it, she began to flip through the pages. "Well, she has all the museum events logged, but nothing seemingly out of the ordinary." She took her time, reading through the past few months along with Ivy's notes written in the margins. It wasn't unusual for the exhibit designer to have a planner in her locker with exhibit dates and times written in shorthand on every page. She flipped it closed and stuck it back in the locker. "Well, that was easy."

"I'm jealous. You got the only easy one." Brock closed the door and Olivia locked it. "What do you think?"

"The receipt and the book on gemstones have me intrigued," Olivia said, thinking out loud. "So does the molding lifter in Graham's locker. He and Simon both have historical artifacts in theirs, so that has me wondering how much is business. I'll talk to Selena or Levi about it."

"Well, shall we go return the keys?" Brock held them up.

Gathering their field kits, Olivia and Brock both returned to the office. As Olivia hoped, Selena stood by Levi's desk, talking over the papers he seemed to have just finished working on. She looked up as they entered.

"Hello. Find anything useful?" She faced them both with open posture.

"Just a few questions," Olivia started out. "Do you know that Simon and Graham have a few historical artifacts in their lockers?"

"Yes, I do." Selena nodded. "They usually keep small projects they're working on, or perhaps souvenirs that don't mean anything valuable that the museum can no longer use. It comes from working here so long. As long as there aren't any diamonds in there that aren't supposed to be?"

Brock chuckled a bit. "We didn't see any diamonds, no ma'am."

"Well, I suppose that's good." Selena's lips lifted in a tiny smile. "So, are you headed out, then?"

"We are." Brock handed her the keys. "Thank you for your cooperation."

"It's my pleasure." Selena's eyes looked weary, but she smiled, nonetheless. "By the way, since you both are doing so much of your work after hours, I thought it would look less suspicious if I put you both on the schedule for later. I'll tell Darren to teach you how to lock down and set the security systems tomorrow sometime so that it looks like I'm putting you both on night shift."

"That works for us!" Brock exclaimed with enthusiasm. "That way we don't have to come up with a cover story for why we stay so late every night."

"Exactly." Selena nodded to him and smiled. "Well. See you both tomorrow at the meeting?"

"We'll be there," Olivia assured her. The meeting was the last thing she wanted to go to. She'd been able to put her sleepless night on hold, but now, all she wanted was to go home and crash into bed.

A few minutes later, Olivia watched the street lights casting shadows on the dash before disappearing under the roof of the car.

"Do you think it means anything?" she asked out loud. "I mean, how easy would it be for either Graham or Simon to slip a jewel into their locker? If they're allowed to keep artifacts that supposedly don't have value any longer, no one would think to look twice. They could easily stash the diamond in there."

Brock shrugged. "It would be pretty easy, I would think. But considering that both Selena and Levi have access to the staff keys for the lockers, it would be stupid for either of them to keep it in there. If I were them, I'd know that as the curator, the first place you'd check would be employee lockers. I don't care how much you trust your employees. You'd think that neither of them would want to keep it in there."

"That's true, I suppose." Olivia let the car engine hum in the silence between them for a few seconds. "Looking forward to the meeting tomorrow?"

"Counting down the hours." Brock paused a few beats. "Till it's over."

Olivia laughed. "Me, too. I've never been one for meetings. It's why I prefer fieldwork."

"You and me both."

CHAPTER TEN

OLIVIA COULDN'T REMEMBER THE LAST TIME AN undercover job had been in such a peaceful place.

She and Brock did their searching after hours for the most part, and during the day, the museum was mostly quiet. Sure, there were patrons here and there, but as Olivia walked through the halls that Thursday afternoon, she thought how lucky the employees were to work in such a calm environment. History had a way of bringing calm to Olivia, even when reading about battles or ceremonies. It was as though the ancient artifacts surrounding her had voices of their own, telling her grand stories of their days in the sun as she paced alongside them. She and

Brock knew they couldn't work together all the time, so they branched out. Olivia worked on doing her rounds, her wayward footsteps leading her into the hall of Chinese vases. She took her time, placing one foot in front of the other slowly and examined each work of art as she passed, pondering the many hands that had previously touched these artifacts, the fingers that painted the symbols, the eyes that beheld them during their time in the Ming Dynasty. What stories could they tell, if they could talk?

A rustling and a clearing of someone's throat behind her turned her attention toward the entrance. Simon entered, clipboard in hand, taking his time as much as she was. It must be nice to have a job where he didn't have to rush. He glanced up to see her. "Doing the rounds, are you?" The sophisticated way he spoke made Olivia wonder if he was from somewhere in Europe, maybe even England itself.

"Always." Olivia looked up at one of the towering vases, black with tiny flowers painted on the side. Her eyes swept up and down the vase. "Beautiful, aren't they?"

"Fascinating." Simon approached her, letting his gaze take in the same thing she was. "Ming Dynasty, from the year 1573. Came to us a few short months ago, and it's been a popular piece."

The awe in his voice was evidence of how he valued the artifacts: for what they were worth. Suspect or not, he took his job seriously. She scrutinized him with a calm gaze, not wanting to wear her thoughts on her sleeve. "You've been around the museum a long time, haven't you?"

"I know each of these artifacts as if they were my children." Simon tucked the clipboard under his arm and reached to adjust the vase so that the flowers faced more outward. "I'm the sort who would rather spend time with old historical artifacts than people who talk about them, I suppose. You can learn much from the actual items themselves."

"I can agree with that."

Simon exuded calm as he stood by her, the opposite of Nick, who was always wired over something. "You'll find that the museum is a place of refuge after a while. Darren has hardly needed to do any work up until recently."

"Recently?" Olivia asked with a tilt of her head. The word caught her off guard, and she wondered if he was referring to the missing diamond or something else that was happening.

Simon nodded. "The theft of the jewel. After it came up missing, Selena commissioned us to check each artifact and make sure that they were all the originals. At least the ones we don't have duplicates of. She's so worried that something like this has been happening under our noses the whole time."

"And is that what you're doing?" Olivia nodded to his clipboard.

Simon nodded. "So far, the only counterfeit I've found among my collections is the Ratnashree. Levi was right. Diamonds reflect rainbows, but not on the inside. It's an eye catcher if you know how to look for it."

Olivia studied him as Simon returned his gaze to the Ming Dynasty vase. "I bet it's a blow to the pride of everyone who works here."

He snorted a laugh. "You can say that again. What's even more infuriating is that someone here betrayed us. It can't be anyone from the outside; we would've seen that. Nick and Darren are always running around the museum, and they spot everything. Especially Nick. He spies poor, unfortunate souls, to unload his favorite historical facts on them daily."

"I've noticed." Olivia grinned.

"The security system is too regulated for anyone to sneak in during the night. So it had to be one of us who knew when and how to snatch it." Simon sighed as he shook his head. "But then again, I shouldn't be talking about this with a new security guard." He looked at Olivia, his eyes heavy with burden. "We were once a family. Now, that family is breached. We just haven't figured out who the traitor is yet."

Olivia couldn't tell him that's the reason she and Brock were around. She had to play the outsider, the one who was called in and had no idea about the inner workings of the family. She nodded in thought. "I understand. For the record, I'm sorry that you all have to deal with that. I can imagine it rattled everyone."

"It did. But we'll soon find out who did it." Simon's confidence rose as he straightened his posture, looking like he was ready to leave her to do her job while he did his. "Sorry for taking up your time."

"I have all the time in the world," Olivia assured him. "After all, as you mentioned before. We security guards don't actually have that much to do."

Simon nodded. "Indeed."

He scribbled something down about the vase in his notes, then turned to leave. His absence left a vacuum of thought for Olivia. She returned her gaze to the vase, studying it as she pondered her thoughts. If what Simon said was true and they were looking at someone on the inside, then he was right. It had to be someone who knew the inner workings of the museum. It had to be one of them.

Brock strode into the room after a few minutes. "Hey."

"Hey." She glanced over at him, nodding to the vase. "Ming Dynasty. Late fifteen-hundreds, Simon tells me."

"Neato. So, you spoke with Simon." Brock settled into a stiff posture beside her and examined the vase by her side. "How did it go?"

"It brought a few things to my attention, things that we already knew." Olivia shook her head. "I know we can't completely throw out the possibility that someone from the outside did it, Brock. But my gut tells me that we're looking at an inside job."

"Your gut is usually right," Brock stated.

"We can't just focus on who had the opportunity. Everyone here has the opportunity, except for a few people." Olivia did her thinking out loud in low undertones.

"Then you're thinking motive might help us narrow things down."

"Motive and character." Olivia side-eyed him. Someone came into the room, a mother with her two small sons. Pen and paper in hand, the mother looked as interested in history as her sons were in their iPads in the stroller. "Let's do some work in the office after hours," Olivia suggested as she stepped away to the exit on the other side of the room. "We'll do our best work there."

CHAPTER
ELEVEN

OLIVIA TOOK A GLANCE AT HER WATCH AROUND 4:45 and started heading to the control room. The museum had more doors than a castle, some of which were hidden from public view. As the guests slowly drifted throughout the remainder of the museum and out the front door, she found Darren and Brock in the control room on the second floor of the museum. "Hi, guys. Sorry I'm running late."

"I'm going to write you up for that," Darren teased a bit. Brock joined him in laughter.

"Come on, at least I was doing my job and not on my phone or something," Olivia joked as she sat down.

"Okay, I'll give you a pass." Darren half-closed one eye, the fun-loving banter dying down a bit. "So, Selena said she was putting you both on the late shift?"

"That's what we talked about," Brock reassured him.

"Well, I feel sorry for you. But also, I'm selfishly glad about it. Maybe I'll get a day off once in a while, then."

"That's always a plus!" Olivia gestured toward him with a flat palm. "Something that doesn't happen often, huh?"

"Well, we have other security guards, but they're more part-time. Trying to schedule them is like trying to herd chickens." Darren sat back in his chair, in no hurry to show them the security lockdown and get out of there. He must've been working late for a while. Olivia hated to think that he'd only be enjoying his evenings temporarily. She and Brock would be gone as soon as they busted the thief. She kept it to herself.

"Well, I guess I'd better show you how this works." Darren wheeled around in his chair and pointed to the wall where the monitors were stacked in a tall column. The elongated table was cluttered with wires, but somewhere in the nest of electronic veins, Darren was able to find a mouse and a keyboard. Olivia looked over his shoulder, studying each monitor and what room they overlooked. She'd come to know the museum well in the last few days, so she took note that nearly the entire facility was visible in black and white on the cameras. Every corner, nook, and cranny of the upper level where the exhibits were on display showed up. Olivia wondered what the cameras would tell her about the week the jewel went missing. Down below in the employee-only area, most of the rooms were visible. The vault had about four cameras covering every angle, one near the locker room and one near the employee break room. Olivia noted the camera on the exit wasn't angled well—it showed more of the corner than the doorway. Since the door opened on the side facing the janitor's closet, someone could slip by unnoticed if they hugged that wall.

Darren pointed, unaware that Olivia had already scrutinized the whole system. "Selena upgraded to the Vanguard Core system last year. So the setup is simple, but I've accidentally triggered the alarm a time or two while shutting things down. The system is pretty unforgiving."

Olivia knew. She kept her venomous hatred of that system to herself.

"At night, the vault door downstairs gets closed and locked with security. Upstairs, the vault behind the main hallway, where we keep the exhibits on display, also gets locked, and the Vanguard Core system activates a laser tripwire system to go across the floor and the hallway leading to the upstairs vault. So here we have the main rooms. We just have to worry about lights and activating the laser security systems."

"Laser tripwires?" Olivia had to ask the question out loud. "Like in the movies?"

Darren chuckled. "Pretty much, yeah. When we turn the security systems on, if anyone walks through the area, the lasers detect motion and set off an ear-piercing alarm. Selena has it wired to her phone, and Levi does, too."

"I see. So if I set the system and forget my lunchbox in the break room, I'd better forget it unless I want ten thousand police to swarm me?" Olivia asked, jokingly.

"The path from the control room to the break room doesn't have any tripwires, just the high security areas like the vault and the main exhibit hall." Darren smiled along with her, chest heaving in and out with laughter. Olivia concealed her true thoughts behind her jokes. If anyone were walking around in the museum where they shouldn't be, they would have triggered the alarm. Someone had to know what they were doing if the diamond was stolen at night. "Got it."

Darren took a few moments to show Olivia and Brock how to activate the system. "I'll go ahead and give you guys the access code that's to be used for emergencies only." With that, Darren typed in the access code to the door to the vault downstairs. Olivia watched the steel door slide shut on the vault, sealing the artifacts safely inside.

"And that's it. That's all there is to it." Darren sat back, satisfied. "I'll go over it with you again tomorrow and let you drive."

"Sounds good," Brock said. "Hey, you go ahead and head on home, man. Enjoy the first night off you've had in a while!"

"Take what you can!" Olivia nodded. "They don't come around often."

"You two are fresh meat, is what this is." Darren chuckled as he got to his feet. "You're the rookies here, so you're going to get the crappy shifts. Can't say I'm jealous, though."

"Thanks." Brock rolled his eyes, mock annoyance in his tone.

"You're welcome. Just remember we're all sticking around late tomorrow night for that meeting." Darren rolled his eyes, but this time, he wasn't joking when he sighed. "I hate meetings. Anyways. So long." Darren gave them a wave and left the room. Olivia and Brock watched the cameras as he made his way down to the locker room, clocked out, gathered his things and left. As soon as his car pulled out of the parking lot, Olivia felt free to talk.

"Well, what do you think?" Brock asked.

"I think that someone had to know what they were doing in order to lift this diamond. I think I want to run a few background checks."

"That sounds good. I'm going to run some security tapes for a bit. I'm curious about this alarm system." Brock studied the cameras for a few moments.

Olivia stood and made her way to her laptop bag she'd carried up with her earlier. "It does raise a few red flags, doesn't it? So what are you going to do? Watch the footage from around the time it was taken?" She pulled her laptop from her bag and sat back down beside Brock. "I'm sure Darren and Selena already did that anyway."

"Yeah, but while I'm here, I'd like to really do an exact search. Levi said he noticed it around October 6th." Brock's weariness stained his tone. "And the jewel's been on display throughout the month of October. So I'm going to start with the 6th and work my way back. It could have been switched out on the 2nd for all we know, and Levi only noticed it on the 6th. It could've been gone for almost a week."

"Not a very comforting thought," Olivia muttered. "Since today's the 11th. The more time it had to circulate, the farther away it could be. It could be halfway across the world by now, sitting in someone's living room, and no one would ever know the difference."

"Let's think positive." Brock clicked through some old footage. "Let's think that the jewel was stolen the night of the 5th or early morning of the 6th. That gives us five days to figure this thing out."

"I like it. Glass is half full." Olivia laughed a bit as she typed in some names. Might as well start with Simon, she thought, as she thought of their pleasant conversation that afternoon. And he'd been here the longest. "I like Simon." She waited until his name popped up on her FBI database. "He's quiet and calm. Very grandfatherly, or like that uncle everyone loves. I hope he isn't the thief."

"You can't get emotionally attached to anyone!" Brock laughed.

Like Abby, Olivia thought. Still, she was glad that she and Brock had worked that case, emotional attachment or not. No one would've ever found out what happened to Abby if not. The local police had all but given up. She scrolled through Simon's information, a smile lifting her lips. "No criminal record for him, nothing that raises a red flag."

"I'm scrutinizing the footage," Brock said over the top of the monitor. "My eyes are already crossing. Wanna switch?"

"Not a chance." Olivia grinned as she backed out of researching Simon's name. She would only dig deeper if a name came back with something. Next up was Graham Holt, the conservator who restored things with care, not likely to tear them down with molding lifters. She still couldn't get that out of her head. "Do you think Graham has found the surprise in his boot yet?"

"If it's even a surprise." Brock chuckled a bit. "Maybe he knows it's in there. If not, then he hasn't yet. He was walking just fine when he left today."

Olivia typed in his name and began to scroll through the details on him. This time, a ping showed up, and her eyes darted to the information. *Graham Holt.* Her eye caught a note under financial history: a civil judgment from a casino three years ago. Unpaid debt on gambling markers. A few clicks deeper, and a pattern emerged. Frequent visits to one local casino and two others across state lines, all logged under his player loyalty card. "Hmm. This is interesting."

"What?"

Olivia rotated her laptop and pointed to the screen. "Apparently, Graham Holt has been dealt a few unlucky hands in life. Looks like he has a rather expensive habit."

Brock stopped studying the footage from the evening of October 6th and looked over. "Really?" Interest clawed at his tone as he read the page Olivia showed him.

She nodded. "Really." She turned her laptop around when Brock was done reading.

"Not a good thing to have on your record when a priceless jewel comes up missing." Brock nodded to her computer. "That's motive. The Ratnashree isn't tiny, but it's small enough that he could easily smuggle it somewhere without anyone knowing. Now, question: Does he have access to the security codes?"

"He doesn't really have to," Olivia pointed out. "He has access to the jewel itself. All it takes is some sleight-of-hand one morning before the doors even open, when they're pushing artifacts in and out. He's the conservator. Maybe he used the excuse that he needed to polish it or something."

"Might that explain the sulfuric acid we found on the silk?" Brock rubbed his chin. "Maybe he was using it to age up a fake diamond? Maybe the color was too pink, so he wanted to make it duller."

"It could be." Olivia nodded. "Graham's a conservator. He'd know what chemicals to use and which ones not to use."

"I'm going to see what he was doing on October 6th." Brock turned back to his work. "Or the days prior."

"I'm going to look at the next one." Olivia saved her search of Graham's history, intending to dig a little deeper when she could. She next pulled up Nick's name. "Hey, here's your pal."

"Who, Nick?"

"Yes," Olivia laughed. "There's not much on him." Really, there wasn't anything on him. He wasn't even in the system, but it did show that he was born in the U.S., despite the Norwegian heritage he flaunted. A quick Facebook search told her that he was proud of his history, and loved his job at the museum enough to call it his passion, not his career. Olivia scrolled through Nick's Facebook for a while, glad that he didn't have anything set to private. She rolled back to October 1st when the jewel was first showcased. Like with all the other historical artifacts, he had a picture posted.

Richmond! Head on over to the Museum of Art History to view this beautiful Ratnashree diamond from India! It goes all the way back to the Gupta dynasty! Don't know what that is? Head on over, and we'll tell you all about it!

Olivia scrolled back a little further to see if he went into detail with every single historical artifact. What she found didn't surprise her. He had just as much enthusiasm for new historical artifacts as someone else might over getting into a relationship. His, Olivia noticed, was single status. Guess girls weren't into nerdy guys anymore.

"Nick put the diamond on his Facebook page, but he tagged the museum," she narrated to Brock. "Not that that's a bad thing. He does it with everything. But what if he unknowingly invited the wrong people to come to the museum? They saw it on his page, wanted it, and planned to come get it?"

"It's possible, I guess. But that's just promotion, right? Lots of museums and zoos and such promote things on social media these days"

"On his personal account, though?"

Brock considered it. "Yeah, that's a bit unusual. I prefer to keep stuff off Facebook. Unlike you with that picture of your cat."

"That was Instagram!" Olivia laughed and rolled her eyes. "And years ago. I highly doubt my life would be endangered over a cat!"

"You never know," Brock smirked as he watched the security tapes. "There's a reason someone coined the phrase 'Crazy Cat Lady.' Someone could have wanted your cat and stalked you to get it."

"If that's the case, then no one should put anything on Facebook," Olivia laughed. "Whatsoever!"

Nick wasn't yielding many more results other than an over-enthused history lover. Which Olivia didn't mind. Not because he'd likened her to a knight of old, but because history was stock-full of lessons modern day humans could learn from. Art was an expression of said lessons. It was better than some video game in his mom's basement, she concluded.

And, onto the next one.

Olivia typed in Ivy Landon's name and waited until the results filled the screen. Once again, there was a lack of a record for her, but the information Olivia did find surprised her.

"Did you know that Ivy only works here part-time?"

"I didn't know that." Brock glanced up from the tedious task of watching the security tapes. His look told her that he would willingly hand over his lunch tomorrow for a chance not to be watching boring security footage.

"She works as a chemistry teacher for the local high school full-time. She's received all kinds of awards, it looks like."

"She must be the coolest teacher around." Brock rubbed the back of his neck. "To work at a museum and teach chemistry."

"But that's all I could find on her." Olivia backed out and typed in the next name on her list, Elliot Ferris. Unlike Ivy, he pinged off a few alerts. Olivia scrolled through his record, seeing a mug shot of a much younger Elliot, probably high school years, wearing a gruff expression. Next to the note of setting off illegal fireworks, Olivia read the words that urged her further into suspicion.

Petty theft. Unauthorized access to a computer system.

Hacking and theft, huh? She read over a portion of the report, detailing how 16-year-old Elliot Ferris shoplifted a DVD from a local store.

"Looks like our friend Elliot may have been a troublemaker in his youth." She glanced up. "Am I bothering you?"

"Sure are." Brock's lip lifted in a smile. "I'm trying really hard to watch nothing happen on this screen. But go ahead."

"Just for that, I will!" Olivia giggled. "They got Elliot for theft and hacking, back in the day. But just because he stole a DVD when he was a teenager doesn't mean that he'd go so far as to steal a diamond."

"But it doesn't mean he wouldn't, either." Brock looked over at her. "Especially if he works one-on-one with the exhibit designer as her assistant. He'd have all the access he needed."

"So we have a few people to keep an eye on," Olivia did her best thinking out loud. "Elliot, with a record of minor theft, Graham Holt, and his gambling problem and debt."

"Technically, still everyone," Brock pointed out. "But at least we're narrowing it down to potential persons of interest."

Potential persons of interest sounded so far off, but Olivia would take what she could get.

Olivia and Brock both slept like babies that night. After such an exhausting night before, when she had gone over the evidence in her mind, Olivia was ready to approach the next day with new eyes. After clocking in, Brock turned to her. "I'm going to go check in with Darren. He's probably in the security room."

"I'll go with you," Olivia said.

She followed Brock up to the security room, where the monitors pointed at each of the guests in the lobby. Darren was nowhere to be found, but a quick glance at one of the monitors told her that he was just returning from the front of house. Olivia took a moment to survey the footage from up there. "So you didn't see anyone going in or out the supposed night of the robbery who wasn't supposed to be?"

"No. I was watching it during the day, too, but nothing seemed out of the ordinary." Brock shook his head as he watched the monitor. "I want to look again, just in case I missed some –"

Suddenly, the door flew open. Olivia whirled around as Tessa came flying through the door. When she noticed Olivia and Brock, her face instantly paled and her jaw dropped.

"Oh!" She stuttered, blinking as if caught in the act of something. "I'm... I'm sorry, I didn't realize anyone was up here!"

Confused, Olivia tried to get words to come. "That's okay. Are you..."

"Sorry, guys!" Tessa retreated, closing the door with a hard slam behind her. Retreating footsteps took her away from the door.

Olivia exchanged a look with Brock and some raised eyebrows. "What was that about?"

Brock's radio connecting him to the front of house crackled, and Levi's voice sounded over the speaker. "Tanner, come in, please?"

Brock held the radio to his mouth. "This is Tanner, copy."

Static. "We need some assistance up front with some crowd control. It's unusually busy and we're shorthanded."

Yeah, Olivia thought. Shorthanded because Tessa was up here doing something she wasn't supposed to do. What could she possibly need in the room where the security cameras were kept? "Sure. I'll be right there." Brock put the radio down and shot a look at Olivia. "We'll talk later, babe. See you tonight."

"See you." Olivia snuck in a quick kiss before he departed.

CHAPTER TWELVE

THE DAY FLEW BY WITH THE SPEED OF A FREIGHT TRAIN. Between rounds and keeping an eye on a few employees discreetly, Olivia barely saw anything of Brock except him running to and fro to do whatever security guard duties were needed at the moment. Did anyone but her notice how good he was at everything? Maybe a little too professional to be an underpaid security guard? Or was she just admiring him because he was the love of her life? Of course he'd do everything well.

Hiding a smile, Olivia went about her own so-called tasks, remembering what it was like in the days before she became a federal agent with the status she had. The rookie jobs, the seemingly small tasks that drove her crazy, but were no less important. Before she knew it, she was helping Darren with a few last duties as the museum closed down. However, instead of the employees heading home for the night, most of them found themselves in the staff meeting room near Selena's office.

Toby, Tessa, and Skylar had gone home for the night, leaving everyone else present around the circular table. Ivy and Elliot had arrived sometime after 3:00 p.m. Olivia found herself watching Elliot with the new information she had on him. He seemed to stay by Ivy's side, almost like she was his mentor more than he was her assistant. Olivia wondered if they were together at all times, or if he ever had an opportunity to be alone with an exhibit, particularly the Ratnashree diamond.

"Thank you for coming," Selena greeted everyone, paying no heed to the idle chatter. The room silenced the moment she spoke, as if merely by standing up, she commanded their attention. "The Ratnashree diamond has garnered much attention, but I feel like over the course of the holidays, as everyone's going on vacation, we need something that will draw in major crowds. We need something that everyone loves, that no one can resist. What ideas do we have?"

Nick's hand was the first to shoot in the air. "What about that Norwegian tapestry? We just got it in, but we don't have a place for it yet."

"As much as I love the idea of a Viking display," Selena countered, "I think we want to save that until after the first of the year. Vikings are good, everyone loves Vikings, but we don't have enough on their art to bring something together in a hurry."

Nick's disappointment could be felt across the room, though his eyes danced with the hope of getting his exhibit next year.

"So what about November through December, possibly January?" Selena's gaze drifted around, meeting everyone's as she called them out.

"I have a few ideas." Ivy stood to her feet, clipboard in hand. "What about Pompeii? I know a few places around that have decent collections, and I think that the murals of Pompeii would really draw in the crowd. Everyone loves Pompeii. It's like the disaster of the Titanic. There's something so macabre about it that it stands the test of time and brings in the crowds by the dozens. They just can't get enough of it."

Ivy didn't pitch her idea with nearly the enthusiasm that Nick did, but her calm voice brought a few nods and agreement around the table. She didn't speak with any less confidence, however, and she seemed to have taught that same confidence to her young apprentice.

"Another thing," Elliot piped up from his position sitting beside Ivy. "You always tell us that your vision is figuring out why an artist does what he does. We could call it the mystery of Pompeii. Did the painters of the murals know that disaster would soon befall them, or were they going with the times, not knowing their lives would shortly be buried under ash and pyroclasts?"

Pyroclasts? Olivia repeated the word in her head. Elliot may have been a troublemaker in his day, but he certainly knew a thing or two about volcanic eruptions.

"I'm intrigued." Selena's lips twitched in a smile. "And Ivy and I have brought up Pompeii before. I was thinking that we would save that for our summer exhibit next year, but considering that we need something to follow the diamond, I think Pompeii is a good idea."

Olivia wondered if Selena meant more by her statement about following the diamond. Perhaps she wanted something that wasn't so easy to steal? Something that people would notice if it were different, not just the sharp eye of the curator's assistant?

"We could host both murals and strips of the walls that were painted." Ivy went on, her voice rising ever so slightly in controlled enthusiasm. "Pompeiians would have the same political posters as we would, only with crude artwork of the politician they wanted everyone to vote for painted on the walls where anyone walking by would see. Pompeii's history is encapsulated in its art. We can tie those two things in together."

Olivia cast a glance at Brock. His look told her he was thinking exactly what she was—what did they hope to garner from this meeting? No one was going to act suspiciously in front of the curator, and no one was going to try and steal something, especially from the Pompeii exhibit. *All for the cover,* Olivia told herself. People might get suspicious if the two new security guards got a pass on a staff meeting.

"John Martin did a painting on the actual eruption!" Nick piped up. "We could use that as our main display."

"And also how the eruption affected art throughout history," Ivy continued. "We can brainstorm a few more ideas, too. As Nick pointed out, many artists were influenced by that event in history. That would give us a good in with the people."

"The Mystery of Pompeii." Nick spread his hand through the air as if showcasing the title. "I can see it already. People are going to love it."

"Then it's settled." Selena smiled. "I was going to have the diamond be our end-of-year special, but I think it's best if we surprise the people with something different. People love surprises."

Olivia fought back a knowing smile. Selena may as well have said that there was a big reason she was cutting the diamond's display shorter. Better to put it away just in case someone other than Levi noticed before they could close their investigation.

"So what do you think about this Pompeii exhibit they're doing?" Olivia chose to drive back to the hotel that night.

Brock was sipping on a soda he'd gotten from the vending machine. He glanced over at Olivia as she asked his thoughts. "It doesn't affect me much."

"Do you think it'll keep everyone busy enough that mistakes and slip-ups will be more noticeable?" Olivia fought to keep the hope out of her voice. "I mean, this thing is huge."

"It's possible," Brock said. "But it also increases the chances of someone doing something without anyone noticing."

"My thoughts exactly." Olivia smiled as she turned up the road that would lead to their hotel. "We just have to catch them doing it."

Brock let the hum of the car's engine fill the silence for a little bit before breaking into vocal thought. "I definitely want another look at the security tapes. I think I'm missing something. A precious artifact doesn't just come up missing—even if it is replaced with a facsimile. I was scrolling rather quickly through them when we were in the security room, but maybe I'll take more time to really pay attention. Maybe we can look together tomorrow night?"

"We could do that. Although you mentioned nothing looked out of the ordinary?"

"No one but employees going in and out, nothing. I really paid attention when they put the jewel back in the secure vault for the night." Brock sighed. "Nothing obvious."

"We'll find something. In the meantime, we have a lot to work with. We just need to piece it together." To Olivia, it was kind of like finding the end of a string. The only thing is, where *did* the string end?

CHAPTER
THIRTEEN

AUTUMN WAS IN THE AIR THE NEXT MORNING, AND Olivia and Brock had been assigned to the museum early. Not for any reason other than two tours had been scheduled for that day. Oh, joy.

When they got out of the car, Olivia took a moment to inhale the smell of crisp leaves that permeated the air. She loved the fall, and didn't care about the chill creeping in to precede the harsh winter everyone was predicting. That's why she dressed in layers.

The museum was packed by 10:00 a.m. It smelled of Friday, with the excitement of school children and the second tour group coming in after them. Apparently, half the city had decided to pick this day to visit the museum. Darren, Olivia, and Brock barely had any time to themselves as they were stationed right away at various parts of the museum.

"Act natural," Darren told them as he climbed the steps to get to his place in the museum. "No one wants a security guard staring at them too hard."

"I wouldn't," Olivia chuckled a bit. Act natural, like he had any idea that she gave herself the same pep talk every day she was here.

"Selena has you in the main exhibit hall during the actual tour, Knight. Tanner, you're dividing your time between there and the music hall. That usually gets a lot of attention."

"I'm on it," Olivia said. Great. She loved nothing more than standing around all day and watching people ogle over historical artifacts. Then again, she could get a glimpse of the clientele. She noted how Selena had positioned herself and Brock to be near the jewel. She must have done that on purpose.

Olivia did a quick morning round before the tour group came in, poking her head in the front of house where two groups of children meshed together, chattering excitedly, happier to be out of the schoolroom for the day than to learn the history of art. Tessa was scrambling at the front counter and Toby sat, his calm the opposite of Tessa's over-eagerness.

"Excuse me." One woman walked up to Toby and pointed over her shoulder. "There's no paper towels in the women's bathroom."

"I'll get the janitor right on that!" Toby reached for something in his pockets, then patted them when they turned up empty. He turned to Tessa. "I left my radio downstairs. Let me run down there really quick and tell Dorian. I'm also gonna grab my radio. Can you hold down the fort for, like, two minutes?"

Tessa looked like he'd asked her to lead the museum into battle against the Vikings. Her face drained to a pale color, but she nodded. "Sure."

"Thanks. I'll be right back." Toby moved out from behind the desk and squeezed around Olivia. "Excuse me."

"That's okay." Seeing for herself that all was well so far, Olivia began her in-house rounds before the crowds invaded. One last glance to make sure everything was okay. She entered the painting hall, where she noticed a man standing near the replica of the Mona Lisa. He had his long, black hair done up in a ponytail behind him and carried himself with the same regality that Selena did. When Olivia entered, he turned to see her and a charming smile lit his face. "Good morning. I haven't seen you around here before."

An old patron, perhaps? Olivia smiled politely. "I'm new to the staff here, but I've been a security guard for a while. I'm Olivia." She left off her last name. Whoever this was didn't need to know that.

"Hello, Olivia. I'm Victor Sterling." The man nodded his head to her and reached out to shake her hand. "I've been in business with Selena for a long time. I collect rare art and supply her with some pieces for her exhibits or to loan to the museum for display. I understand that you all are planning to do a Pompeii exhibit on the art that was excavated there?"

"We are." Olivia brightened a bit.

"May I speak with Simon Westbrook?" Victor released her hand and straightened himself back up. "I have some murals I'd be happy to donate to the museum during their display."

"Certainly. I'll get right on that." Olivia turned aside and held the radio to her mouth. "Simon, come in, please?"

A crackle and Simon's voice met her ear. "Whatcha got, Knight?"

Well, great, now the stranger knew her name. But if he worked with Selena often, no doubt he'd be seeing her again, so it didn't really matter. "I have Victor Sterling here requesting a meeting with you."

"Oh." Recognition brightened his voice. "I'll be right there. Where are you?"

"Art hall."

"I'm on my way."

Olivia lowered the radio and Victor shot her a grateful smile. "My dearest thanks, Ms. Knight. I'm sure we'll be seeing each other more. It was good to meet you."

"It was good to meet you, too." Olivia waited with Victor until Simon came in the door. He greeted Victor like an old friend. "Come on, step down to my office. I'm eager to hear about these murals you told Miss Vance about."

Olivia watched as they disappeared and glanced at the clock. Figuring it was time to move to her station, she hurried to the exhibit hall.

By noon, the exhibit hall was packed with nothing but noise and shouting children. The first tour group had arrived, crowding into the rotunda and speaking over the voice of the teachers shouting for them to be quiet.

"Quiet! Quiet, please!"

Olivia smiled to herself. Being an FBI agent wasn't always easy, but it sure seemed easier than herding children around all day.

She watched the activity closely, but even as the tour director gave a presentation of each exhibit in the hall, including the diamond, no one seemed particularly interested. Olivia remained by her station until the tour finished, each of the rooms in an hour, and retreated to the bus for lunch. She moved to the front of house to make sure all was well before the second group of tourists came through.

She paused by the front desk, noticing that Skylar in the gift shop was busier than Olivia had ever seen her. Everyone wanted something, it seemed. Olivia paused by the front desk. "How are we doing up here, Tessa, Toby? Everyone behaving themselves?"

"So far," Toby answered.

Tessa rolled her eyes. "Sort of. Have you seen Dorian around?"

Olivia fought to remember which one was Dorian. "I'm sorry, which one is that?"

"The janitor." Tessa sighed. "He was supposed to come restock the towels this morning, but he never did. I had to go to the men's bathroom and grab some of theirs and do it myself." She shuddered, an adorable blush igniting her face at the thought of going into the men's restroom at all. "We're too busy for this!"

"Don't worry, I'll see if I can get a hold of him." Olivia assured her. Another tour group piled through the door, so she grabbed her radio and hastened back into the exhibit room just ahead of them. She held the communications radio to her mouth. "Dorian, can you come in, please?"

Static and silence.

"Dorian, can you come in?"

Still, more silence. Olivia didn't have time to go down and check on him. After a few minutes, the doors burst open, and a bunch of loud people all in their sixties drowned out whatever noise the radio would make. One of them instantly put their hands on a nearby exhibit while her friend snapped a picture.

Those towels would have to wait.

Looks like this group was going to be more problematic than the children. "Ma'am?" Olivia rushed forward, wondering where her FBI agent ended and the security guard began. She realized in this moment that she cared about these artifacts as much as if she actually worked here. "Ma'am? You can't touch the exhibit. Please, get your hands off the exhibits."

"You can't?" The woman pulled her hand back. Olivia fought the urge to sigh.

"No, ma'am, the oils on your hands can be detrimental to the artifacts. Please refrain from touching anything."

Across the room, she heard Brock admonishing someone for something similar. This was going to be a long day.

CHAPTER FOURTEEN

WHEN THE MUSEUM FINALLY CLOSED FOR THE DAY, Olivia bit back all the comments she would've made to Brock about never imagining she and he would be babysitting patrons at a museum. The relief that washed over her once the museum doors were closed made her take a moment to breathe in a sigh of relief. Darren tugged at the doors beside her to make sure they were locked. "Talk about a trial by fire, right?"

"You aren't kidding." Olivia didn't tell him that she'd seen worse, much worse. Shootouts, cat-and-mouse games, stake-outs... she'd take today's chaos any day. She pinched her lips together in a tight smile.

Darren started walking back toward the exhibit room, Olivia in his wake. Brock was already inside, working to push one of the other displays back toward the upstairs vault. Olivia paused and looked around the rotunda. "This place is trashed," she remarked. Paper cups lay strewn, sitting on the stone wall that surrounded a small fountain in the center of the room. Dirty footprints, leaves and pieces of paper lay scattered on the floor as if a strong wind had blown right through.

"Where on earth is Dorian?" Darren sighed. "Never mind, let's get these back where they belong."

He and Olivia chose to push the jewel display case back into the room while Brock worked on some of the other displays.

"What did you think of that last tour group?" Darren asked Brock, his voice teasing as if he already knew what he was going to say.

Brock blew out a breath through loosely closed lips and shook his head. "Man, that was something else. I've never seen a group of adults act so unruly before. The children behaved better than they did."

Olivia snickered. "I was thinking the same thing."

Suddenly, a scream ripped through the still air of the museum, startling them. Olivia and Brock paused to exchange glances between them and Darren. It was almost like they were asking the unspoken question: *Did you hear that?* Brock was the first to take off running, with Darren bringing up the rear. Olivia followed the direction of the scream as the museum employees poured out of their places. Levi came running from the office as Skylar came up the stairs that led to the employees-only area, her face stricken with panic and sheet-white with terror.

"Skylar?" Brock rushed up to her, slowing his pace a bit as he approached. "What's wrong?"

"He's... he's... dead ..." Skylar hiccupped her words and started to flail her arm toward the downstairs.

Brock took her shoulders, speaking in a trained, calm voice. "Slow down, Skylar. Breathe for me. Who's dead?"

"Dorian!"

Dorian. Is that why he hadn't attended to any of the calls so far that day? Olivia couldn't wait. She started down the stairs, reflexively reaching for her gun and hating that she only had a nightstick hanging by her side.

"Stay with her, Brock!" Darren called to Brock as he followed Olivia down the stairs. Simon was in their wake, as was Levi. Olivia sought to control the situation as she made a sharp turn left and ran toward the janitor closet. She rounded the corner, her eyes scanning for Dorian. He wasn't easy to miss, lying half-in and half-out of the janitor's closet. He hadn't fallen over with a heart attack or a stroke. Olivia noted the color of the huge blood pool spreading out under Dorian's chest. Dark red. Probably meaning he was stabbed in an organ or he'd been there a while. Even though he lay face down where she couldn't see the wound, Olivia figured that he'd been dead for some time. He'd been radio silent all day.

"Stay back!" She called out of habit, before remembering that, to Darren, she was just a security guard. "We need the authorities," she added quickly.

"I'm on it," Levi said from behind her, calling 911 as quickly as his fingers could dial. He looked up and around at everyone present. "Everyone, stay back. We can't contaminate the crime scene!"

Olivia, Darren, and Simon took a single step back, like a wave. Graham came out of his office and gasped at the sight. Olivia observed what she could, even though she wanted to dig in, elbows deep into the crime scene. No exit or entry wounds to the back, she noted. So the fatal wound had to come from the front. From the position of the blood pool, it looked to be leaking from his torso somewhere. Her eyes scanned his closet. There was an emergency exit directly beside the janitor's closet that led to the outside of the building. Olivia also remembered from what she'd seen of the camera that anyone could slip in and out unnoticed if they stayed close to the wall. To the right of the closet was a room that Dorian occupied as well. A quick glance inside told Olivia that was where they kept what wouldn't fit in the janitor's closet. Shelves stacked with objects too dark to see, a good place to hide if someone wanted to. It also appeared to be the HVAC room.

So had the assailant hidden in the HVAC room or the janitor's closet? Olivia stole a glance in the closet, big enough for two people to fit inside. Hanging in the back were some raincoats. Was it just her, or did it look like they were pulled aside a little bit, with a little bit of a gap between them? Was someone hiding in there?

"Cops are on their way. Everyone, out," Levi's calm voice instructed. "We need to leave the scene and let the authorities do their work."

CHAPTER FIFTEEN

66 I WANTED TO GET IN THERE AND PROCESS THE SCENE SO badly," Olivia complained to Brock as she sat helplessly in her hotel room. "The museum was a mess. Everyone was hysterical, the police were everywhere asking questions."

"We can access the police reports and coroner's report tomorrow." Brock reached across and set his hand on her knee. "You couldn't do anything, Olivia. We can't blow our cover. An everyday security guard is not going to be allowed to process the crime scene."

"I know!" Olivia cried in frustration. "We're there to keep people from touching hundred-year-old exhibits while keeping an eye out for a potential thief. I feel so helpless. What if the police missed something?"

"They're not going to miss something." Brock gently tried to redirect her thinking. "Besides, you saw what you needed. Tell me. What did you see?"

Olivia sighed, feeling herself calm down a little bit. She knew Brock was letting her work this out verbally, and she took a moment to be grateful for that before replaying the day over in her head. "Toby called Dorian earlier this morning before the kids were allowed inside to tour, saying that there were no paper towels in the women's bathroom. By the time the second group got around, there were still no towels. We were busy, so no one bothered to check on Dorian to see why he wasn't doing his job." Olivia remembered hearing the radio silence on his end before the second tour group came in. Why didn't she think to check then? Surely she could have slipped away at some point or got in touch with one of the other guards to go check on him. "The one who found him was Skylar. I don't know why she was down there. Maybe she was clocking out and happened to notice him lying half in his doorway, half out of his doorway to the janitor closet? He was down there in the employee's area with all the offices, so how did no one notice him?"

"It was a busy day, like you said. The hallway is dark. But, go on," Brock encouraged her. "What about the crime scene?"

"Blood." Olivia pictured the scene in her head. "My guess is that it came from his upper torso. His arms were out, sort of in the *I surrender* position, your typical chalk outline you see in murder mysteries."

Brock nodded as he listened, his gaze set intently upon her.

"My guess is he might've fallen forward and just," Olivia demonstrated by bending her body forward a bit. "Flopped. The raincoats were disturbed in the back. You know how they hold the shape of something?"

"Yes."

"They looked like they were pushed aside. That's all I could see before Levi shooed us out. Oh, there was also no entry or exit wound visible on his back."

"We'll get all the reports tomorrow." Brock settled back onto the bed. "It's okay, Olivia. We aren't going to let this go. While it's probably not related to the case of the missing jewel, it happened while we're there investigating a case. We're going to look into it."

"I know. It just frustrates me that I can't get to the evidence because everyone thinks I'm a security guard." Olivia hung her head. "It's like seeing an ad for a cookie or cake on a diet. It drives me nuts!"

"I know, baby. But we will." Brock drew her into his arms. "Hey, come here. Come here. Why are you so frustrated? We're doing what we can, Olivia."

Olivia huffed a sigh. True, why was she so frustrated? Brock knew how to read her so well. He knew that she wasn't typically so keyed up over something like this. Why was she so intent on getting to Dorian's crime scene when she knew they'd investigate what they could tomorrow? She thought long and hard, bitterly admitting it out loud. Both to him and herself.

"You know what I think it is? I think it's because Dorian was so overlooked. I saw it that day that Darren was going around and introducing us all. He nearly crashed into him as Dorian was going by, and all he said was a quick 'I'm sorry.' I could see it in Dorian's eyes... he was used to it. He looked so sad, Brock. And no one noticed he was dead until he stopped answering everyone's radio calls to come clean up their messes." Even as she said the words, her heart sank. "What kind of people are we?"

"I know," Brock sighed. "You were kind to him, though. You made sure to greet him every time you saw him and lighten his day in any way you could."

"It still wasn't enough." Olivia felt like crying, but she refused to let her tears weaken her. She was here to do a job and to find out why Dorian had been killed. And by whom? Who felt he was unimportant enough to dispose of, or important enough to snuff out his life? "He died lonely."

CHAPTER SIXTEEN

THE NEXT MORNING, THE TEMPERATURE HAD DROPPED under thick, heavy clouds and precipitation. Yesterday had been bright with promise, but today, as befitting the mood, it was gray and gloomy.

Olivia and Brock chose to dress in everyday clothes rather than their usual business suits, but still opted for nicer wear. They had work to do, but should they run into anyone from the museum, they wanted to make it look like they were out, running errands. Not that most people had errands to run at the local police station or the coroner's office. But the pawn shop made more sense.

"Let's stop by the police station and coroner's office around the afternoon sometime," Brock suggested as he grabbed the keys to the car. "Give them time to process as much evidence as they can and maybe get that autopsy figured out. I was thinking we'd hit the pawn shop first. What was the name on the receipt in Skylar's locker?"

"Miller's," Olivia repeated from memory. "So, what's our story for poking around the pawn shop?"

Brock grinned. Olivia couldn't help but notice how mischievous it was.

The pawn shop was tucked away on the corner of one of the strip malls a few blocks from the museum. It was also the definition of a dumpster fire. Maybe this Miller ran a good business, but he could invest some time into cleaning the place up a bit to make it look less like a tornado destruction zone. Shelves packed with more items than could fit on their wobbly surfaces weren't even lined up; they were placed wherever there was room. Olivia could barely see anything on display in the glass case. It was hard to pick out anything through the fingerprint smudges and oil smears. As she walked through the front door, she kept her elbows tucked to her sides. Brock, however, strode into the pawn shop with the confidence of a man who loved pawn shopping. With a smile on his face, he turned to Olivia, gently setting his fingertips on her elbow. "Honey, why don't you have a look around?"

"Okay, sweetheart." Olivia cupped his elbow back and squeezed. As Brock walked toward the front counter, she drifted around the pawn shop, scanning for something that might catch her eye. So it seemed. She highly doubted the Ratnashree diamond—if it were here—would be showcased out in the open, but in a disaster like this? There wasn't any telling.

Brock strode up to the counter, aiming a smile at the man who worked there. "Hello, my good friend." He turned on the charm he was so good at, and Olivia hid a smile as she turned her back to the counter.

The man looked up. "Why, hello!"

"Are you the Miller on the sign out front?"

"That'd be me, yes! Tom Miller, at your service."

Well, at least Brock had identified the owner of this fine establishment. Olivia wandered up one of the aisles, peering over the top of it through the dolls on stands and stacks of puff pack VHS tapes that looked like someone had been playing a risky game of Jenga.

"What can I do for you?" Tom asked cheerily.

Although Brock kept his tone hushed, Olivia could still hear him clearly. Maybe it was because she was trained to, or maybe Brock wasn't that good at being discreet in situations like this.

"Well, I'm in search of a special item," Brock murmured to the man. A mischievous lilt to his voice made the corners of Olivia's lips raise in a smile. Despite her frustrations from last night, she was fully immersed in the case at the moment. She would get to Dorian later. For right now, they were back on the search for the missing jewel. And she was enjoying watching Brock work by charming his way into the pawn shop owner's space.

Brock went on. "See that girl over there?" His voice rose a bit, indicating that he swung his head in Olivia's direction. "That's the love of my life. I'm looking for something very special for a certain," he paused, "proposal I'm planning."

Proposal. It brought back memories of Barcelona, where he'd gotten down on one knee and asked her the question she couldn't answer *yes* fast enough to. Had he been like this when he'd actually been ring shopping for her? Sly, giddy, maybe a little nervous? Or had he known exactly what he wanted?

"Ah, the big question, eh?" The pawn shop owner's voice lowered a bit as if he were in on some great secret. "Do you have anything in mind?"

"I do," Brock replied. "My woman loves pink. Do you have anything pink and flashy? Something big? I'd like to see everything you have that might be pink, even if it's not set in a ring. I've been thinking of doing a custom band, so I'd like to see your options."

"We don't have a lot of pink," the pawn shop owner warned. "But I do have something really special that just came in a week or so ago."

A week or so? As in, right around the time that the jewel went missing? Olivia felt her senses heighten. Were they going to have to conduct an investigation right here and now? She cast a look around her at the pawn shop, scoping out whether or not they'd need to call the man to the back room privately to look at his records or if anyone was thinking of stopping by.

But certainly not, right? What kind of expert thief would swap out a priceless diamond for a near-identical fake and then just send it off to the nearest pawn shop? Olivia almost felt ridiculous even being here. But this was where the investigation had led her so far, and she had to keep her mind open to any possibility.

"Ah, something fresh? I'd love to see it." Brock managed to keep the eagerness in his voice. If he was suspecting the same thing she was, he did a good job of hiding it.

Olivia fought the urge to look over her shoulder, so she ducked behind a shelf. Pretending to examine a dusty case of flutes and other instruments stained with oily fingers, she cast a sly look over to the counter as the man went into the back. Brock looked back at her and raised his eyebrows, a hopeful and curious expression on his face. Olivia nodded in return. When the man returned, she went back to examining the flutes as if she had a concert coming up and was looking for the best.

"Here we go. Here's everything I have that's pink."

"This is all the pink you have?" Brock asked after some hesitation. Olivia chanced a glance over at him. Half of them were cheap costume jewelry, and the jewels that were real were small and tacky. Olivia was pretty sure most of them were amethyst or rose quartz anyway. "I was looking for something a little bit bigger."

The man sucked in a breath through his teeth. His head slowly shook from side to side. "I'm sorry, man, but I don't have anything. Most people hock their engagement rings, which are plain diamonds or some other type of stone. I could put your number on a list if anything were to come through."

"That's all right," Brock shook his head. "I can always stop back in. But I'm planning to pop the question sometime soon, so I'm looking for something kinda immediate."

Olivia returned to browsing the pawn shop and let Brock talk his way out of this one. When he got back to her, she smiled innocently up at him. "Are you ready?"

"Sure thing, honey." He put his hand to the small of her back and guided her out of the pawn shop.

"How sure are we that the diamond wasn't there?" Olivia asked on the way to the police station.

"The guy actually was working on his logbook when I showed up at the counter." Brock got off at the exit which would take him to the police station. "I got a quick peek at it and nothing like our diamond has come in. I suppose it is possible he has it, but I just don't get the idea that our mastermind jewel thief would hock it for petty cash at the pawn shop down the street, you know? That diamond is worth millions. Pretty far above ol' Tom Miller's pay grade, by my estimation. And the state of things in there."

"Yeah... I wonder what that receipt in Skylar's locker was for," Olivia mused as she looked out the window. "The date was recent."

"Who knows." Brock shrugged. "There was so much dust and junk in that pawn shop, I was starting to get claustrophobic."

"Maybe he does have the diamond, and it got lost in that giant pile of teddy bears stuffed on that back shelf." Olivia laughed.

"That would make sense."

Brock drove to the police station first. He'd made all the phone calls that morning and explained the situation, so they were expecting them. He and Olivia got out of the car at the same time and strode into the police station. Making their way through the maze of desks, they approached the office set aside by itself, surrounded by glass. A man sat behind the desk with a sagging posture and sunken eyes. Olivia tried to look alert behind Brock as he knocked on the open door. "Detective Morgan?"

The man looked up. "You the FBI people?" he asked wearily. "Come on in."

He gestured for them to sit in a pair of ratty chairs across from his desk. Olivia took a quick glance around at the place as she did. The office was not quite as dusty and cluttered as the pawn shop had been, but it was close. On the wall behind the detective were several framed awards and certificates for exemplary service, along with photographs of the man with his wife and children. The man in those photographs, though, seemed an entirely different person. The John Morgan in the photographs smiled brightly and dressed neatly, beaming in pride at his son's baseball game or his daughter's ballet recital. It was a stark contrast to the John Morgan who currently sat across from them. The dark circles around his eyes were so prominent it almost looked like he had two black eyes, and the five o'clock shadow he sported seemed to Olivia more like a three-day-later shadow. Coffee stains littered both his rumpled, unbuttoned shirt and several of the scattered papers on his desk, and his hair obviously hadn't been combed in days, maybe weeks.

Olivia's heart broke a bit at the sight. She had no idea what had happened to turn this once well-regarded detective and handsome family man into such a wreck, but she knew the feeling well. She hadn't been too far from this feeling when first moving to Belle Grove so long ago, before even meeting Brock. That felt like a different lifetime, now. They'd been through so many ups and downs since then that she'd come out a better person and a better agent for it. She could only hope that Detective

Morgan was dealing with a difficult case and not other life-shattering circumstances.

Brock gave a polite smile and reached his hand across to shake, but Morgan refused it with a grunt. He traded a quick glance with Olivia and cleared his throat. "Agent Brock Tanner, this is my partner Olivia Knight. I called earlier…"

"Museum case, right?" Morgan grunted, pushing a file folder toward them. A coffee ring stained the manila envelope, but thankfully the papers themselves seemed clean. "This is all I've got. Sorry if it's not up to *federal standards*," he said, a little too pointedly.

Brock let the comment slide with as polite a smile as he could muster. "Thanks." Brock picked them up and thumbed through the crime scene photos.

Olivia had already seen the crime scene, so she decided to ask a few questions. "I'm sure it's all in the file, but did you notice anything important about the crime scene that we need to be aware of?"

"No murder weapon was recovered at the scene." Morgan sank back in his chair. "Coroner ain't ready yet. He said it would be done around this time." He sent a glance up at the clock, which read 2:00 p.m. already. Where had the day gone? "No footprints in blood, no fingerprints, fibers, anything like that. We got a statement from the girl who found him, Skylar Gray. She wasn't much help; she was pretty hysterical. She kept saying that she found him like that, that she'd gone down to look for him because of a broken shelf in the gift shop or something and found him like that."

"She was pretty shaken when she came upstairs." Olivia wondered how she was doing emotionally. For a girl her age to witness something so morbid, it had to take a toll on her mental well-being. "Anything else important enough to tell us?"

"It's all in the report," Morgan said tersely.

"Well, I look forward to reading it, then," Olivia said. She felt bad for the harried detective, but not bad enough to sit and act as his therapist. "We'll be in touch with any questions."

Morgan grunted under his breath again, sounding somewhere between "sure" and "mhm."

"Well, we won't take up any more of your time," Brock said, getting to his feet and subtly nudging toward the door. "And, uh, good luck."

"Mhm."

The second they were out of the police station, Olivia let out a breath she hadn't realized she'd been holding. "What was all that about? Guy was on another planet."

Brock shook his head. "Guess the job has gotten to him. I heard he is a pretty well-respected detective in the department. Or was, at least. But if this is what's happened to him…"

"Promise me that if I ever get that low, you'll snap me out of it."

Brock laughed. "You won't get that low, Olivia."

"I'm serious!"

"I am too. I've *seen* you low. I've been there, too. But that's why we're so great together, isn't it? We have each other to lean on, to make sure we can always get back on our feet. And we always will."

"I could kiss you for being so sweet," Olivia said.

"I like the sound of that. But wait until we're in the car, at least," Brock countered as they continued their way through the parking lot.

On the way to the coroner's office, Olivia flipped through the crime scene photos, happy that she could actually see them this time. The wound in the left side of the chest was the most obvious cause of death, but it intrigued her that no weapon was left behind. "I can't wait to see what the coroner has to say."

"You don't have to wait much longer." Brock pulled to a stop and turned the engine off. "We're here."

Olivia looked up, studying the dreary mortuary building looming ahead. "Weren't we here before?"

"Yeah, for that gang leaders case we did a few months back," Brock nodded. "If I remember, the coroner was very thorough."

"Let's hope that's the case this time." Olivia took off her seatbelt and stashed her folder away, securely.

They recognized Dr. Englewood right away and Olivia breathed a sigh of relief that it was the same coroner she was thinking of. She remembered him by the calm and quiet air he exuded. Unlike Morgan, he carried himself in a professional manner, taking obvious pride in his job and treating the victims with the respect and seriousness they deserved.

Englewood greeted them both with his quiet voice. "Agent Knight, Agent Tanner. Good to see you again."

"You as well." Olivia nodded to him.

"Right this way, if you please."

Olivia appreciated that he always cut to the chase. She and Brock followed him down the row of drawers. Englewood read each carefully, then chose the one that read *Hale, Dorian*, in his chicken-scratch handwriting. He pulled the drawer out, revealing the work he'd done so far on Dorian. "Cause of death was a single puncture wound to the heart. The weapon was never recovered, but what I can tell you is that it was a serrated edge about four inches long that reached the heart between these two ribs." He flipped the covering back and pointed. "Estimated time of death was around 10:00 a.m. that morning."

"So he'd been dead all afternoon." Olivia stepped forward, examining the body. Even with eyes closed in death and pallor blanketing his face, Dorian's expression appeared lonely.

"It appears that way, yes."

Brock studied the wound as if it were his final exam at the Academy. "It's not messy," he remarked, glancing up at the coroner. "It looks like it was in, then out again."

"That's what the internal damage suggests. The precision of the wound indicates that someone either got very, very lucky or they knew what they were doing."

"Element of surprise," Brock stated again. He leaned forward, examining the stab wound that centered over the man's heart. "Agent Knight mentioned that the raincoats looked like they'd been moved aside, as if someone was hiding inside of them. He was lying face down out the door, so he may have been surprised from behind."

"That's for you guys to figure out." Englewood stepped back, reading over his notes. "Hale's charts include depression medication and a small prescription for arthritis, but other than that, it doesn't appear that he had any underlying health conditions."

Depression. Of course. He was a man in his late fifties, working as a janitor in a museum that pushed past him as if he were just another old, ancient artifact. Olivia's heart went out to him, regretting that he probably died miserably. "Thanks, doctor."

CHAPTER SEVENTEEN

O LIVIA DIDN'T SAY MUCH AS BROCK DROVE BACK TO THE hotel. When they pulled into the parking lot, she stayed quiet, deep in thought, not ready to get out of the car. Brock sensed it. He turned off the engine and leaned back, looking at her. "You're thinking about Dorian, aren't you?"

"That, and his manner of death." Olivia listed off her thoughts on her fingers, counting them off. "Stabbed in the heart, possibly frightened from behind. Like you said, the wound was precise. It sounds too much like a professional hit." She paused, then went on. "I remember how the raincoats were shaped. As if someone had been hiding there. So, my theory is that someone was lying in wait for him. My question is: Who lies in wait for a janitor? What did he do to deserve that?"

Brock pondered this for a moment. "Did his record indicate anything in his past that might have chased him here? Any witness protection, any indication that he may have gotten tied up with the wrong crowd at some time in his life?"

"When we were doing background checks that night, all I remember learning is a few things. He's lived in Virginia his whole life. Married young and lost his wife about ten years ago." Olivia shook her head. "He's been working at the museum for over a decade. So unless he was really good at hiding something, nothing on the surface indicates that he was in any kind of trouble. I'll have to dig a little deeper."

Brock sat back, thinking out loud. "Dr. Englewood mentioned he was on depression medication. What if he wasn't so much clinically depressed as he was circumstantially? Think about it. The guy lost his wife, and it sounds like they were married for a long time. He's working at a museum with people who don't appreciate his work until he's not there to do it anymore. What if he was planning on getting out? What if he sold the jewel to the wrong people, or told them how to access it?"

Olivia wasn't sure she fully bought the story, but she wasn't dismissing it, either. "Do you think he'd know how to access the Ratnashree diamond?"

"I'm not saying he did. I'm just throwing out possibilities." Brock drummed his fingers on the steering wheel. "He's the one person we haven't had a chance to look into yet. And what if whoever has the jewel now caught wind that the FBI might be sniffing around, or the new security guards were making them uncomfortable?"

"Or he changed his mind," Olivia completed his thought. "Maybe they wanted to silence the guy who did it. Or, a witness. What was Dorian doing on the dates of October fifth and sixth? Is it possible that he saw something he shouldn't have?"

"I don't remember. I'll have to look again," Brock said.

Before Olivia could follow up with another question, Brock's cell phone cut into the conversation. Brock reached into his pocket, frowning at the caller ID. "Levi, what's up?" He swiped the screen and held the phone to his ear. "What?"

Olivia could sense the heavy seriousness in Brock's tone and read it in his eyes as they grew a little bit wider. "You're kidding me."

Never a good thing to say to someone on the other line.

"Of course. We'll head over there now. What hospital is she in?"

Hospital? *She?* Had there been an attempt on someone else's life?

"Got it. We're on our way." Brock hung up the phone and turned to Olivia. "Selena Vance was just in a car accident. She's currently unconscious."

"No!" Olivia gasped.

"Levi's at the hospital with her now. Let's get over there."

Olivia re-buckled her seatbelt. "Did he say anything else about it?"

Brock turned the key in the ignition and backed out of the parking space again. "He didn't give details. He said he'd fill us in on everything when we get there."

Levi stood waiting for them in the waiting room and spotted them immediately. He approached them with a nervous gait, his eyes wide with concern. "You were the first ones I called." He glanced between them. "I haven't called any of the other staff. I didn't want them to see you here and get suspicious."

"Good thinking," Brock commended him. "So, what happened, exactly?"

"Come on up to the room and I'll tell you." Levi led them toward an elevator. Once the doors had closed them inside and any hope of being overheard was gone for the moment, Levi pushed the floor button and stood back. "The local police recognized her and got in touch with me. Selena lives out in the woods in the country, about forty-five minutes from the museum. There's a bridge that she has to cross in order to get home. When they found her, she'd rolled her car into the ditch a few times. Something happened, and her tires skidded right off the highway, as if she was braking for something. The car hit the ditch and rolled. By some miracle, she's still alive, but she's in critical condition."

The doors dinged and Olivia and Brock stepped out. "Any signs of foul play other than the possible tire marks?" Olivia asked.

"They didn't say. They won't talk to me. They stationed someone outside her door, though. They might be able to fill you in."

Levi led them past the nurse's station to the ICU room. Standing in front of a closed door was an officer speaking with his detective. "Gentlemen," Olivia and Brock showed off their badges. "Agent Knight, Agent Tanner, FBI." She fired off questions as she put her badge away. "Can you tell us what happened?"

"We're still investigating all of it, but we had a call come in from a group of teenagers who were driving into town. They saw the tire tracks and the car in the ditch with no one else around."

"Any sign of a second car?" Olivia asked. "Paint transfer, unusual damage that doesn't appear to be from the rollover?"

"None whatsoever. We checked each dent for paint transfer, but we couldn't see any. The tire tracks on the road showed that she braked hard, then swerved and got into the soft soil of the shoulder before rolling over a few times. She was wearing her seatbelt."

"Was anything collected from the scene?" Brock asked. "Her cell phone, by chance?"

"We have it all down at the station," the detective answered.

"We believe it might be connected to a case we're investigating involving the museum, and another recent death of an employee there," Olivia explained. "We're going to have to take a look at the evidence you collected from the scene of her accident."

The detective nodded. Olivia was glad he didn't put up a fight. He seemed much more on the job than Detective Morgan, anyway.

"I'm working her case. I'm Detective Jim Cade. I'll have her things collected for you."

"That would be great, thanks." Olivia turned to look inside the window. "May we see her?"

Levi nodded. "They said she's stable. For now. She has a concussion. The doctors said something about an ICP – brain pressure, I think? She hasn't been breathing on her own consistently, so they've put her on a ventilator."

Well, that was far from good. Olivia nodded as she pushed through the door. She and Brock walked gingerly across the hospital room. Selena had more tubes than a scuba diver, spreading her dainty mouth wide open to feed her air. She didn't look anything like the regal queen Olivia and Brock had met the day they first stopped by the museum.

Levi's eyes were heavy with sorrow as he approached the bed. "The next seventy-two hours are critical." He reached forward, gently taking her IV-ridden hand within his. "If she can hold on that long, then her chances of survival go up. If not..." his voice trailed off.

"I'm sorry, Levi." Brock lowered his voice to fit the situation.

"It's just not right." Levi shook his head.

"Where were you when you got the call? You said the local police identified her?" Olivia asked.

"I had just sat down to dinner. I was meeting with my fiancée at the Italian restaurant downtown."

"What a great way to ruin dinner," Brock sympathized.

Levi breathed a humorless laugh. "Tell me about it."

What had happened? Selena was too smart to text and drive. At least, that's the impression she gave. Olivia would still take a look at her phone, but she felt like it was a shot in the dark. The accident happened near a bridge, they said. Was it possible she was swerving to avoid some kind of wildlife? Fell asleep at the wheel?

Olivia kept her thoughts to herself until she and Brock were on the elevator, heading back down to go home for the second time that night. "We need to kick this investigation up several notches the minute that the museum opens."

Brock side-eyed her. "You think this is related?"

"I don't know what to think. But between Dorian's death and now Selena in the hospital, we need to do them justice. Something tells me this is all far more than a simple jewel theft."

"You can say that again."

"There's something going on at that museum, even more than the theft of the jewel."

"It can't be a coincidence that sudden tragedies have befallen two of the employees," Brock said as the doors opened. "Somebody must know something. I don't know who, and I don't know what, but it's clear the picture is much bigger than we thought."

"Well, one thing's for certain," Olivia said. "Guess we'll be undercover a little longer."

CHAPTER EIGHTEEN

"**H**AVE YOU SLEPT MUCH SINCE WE STARTED THIS CASE?" Brock asked Olivia the next morning on their way to the police station.

Olivia stared out the windshield, grateful for the light traffic. Not that she enjoyed working on weekends, but it did have a few perks, such as little traffic. "It's been hit or miss. I have too many questions and not enough answers, so sometimes that drives me crazy and keeps me awake at night."

"Sometimes?" Brock raised an eyebrow. "The Olivia I know usually lets cases consume her life."

"Hey, I've been getting better at that. I slept for a good solid six hours last night!" Olivia teased.

Brock buzzed his lips. "Six hours. Wow. Are you groggy from getting so much sleep?" he added, sarcastically.

"I'm wide awake, actually." Olivia sighed. "I keep thinking about Selena. My heart goes out to her and to the whole museum staff."

"So does mine." Brock parked. "Let's see if we can find some answers."

Detective Cade seemed more than happy to sign over the case and all of Selena's personal belongings to Olivia and Brock. Maybe he was overbooked or maybe he thought it was a dead-end case that he didn't want to get hung up on. Olivia stared at the evidence bag containing her keys, phone and a few random items from the car, along with Selena's purse beside it. "The purse dumped out, but we tried to collect all the contents and put them in the bag." Cade nodded to the evidence bag.

"Thank you." Olivia lowered it. "We also need to see the car."

"What's left of it. Right this way." Holding his coffee in one hand, Cade led them through a maze to the downstairs garage. When he flipped the lights on, Olivia cringed at the sight. Selena's black Mercedes was little more than a crushed can at this point. "She's lucky she survived this," Olivia remarked.

"Well, I'll leave you to it. I'll be upstairs in my office if you have any questions." He turned to leave, but Olivia held up a hand to stop him.

"Hey. I wanted to ask you something."

Both Brock and Cade gave her looks of confusion, but she pressed on. "It's nothing bad. I just… well, we were working with Detective Morgan earlier, on another related case to all this. And I couldn't help but notice that he seemed a little…"

"Down in the dumps?" Cade supplied.

"Yeah. Is he okay?"

Cade ran a hand through his hair with a sigh. "Wish I could tell you. John's been one of the best on the force for a long time. He still gets results, but… I don't know what's changed over the last few months. It's like he's not taking care of himself anymore.

Everyone's noticed, but nobody wants to say anything about it. So me and the boys have been bringing in extra lunches for him. Even then, it's like pulling teeth to get him to eat anything other than coffee and cigarettes these days."

"That's good," Brock said. "It's hard, being in this line of work."

"I really don't mean to cast any aspersions on him or anything," Olivia said. "I'm just looking at both of these cases as definitely related, and, to be completely honest, you've been a much bigger help in the last twenty minutes than he has been at all. Again, it's nothing against him personally, it's just that—"

"It's just that you worry about how much he seems to care about this case?"

"I wasn't going to say that, but yeah. Sort of," Olivia replied.

"I know. I've been worried about it, too. Well, I'll see if there's anything else I can help you with. But between you and me, don't let it get out that you've been asking about him. It's a pretty touchy subject around here."

With that, he gave them a wave and headed off, leaving the two of them alone. Olivia approached the car, pointing to the roof. "Looks like the fire department cut her out."

Brock sighed and shook his head, letting the weight of what they were seeing get to him. "Selena, you better pull through this. It would be a miracle." After a moment of quiet, he nodded to Olivia. "You take the front, I'll take the back."

"Oh, sure, give me the evidence overload." Olivia knew this wasn't a time to joke, but the job would drive her nuts if they didn't try once in a while to keep things light. Her worst nightmare was to end up like Detective Morgan, so buried under the weight of the job that she couldn't see any light at all. She held onto the hope that Selena would be okay, and for that, she could show her a little enthusiasm. *I've got you, Selena. We're going to figure out what's happening all around.*

"The question is, was she targeted? Was it an accident? Or… you don't think she was suicidal, do you?" Brock asked as he jimmied open her trunk.

"Why do you say that?" Olivia stepped out of the way as the damaged door flew open. She poked her head inside, careful of the broken glass scattered on the seats. How ironic that it reminded her of diamonds, when that's what brought her and Brock here in the first place.

"She has a lot going on. She's got this jewel on loan from India, and under her watch, it was replaced with a fake. If we don't find out who did it, she's got that heavy burden to contend with. She's got to call it in and admit that she lost one of the most precious artifacts in history. Talk about a hit to the reputation. How do you admit that you lost something that goes back almost two thousand years? Something so carefully preserved until then?"

Olivia kept listening as she examined the front of the car for any evidence. She turned the key in the ignition, surprised that the battery still powered it up. Soothing classical music drifted from the speakers. It didn't surprise her that it was Selena's music of choice.

"Then, Dorian dies," Brock went on. "Maybe she was feeling like a failure."

"I get it if she wanted out of a conversation with Indian authorities. On top of it all, the ruin of her reputation. But do you think Dorian's death was just the straw that broke the camel's back?"

"I suppose it's possible." Brock slammed the trunk. "Checking the right side for paint transfer."

Olivia knew that she wasn't going to find anything in the front seat; she wasn't meant to. No one was found in the car with Selena. So, she examined the left side of the car for paint transfer.

"I'm not seeing any signs of a second vehicle," Brock called to her. "No paint transfer at all."

"Same." Olivia went over it twice. No paint transfer. No strange dents in either bumper or the side of the vehicle to explain someone ramming her, thus pushing her off the road. Maybe Brock was right and it hadn't been someone targeting her.

Maybe Selena just tried to take the only way out she could see. The thought was unnerving. "How are the tires on your side?"

"Banged up, but not flat. And the suspension is twisted and messed up. Yours?"

"Same." Olivia examined them both. "So it wasn't a flat tire. So maybe she was suicidal. Or fell asleep behind the wheel. Or was distracted. Or there was wildlife." She checked Selena's dash, hoping for a dashcam or something to point to what might have happened. Nothing.

"What does her phone say?"

Olivia took it out of the package and fired it up. "It's locked with a password. I'll have to hook it up to the laptop to open it."

Olivia hoped that something on the phone would lead them to figure out what exactly had happened. But if this was just a freak accident, and she'd been swerving to avoid some wildlife or had fallen asleep at the wheel, then they'd never know unless she woke up. But that wouldn't stop Olivia from trying.

Back in their hotel room, Olivia plugged the phone into her laptop and had it open within fifteen minutes. She scrolled through Selena's messages and phone records while Brock scooped out slices of pizza for each of them on paper plates. "The last text she sent was at three that afternoon. She was still at the museum."

"Who was it for?" Brock called back as he shook a mountain of red pepper flakes on his plate.

"To some guy named Bob."

"Oh, that narrows it down. Pretty distinctive name."

Olivia scrolled through the conversation. "Looks like he's a newspaper reporter she talks to. She was telling him about an article she wants in the paper about the Pompeii exhibit."

"And the call log?"

"Her last call was an hour later, at four." Olivia checked everything else, but Selena didn't have any social media on her phone. It looked like she had no life outside of the museum, which was somewhat sad, but also made Olivia's job easier. "So she wasn't on her phone on the way home."

"That rules that option out, then. Parmesan?" Brock asked as he passed her a plate.

"Sure, thank you." Olivia took the packet and closed her laptop lid before digging into her dinner. "So what do you think?"

Brock chewed a small bite, probably treating his thoughts the same way. "I think that maybe it's time to ask a few questions around the museum. Someone somewhere has to know something. Levi informed them of Selena's accident. We'll know tomorrow if she's made it past the seventy-two-hour window or not."

"That's good." But how to get these people to talk without being suspicious? For some reason, Olivia's mind flashed back to Nick. How over-eager he was for everything, and how happy he'd be to be back at his job. Suddenly, it hit her.

"I think I know how to ask some questions without being overly suspicious."

"How's that?"

Olivia leaned forward. "I think that I'll pull the over-eager security guard who wants to be the hero. Maybe I'm a girl who had to earn my place in the security field, and now I want to be the hero in figuring out what happened."

"You're really going there?" Brock teased with a raised eyebrow.

"Why not?" Olivia shrugged. "It would give me an excuse to be going around and asking things. As long as I don't ask anything *too* professional sounding. You know, the verbiage of the Bureau."

"I think you'll rock that part." Brock grinned at her. "So, am I supposed to treat you like my underling from here on out? Since you had to," he made air quotes, "'earn your place?'"

Olivia glared at him. "Don't make me kick you to prove a point."

CHAPTER NINETEEN

A RMED WITH A NEW PLAN, OLIVIA STRODE INTO THE museum that Monday morning, slightly ahead of Brock. As Brock took his time getting his badge and clocking in, Olivia hurried through the process, then raced upstairs.

The air in the museum hung heavy that day. The artifacts had already been moved out, and Olivia couldn't help but glance over at the fake diamond that had started this whole thing. Selena's accident weighed on everyone's minds, and it showed in their long faces. Brock came up behind her after a while, and everyone filtered their way into the main exhibit room. Even Nick's usual bright cheer had dimmed as he traced one of the glass display cases in deep thought. Simon and Graham divided their time between looking out the window, then looking back at the barren room, which seemed so empty without Selena. Darren tried to look busy by pacing to and fro, in and out of the exhibits, but clearly he was just working things out.

Finally, Simon broke the silence with a sigh strong enough to cause a storm. "All right, guys. Look, I know that we're all down about Selena. But she's still alive. And she's a fighter. If anyone can pull through, she can. In her honor, let's try to make today a good day, huh? We're not going to keep this museum running like a top if we walk around all mopey." He said the word *mopey* with slumped shoulders, a throaty voice and an overexaggerated turn down of the corners of his lips.

Brock glanced around, filling his role as a new security guard. "Simon's right, guys. Selena wouldn't want this of us. Let's just buckle down and make the guests have the best day at the museum. They have no idea what's happening, so let's keep it that way."

Of course, not surprisingly, Nick was the first to break into a smile. "The Tanner's right, guys! Selena's strong. She's gonna pull through, and when she does, let's make her proud when she comes back to work!"

Olivia shot Brock a teasing glare, now that Nick had resorted to calling him *The Tanner*. For once, Brock didn't seem to mind. Maybe the name was growing on him.

"I'll go tell Tessa to open the front of house, and we'll get this show on the road," Darren announced, heading toward the front. "Gotta do it eventually…"

And just like that, each employee scattered to do their jobs.

Brock managed to squeeze Olivia's fingers subtly before taking off to start his rounds in the hall. Nick scurried off, whistling *The British Grenadiers* as he did. Olivia lurked in the exhibit hall until Darren came back, followed by the voices of patrons who had gathered in the front of house. Olivia took in a deep breath and approached him. "Hey, Darren. Can I talk to you?"

"Sure." He nodded downstairs. "Levi wants us to log the climate control and alarm panel readings for the vault downstairs. Care to join me? We'll leave Tanner up here."

"Sure." Olivia fell into eager step behind him. Darren waited until they were downstairs and approaching the gaping vault before letting her talk. "What's up?"

Olivia looked around as if she didn't want to be overheard. "Can I ask you something? Something kinda personal?"

"Sure can. I'll try to have an answer." Darren smiled slightly.

Olivia huddled by his side as he opened the panel to the vault's security system. "I know it's only been a few days, but... do you think I do this job well?"

He stopped and looked over at her. "Yeah. There's really nothing to it, though. Why do you ask?" The edge to his voice made her wonder if she was going at this the wrong way. He pulled the meter out of his pocket.

"I know there's nothing to it," Olivia brought her voice down a notch. "And that's why I want more. See, I'm tired of the jobs that don't require anything but an occasional escort out and keeping people from going where they shouldn't. I've had to fight my way into the position I have today, and I can't tell you how draining that is."

A smile teased the corners of his mouth as he watched the meter for the reading. "Had to work your way up the ladder, eh?"

"You have no idea." Olivia rolled her eyes. "You'd think we're in the 1920s instead of the 2020s sometime."

"Don't say that around Nick," Darren chuckled. "He'd launch into an entire history lesson about the women's suffrage movement and insist that the 1920s were actually a good year for you guys. Gals. Whatever."

"Good point," Olivia laughed. Okay, making jokes, they were on the same page. "I'm so tired of fighting, Darren. And I haven't said anything, but all this talk about the missing Ratnashree diamond and all? I thought..." She paused, then hung her head. "No. It's silly."

"It's not silly." Darren logged whatever the meter read, not bothering to train her how to do it. "Unless, of course, you're going to tell me you're a superhero in disguise."

Olivia laughed. "If only."

"What were you thinking, then?" Darren put the panel back together, carefully.

Olivia licked her lower lip. "Do you think I have a chance of figuring out what happened to the missing jewel? It seems like no one around here is doing anything about it, and I thought, maybe I have a shot at being something better. You know, like a detective or something. It might earn some respect or, I don't know. Maybe give me a confidence boost?"

"Tanner seems to respect you," Darren pointed out. He turned and started heading into the vault.

Olivia shadowed him. "Yeah, but he respects everyone. I'm talking about everyone else."

"Understandable. But I doubt you'll solve anything. I'm sure Selena was working with someone to find out what happened; she's not going to let something like that go. I mean, it even went over *my* head." Darren paused and sighed, then turned to face her. "But I'm not going to tell you no, either. Just be careful. You can't be too obvious with asking questions or finding things out because people will start to figure it out."

"Oh, I know. I'm a huge Agatha Christie fan," Olivia grinned. "So I know how to play the detective while still being subtle. I learned from the best."

"Oh, *And Then There Were None*?" Darren lifted an eyebrow. "Don't jinx us, now, Knight. Too many people have already had things happen to them."

"I suppose you're right," Olivia laughed. "So you're a security guard. Noticed anything I don't know..." She inched closer to him, grinning. "Different around here?"

"Around the time the Ratnashree went missing?" Darren shook his head. "Unfortunately, no. Everything was as it should be. We didn't even know it was missing until word spread the next day. And I scrubbed every inch of footage about a hundred times to figure it out."

"Who leaked it? Do you know?" Maybe the person who leaked it was the one they needed to keep their eyes on. Olivia didn't see Levi or Selena telling anyone in the museum that the jewel was fake. So if they'd kept it to themselves, who leaked the information?

"We don't know, exactly. Selena told me when it happened, but my lips were sealed. Problem is, not an hour later that same day, I heard it from Nick, who heard it from Simon. And of course, once Nick hears something, everyone will know within a few hours."

"Isn't that the truth?" Olivia chuckled a little bit. Well, it made sense that Levi or Selena might have told Simon. He was the collections manager, after all. "Huh. So maybe someone took it during the daytime?"

"It would be nearly impossible for one of us not to notice," Darren countered. "I do the rounds every day, and when there's a large tour group, I'm always in with the exhibits. Someone would have noticed a patron messing with the case during the day. Nick is always running around, Simon and Graham come to and from their offices whenever they need a break from their work, so if someone took it during the day, they'd need access to the keys. You can't just open that case, Knight."

Olivia knew. She'd even had to play with the lock a little bit the night she and Brock searched the display case.

Darren went on, proving his point. "It would take too long to try and steal it during the day. And it would be too risky. *And* it would have shown up on the cameras."

"I see. So it has to be one of us. Well…" she gestured. "One of you."

"Unfortunately, that's most likely the case." Was that betrayal Olivia heard in Darren's tone? "The Vanguard Core system I told you about? No one can get past that. It's not the kind of system a petty thief can just crack."

Olivia knew that was the truth, reflecting on her failed test. But this conversation only confirmed what she already knew. It had to be one of them. She wanted to ask about his fingerprints on the display case, along with Simon's, but she had to do it subtly. "So, who puts the artifacts back in the vault most of the time?"

"Simon and Graham, mostly, but we're all a family here, so if we've had a large tour group that hung out in the gift shop till five minutes after closing, we'll all pitch in with the cleanup process afterward. Simon and Graham will check them and make sure they're still in good condition, which is another reason why it has to be someone on the inside. They would have noticed if something was off right away."

Maybe, Olivia thought. She chewed her lower lip and nodded. "So security guards help?"

"We do." Darren nodded. "But I'd never lay a finger on any of these artifacts. Do you know what the repercussions would be if I were ever caught? Not to mention, I respect the museum too much for that. I've been here longer than any other job, I can't do that to Selena or the museum, or the community. And the other security guards?" He chuckled a bit. "Let's just say, they're not like you, Knight. They're great to work with, but let's just say some of these folks aren't the sharpest blades in the toolbox. I feel like they're around more as a deterrent than anything. You know. A patron sees them standing near an artifact, they're not going to go near it with the security guard standing there."

"I see." Olivia smiled. "Don't worry, your secret is safe with me."

"I appreciate that." Darren grinned. "You really *do* ask questions like a detective. And you said you had to *fight* for your position?"

"You know how it is," Olivia shrugged laughingly.

"Well, if you keep it up," Darren half-closed one eye, reassuring her. "You just may track down something that all of us have missed, after all."

With that, he turned and strode out of the vault. "Let's head back upstairs. If we're down here too long, people will wonder. And you certainly don't want to look suspicious."

"No way." Olivia followed him out of the vault. "Thanks for talking with me. And for, you know. Understanding."

"Any time, Knight. I know what it's like to be stuck in a dead-end job," Darren said as he climbed the stairs. "The difference between us is that I *love* my dead-end job. You want to go places. And with an attitude like yours, you should."

Olivia grinned at the compliment. Little did he know that she had.

CHAPTER TWENTY

S HORTLY AFTER CLOSING, OLIVIA FOUND TIME TO SNEAK away to the control room where Brock sat, once again staring at the monitors. "How did it go today?" Brock asked.

"Fine. I got a little buddy-buddy with Darren, telling him my sob story about how I had to work my way up in the security industry, how no one appreciates me, you know the drill." Olivia grabbed a cup of water and sat down beside him. "What about you?"

"Got stuck doing rounds today, and I've only been up here about five minutes." Brock sat back and looked her way. "I thought we could look over them together. You know, balance each other out. You may catch what I miss and vice versa."

"Sounds better than reading a bunch of boring background checks on people." Olivia plopped down beside him and eyed the screen "Okay. Where are we starting?"

"October the 5th. The day before Levi noticed the jewel missing. Are you ready?"

"Yes."

Brock started the footage and scrolled through it, stopping only when someone would stand too close to the jewel's display case. Which took forever, since the Ratnashree diamond was the talk of the town and numerous patrons stopped in to examine it. Olivia took her time scrutinizing, but no one showed any signs of being overly interested. No one dug into their pocket or looked around to see if anyone was watching. She watched until the displays were pushed back into their original places at the end of the day. During the time of watching the footage, she made note of every employee that appeared and disappeared on the screen. Ivy Landon by herself going in to meet with Selena, then heading into the back area also by herself. Nick scurrying around and talking to people as he attempted to do his job. Olivia wondered how much work he actually got done during the day. Simon and Graham kept to themselves downstairs in their offices the whole day, and Darren did his rounds with the other security guards he mentioned. Other than Selena's meeting with Ivy toward the beginning of the day, both Selena and Levi never appeared in the footage.

Brock let the footage play for a little bit into the evening of October 5th. "This is the best part of the job, isn't it? Rewatching boring 24/7 footage in order to catch that one toothpick-sized clue that's out of place?"

"But when you find it, nothing can compare to the rush!" Olivia replied cheerfully.

"Sure," Brock mumbled, eyes on the screen. Olivia glanced over at the clock for just a moment, but long enough for Brock to perk up and sit straight in his chair. "Wait... did you see that?"

"Sorry, no, I looked up for a moment." Olivia leaned toward the monitor. "What was it?"

"Watch this! The footage glitched." Brock went back a few seconds and pointed to the camera near the upstairs vault where the diamond was kept. The cameras aimed at the artifacts from three different sides. He typed in to play the footage in slow motion and hit play. Olivia watched the one with the full display of the jewel... but sure enough, sometime after eleven that night, the footage jerked for a single frame—a tiny, thin white line running down the screen as if the camera had been adjusted.

"I did see it." Olivia raised an eyebrow. "Does that mean this footage has been tampered with?

Brock was already hot on the trail of the new clue he'd discovered, watching the footage of the other two cameras aimed at the jewel. "You watch this one, I'll watch this one. Same time, after eleven?"

Olivia nodded. She noted the time at 11:03. Sure enough, at the exact same moment, the footage she was watching glitched. "Yep. God, how did Darren not notice this?"

"I've been over the footage like three times and I've never noticed it either. Literally blink and you miss it, it's only there for..." he checked the time stamp, "sixteen milliseconds."

"If you didn't know it was there, it would just blend in with the rest of the footage."

"Let's check the other cameras," Brock said. "Maybe there was a power glitch or power outage?"

"I'll watch the ones in the employees-only area around 11:03."

"I'll cover the upstairs. And the rest of the museum."

Olivia watched for a good solid fifteen minutes after 11:03. "I got nothing." She paused. "Let me check something." She scrolled back to a little before 11:00. She watched the footage long enough to see a shadow move across the camera, which pointed to the exit by Dorian's closet. "Okay, the light changed a bit. I think someone came in through the back exit. But I can't see who. The camera doesn't show that."

"Interesting. I only had one glitch on my end," Brock answered.

"Which one?"

"The one facing the parking lot."

"Really?" Olivia hummed as she looked over his shoulder, seeing the same glitch. Her eyes drifted down to note the time: 11:41.

"So almost forty minutes later," she noted. She sat back, chewing her lower lip in thought. "This footage was tampered with. Someone came in that back door and erased the footage from October 5th."

"And Levi noticed the morning of October 6th that the jewel was fake." Brock pulled up the footage from after 5:00 p.m. the night before. "Let's see who was still at the museum after closing."

Eagerly, Olivia watched right along with him. But each member of staff left through the front door and was seen walking down the street. Toby, Tessa, and Skylar left together at 5:03, Nick left at 5:30, Simon and Graham both clocked out at 6:00, and shared a talk in the lobby before taking off and going toward the parking lot. Elliot wasn't seen that day, but Ivy was, so Olivia watched for her, seeing that she left around 5:25. Darren was the last to leave, but he disappeared out of frame shortly after Simon and Graham did, right after the alarm was set. Watching the footage frame-by-frame was exhaustingly slow, but finally, Olivia definitively proved it: the footage never glitched again at any point before 11:03.

"Selena and Levi, when did you see them leave?" Brock asked.

"They left together around four, I think?"

Brock scrolled back in time to 4:00, when sure enough, both Selena and Levi left, looking like they were intently talking about something on the way back to their cars.

"So no one was ever seen coming back. How did they get around the cameras on the outside of the museum?" Olivia mused out loud.

"I don't know," Brock shook his head. "Whoever it was knew that the camera doesn't cover the whole back door. They know it has a huge blind spot back there."

"Who would know that and how to tamper with the security system?" Olivia hummed. "They'd need the knowledge to shut down every single security camera that points to the jewel and their existence within the museum, kill the security system, then sneak in and steal the jewel without leaving a trace, and *then* splice back together the footage seamlessly."

"Darren knows the security system," Brock pointed out. "Darren was the one who supposedly scoured every inch of footage before we got called in. So your little friend is the one that my mind is going to."

Olivia grinned. "Not my little friend. Just a mark."

"Whatever," Brock teased her before returning to being serious. "Simon and Graham both have access to the case. Simon's been here the longest, so the possibility of him knowing a thing or two about security isn't unreasonable."

"And Nick?" Olivia thought out loud. "I didn't see any flags in his record, but is it possible that he knows a thing or two about hacking? He certainly would know more about computers than most of this lot."

"It's possible. And as obsessed as he is with history, I wouldn't put it past him entirely to pull something like this. Maybe he wanted it for his own collection and figured it would be the artifact least likely to be flagged as fake."

"Didn't stop to think about the ramifications it would have when India gets a fake jewel back," Olivia remarked.

Brock pushed his hands through his hair. He let the silence of the humming monitors fill the air for a few moments. "Let's take a look at the footage of the day Dorian died. Maybe there's a connection."

Olivia nodded. "Let's do it."

She patiently waited until Brock called up the correct footage.

"Englewood said TOD was around 10:00 that morning. But he never restocked the paper towels when he got the message. So let's start with 8:00 a.m. that morning, shall we? It was a crazy day, so let's just watch the employees."

"Sounds good." Olivia nodded.

Tessa, Toby, and Skylar showed up on time, along with Simon, Nick, Graham, Dorian, and Darren. Once the museum was open for business, Olivia caught a glimpse of herself, Brock, and Dorian walking upstairs from the employees-only area. Tessa, Toby, and Skylar stayed busy near the front while Simon and Graham stayed out of sight until Simon came up for his meeting with Victor Sterling that morning, then took him back to his office. The meeting lasted about three hours, Olivia noted as Brock scrolled through the timeline. There was Ivy, coming and going as she worked with Elliot on the exhibit, going up and down the stairs as part of their job.

"Nothing!" Olivia shouted in frustration. "It's as if we're looking for a ghost!"

Brock nodded. "I know we just skimmed through as much as we can, but no one came in or out who wasn't supposed to." He and Olivia both sat in silence for a few moments until he shifted to face her better. "Let's keep doing what we're doing. Maybe the answer is in the security footage, but we won't see it unless we know where to look for it. Someone tampered with the footage the night of October 5th. But no one tampered with it the day Dorian died. The question is, what are we looking for?"

"I'll keep asking things under the guise of a security guard who wants to be more," Olivia said. "What are you doing in the meantime?"

"Scoping the place out." Brock stood. "I think maybe I'll hang out in the employees-only area for a while tomorrow and see if there's anything out of place."

"Good call."

CHAPTER
TWENTY-ONE

O LIVIA COMMENDED THE EMPLOYEES OF THE MUSEUM of Art History for going about their duties. Ivy and Elliot worked tirelessly to prepare the main room for the Pompeii exhibit, receiving murals and other art pieces to add to their collection. The excitement over a new exhibit buzzed in the air and kept the environment looking alive.

Olivia let Brock perform his investigation downstairs as much as she could, while she kept an eye on things in the museum on the first floor. As she paced one morning, Nick strode into the area, all smiles as usual. She found a smile of her own as he approached her. "Hey, Knight."

"Morning, Nick." She nodded to him.

Nick stopped in front of her and cast a look around him before leaning in. "Say, I was wondering. I know that it's not exactly protocol, but I've been worried about Skylar. She hasn't been the same since Dorian was, you know. Killed."

"What's been going on?" Olivia didn't have to fake concern, she often wondered how Skylar was doing. But her antenna did perk up a bit.

"Well, she's been really jumpy, like she's off in her own little place. She hasn't been doing her job as well and is barely eating. I know this, because I keep an eye on everyone here."

"You do?" Olivia asked. Why did Nick watch everyone so closely?

"Of course!" Nick spread out his hands. "The museum is my life! This is my job, my happy place. The people I work with, we're all family here, but I wouldn't want anyone to be doing something they're not supposed to. I know I'm just the archivist, but to me, I'm much more than that. History is a treasure, and it's up to people like us to keep it alive."

It occurred to Olivia that maybe there was something more to Nick's constant surveillance of the museum than there ought to be. He could say he loved history, but what if that was something he used to hide his real motives? "Have you seen anything unusual? Out of the ordinary?"

"Not really." Nick shook his head. "Everything's been in an uproar since the Ratnashree got pinched."

Olivia tried not to laugh at all the verbiage from different cultures and times he managed to cram into any conversation she'd had with him. *Pinched* wasn't one she'd heard in a while from someone younger than thirty. "Everyone's probably on edge."

Nick sighed, his face falling a bit. "Still. I know that you're just a security guard and not a nurse or anything, but I was thinking you could check on Skylar?" He pinched air between his fingers. "A little bit?"

"Sure." Olivia smiled, reassuringly, and nodded. "I'll check on her. Thank you for looking out for everyone, Nick. It really shows that you care."

"Thanks, Knight!" Nick held two thumbs up. "You're the best. Chivalry, am I right?" He pointed at her and winked.

She laughed lightly. "Chivalry, Nick."

Nick swiveled and returned to whatever it was he was doing. That is, until he spotted a couple admiring something in the corner. "Hey! How're we doing today?"

Olivia watched him for a while, not sure why she was so fixated on him at that moment. Nick really did seem to love his job. She didn't put it past him that he'd want to preserve what he could. But still. Maybe it was just his chipper, over-eager demeanor that put her off.

She turned, leaving him behind to talk with the person he'd snagged and headed toward the front of house. When she pushed through the open doors, she glanced at Toby and Tessa. Tessa had the phone plastered to her ear, patiently answering questions about a tour and Toby sat at the computer, scrolling something. "Everything good up here?" Olivia asked.

Toby glanced up and nodded to her. "Oh, hey. Yeah, we're cool. Just working."

"Great." Olivia shot them a smile. "I'm going to go check on Skylar for a bit."

Toby nodded. "Sounds good, she'll appreciate it. I'll let you know if we need something."

Olivia slipped inside the gift shop, realizing she hadn't been inside this part of the museum yet. She took a moment to glance around at the various iconic paintings and artworks being sold as keychains, cups, pictures, postcards, and tiny stuffed animals. Wind chimes hung from the ceiling, tinging a sweet sound. The shop was rather inviting, and if Skylar was in charge of keeping it organized and not just the cashier, she was doing a fine job.

Olivia waltzed up to the counter where Skylar sat. She had slid open the doors to the cupboard that formed the counter, and both of her feet were tucked inside. The book on gemstones that Olivia had spotted in her locker lay open on her knees as her eyes scanned the page. "Hey, Skylar."

Skylar jumped and looked up rapidly before breathing a sigh of relief. "I'm sorry."

"No... *I'm* sorry. I didn't mean to startle you." Olivia cooed gently as she stepped forward and leaned on the counter.

Skylar shook her head. "No, I've just been really jumpy lately. It's not your fault. Toby has jump-scared me twice, until I yelled at him to stop. So I appreciate you being sensitive."

"Of course." Olivia leaned on the counter. "Hey, speaking of, I never got a chance to ask how you were doing. It must've been pretty scary, you know. What you went through the last couple of days. Are you doing okay?"

Skylar glanced down and studied the book, smoothed open on her lap. She ran a flat palm across the page and nodded. "You see it on TV all the time, you know?" She began in a monotone. "You know, people getting killed and the bl..." she gagged on the rest of the word and swallowed. "You think you're ready to see it in real life, but when it actually happens..." she sighed. Her head shook back and forth, and she couldn't meet Olivia's gaze. "I just can't get that image out of my head. Dorian lying there. He was always such a gentle guy, you know?" She finally looked up, and her eyes moistened with tears she hadn't shed.

Olivia nodded, humming softly under her breath. "I know."

Skylar sniffed and looked away, but not before a juicy tear rolled down her face. "I'm sorry. I know you don't know me, and here I am, dumping all this," she waved her hand, "stuff on you."

Olivia shook her head. Somehow, this reminded her of when she had connected with the teenagers in South Carolina. She remembered Susanna, how the mature seventeen-year-old had opened up to Olivia along with her friend, Mae. Was this another one of those moments where she could find a way to connect with a witness?

Olivia was chasing the trail of the case, but right now, it mattered more to her that Skylar was okay. She decided to kill two birds with one stone and shifted her place on the counter. "I remember the first time I ever saw a dead body."

Skylar glanced over at her, her eyes wide with amazement. "You saw a dead body before?"

"Oh, yes." Olivia wasn't about to tell her that it was a dime a dozen every time she stepped out the door. "Being a security guard doesn't always mean that you don't see tough stuff, especially growing up in the city." She sighed, letting a far-off look come into her eyes. "I was young. First starting out on the job." FBI Agent, security guard, did it matter? The feelings would have been the same. "I thought I could take it, you know? Being all tough and weathered against the stuff you know you'd see in a job."

Skylar nodded, understanding dawning in her eyes.

"But then I came around the corner and saw him. It was the lifelessness that got to me, you know?" She pressed her fingertips together as if somehow she could show what his soul had once looked like, dancing on the peaks of her fingers. "The fact that he was human, but he wasn't moving, wasn't breathing. Just staring lifelessly up. It unnerved me, not going to lie."

"It's unnatural." Skylar hung her head low to look again at her book. She was quiet for a long time, then quietly asked, "How did you cope with it?"

Her quiet voice nearly broke Olivia's heart. This poor girl had no idea what she had seen or how to process it. "I saw things I couldn't forget. His face, mostly. At night, it would flash in my head like he was still alive, or something. I used to think that if I shut stuff like that out, it'd make me cold. Harden me. But it's actually the opposite. The more I let it eat me, the less useful I was. So I focused on some things that reminded me that life goes on. Farm animals, for instance. I'd picture chickens pecking and scratching the ground. Horses running in the pasture. Puppies, kittens. I'd acknowledge what I'd seen, and how it was awful. Then move on."

Skylar looked up and locked onto Olivia's eyes, listening intently. She had the girl's attention now.

"I learned from some research that I did how redirecting your thinking can make a huge difference," Olivia went on. "Don't ignore it. You never forget what you saw, and pretending it didn't happen is the worst thing you can do. But you can't let it get you down, either. Sometimes, for me, writing about things helped. As long as I burned it afterwards."

She shared a tiny laugh with Skylar.

"Do you have someone you can talk to about it that you trust?" Olivia asked, making it personal. "It's okay to talk about it, you know."

Skylar shook her head. "Not really. My mom and I aren't on the best terms. We live together but she and I haven't been close since she left my dad and gained custody of me. I have friends, but they're mostly Tessa and Toby and their friend group. And the last thing I wanna do is talk to them about… this."

"You're all pretty close, huh?"

Skylar nodded. "Yep." She sighed.

Olivia chose her words wisely. She leaned closer, then asked in a hushed tone. "Do you wanna talk about it or talk about something else? Because I can start talking about any number of random things if you want to."

Skylar bit her lower lip and shook her head. "There isn't much to say, really. I was trying to get a hold of Dorian all day because the shelf of snow globes broke. Thank goodness they're all plastic." She pointed where she had two studs of wood propping up a shelf with two or three snow globes on it. "When he wasn't answering, at the end of the day, I thought his battery on his radio was dead or something. So I went downstairs to look for him, and when I came around the corner," she bit her lip. "He was just… lying there."

Olivia studied Skylar for a few moments. Not wanting to cause her to break down at work, she reached across and tapped the space between them to bring her point home. "Skylar, listen. What you saw would scare anybody. It's not your fault."

Skylar sniffed. "Are you a mind reader?"

The corners of Olivia's lips lifted in a smile. "Just good at reading people and knowing what goes through their minds. See, I want to be more than," she lifted her nightstick, then let it fall back down to tap her leg, "this. A security guard with no name except one for Nick to rave over because it has historical significance."

That tickled a laugh out of Skylar. "Try having the last name *Gray*."

"I'm so sorry," Olivia laughed with her for a few moments before growing serious again. "So I study people. I know what goes through a lot of people's heads. I remember what went through mine when I saw my first D…" Did she really almost say *DB*? The shortened version of *dead body*? Dead giveaway, is what that was. "The deceased person. I had this strange feeling that I was somehow responsible, even though I knew nothing about it twenty-four hours earlier. You just gotta remember that it's just that. A feeling."

Skylar's lips slowly broke into a smile. "You don't think I'm crazy?"

"Crazy?" Olivia straightened from her position on the counter and tossed her hand in the air. "Girl, you experienced something traumatic and still came to work and are killing it a few days later! You're here, you showed up, and that shows that you have more resilience than I did when I was your age." Not entirely true, but Skylar didn't need to know that. "If anything, I think that speaks volumes to your character. No, I don't think you're crazy. I think you're human."

Skylar beamed. "I hope you stick around for a long time, Ms. Knight. Thanks for talking to me like I'm a person."

"You *are* a person." Olivia leaned closer and let her smile take over her face. "Hey, listen. You're doing great. But if you need me, I'll be around. Okay?"

"Thank you again." Relief flooded Skylar's tone.

"Skylar was terrified over what happened with Dorian." Olivia walked briskly beside Brock, later that night. It had been his idea to walk around the block where the hotel was for some regular exercise. Not that they didn't walk around the museum a million times a day. At least they could do it with some fresh air this time.

"I can imagine she was," Brock said. "She's only, what, twenty?"

"Something like that." Olivia sipped her water as she walked. "Slow down, would ya? I worked all day."

"And I didn't?" Brock snickered, but slowed his pace.

"You were hanging out in the break room all day." Olivia rolled her eyes.

"No, I wasn't! I only went down there a few times! And I was scoping the place out! Do you know that Simon and Graham hardly ever come out of their offices?"

"M-hm, listen to you changing the subject! How would you know that if you weren't down there the whole time?" Olivia shot him a teasing glance and sipped more of her water.

Brock glared playfully at her. "Well, at least I wasn't having girl talk the whole time, either. Did you talk about your favorite shade of mascara?"

"I think you're thinking of *eye shadow,* and no, we just talked about guys."

"Should have known."

"So it's true, though, that they hardly ever come out?" Olivia asked, slowing her pace to be more even with his.

"Hardly ever. That's not to say they don't, though. But it would explain why they didn't notice that Dorian was dead."

"You'd think one of them would notice that there's a man lying face down, bleeding. Not that they could have helped him, but still." Olivia stopped in front of the hotel and looked up at the building. It always seemed like the tall buildings were slowly falling over with the backdrop of the moving clouds behind them. Or was she just tired? Something else snagged her attention. "Wait a minute. Darren said that one of the reasons that an outsider stealing the jewel during the day was impossible was that Simon and Graham come and go from their offices. You said they hardly come out."

"Maybe they were just overloaded with work for the day?" Brock suggested. "I don't know, Olivia."

Olivia chewed her lower lip in thought. She needed to see what they were working with. Touch it. Feel it. "Do you want to piece this together again? Like we did in Cape Fremont?"

"What, that wall art you did?" Brock chuckled.

Olivia nodded. "I need to see a visual." She spread out her hand as if she could already see it.

Brock glanced back up at the room. "Let's try it. It wouldn't hurt to see what we have to work with."

CHAPTER TWENTY-TWO

"LET'S START WITH OPPORTUNITY."

Olivia stood in front of the wall where she had gently taped up index cards with all the information on her suspects. "Who had the opportunity to get to Dorian?"

"Are we talking Dorian's murder or the missing jewel here?" Brock sat back on the footstool and examined Olivia's masterpiece.

"Both. I think it's related. It… technically might not be. But while we might be looking at it too hard, it helps to examine from every angle."

Brock nodded. "Okay, I follow."

"Right. So here, we have," Olivia pointed to the index card with the receptionist's name on it, "Toby. He was the last person to see Dorian alive, as he went to go tell him that the paper towels were out. I saw him leave; he pushed past me. This was shortly before the tour group with the children came in."

"The most well-behaved ones," Brock chuckled.

"Oh, my gosh, I couldn't believe that! Some of those adults obviously have forgotten how to behave." Olivia loved the casual setting where she and Brock could pause to talk about a mutual amazement over something that happened before diving right back into it again. "But, yes. That one."

"That doesn't mean Toby's the killer. Even though he was the last one to see him alive." Brock shrugged. "Would he—or anyone—even have motive to take out the janitor on the busiest day of the week?"

"Not a good one, that's for sure." Olivia shook her head. "We'll circle back to him. Simon and Graham are downstairs all day with him. And I'm sorry, but I find it both sad and suspicious that neither one of them noticed he was dead. Simon had a meeting that day, so he had to walk by the closet to get to the upstairs. And Graham had to come out sometime."

"Their offices are very far back," Brock mentioned. "They're down the hall a bit."

"Still, they have to walk to the staircase, and the janitor's closet is a straight shot to the stairs." Olivia bit her lip. "One of them had to have noticed. And either they didn't say anything— which my question is, why? Or they weren't paying attention. Or maybe, they didn't want the janitor around anymore."

"And both of them, especially Graham, are people we're watching closely." Brock shifted positions. "Even though we have minimal evidence on both of them. Simon just has prime opportunity, and Graham had a pretty hefty tool in his locker. Neither of which are enough to pin anything more than wild theories on. The DA would laugh us out of the courtroom and have our badges for that evidence."

"But it's the little things that stack up." Olivia tapped her pencil against her lip. "The only other person known to have seen

Dorian the day he died was Skylar, and she found him. The time she found him also doesn't line up with his TOD. He was killed around 10:00 a.m.; she found him closer to 5:00. And believe me, Brock, she was rattled. She could be a really good actress and faking it, but I don't see her stabbing him in the heart. Which leads me to another thing. You don't just stab someone and walk away with no blood transfer on your clothes. So someone, somewhere, has to have blood on their clothes."

"What if they were wearing a raincoat and tossed it when they were done?" Brock suggested. "You said yourself the raincoats looked like they were moved. What if someone was not only hiding in them, but they were also using one as a disguise, too?"

Olivia hadn't even thought of that. She snapped her fingers and pointed at Brock. "That's right. We should check the trash cans tomorrow!"

"Oh, goody. I love dumpster diving." Brock rubbed his hands together. "But anyway, back to what we were talking about. Like you said. Simon and Graham are down there all the time with Dorian. They could have done it and gone back to work, and that's why no one noticed. The cameras aren't good at covering that portion of the downstairs. There's only one camera, and it points to the door. And it doesn't do a very good job of monitoring it, either."

"But all this is circling around Dorian's death. We haven't even mentioned the jewel yet, which is why we're holding this discussion in the first place. The FBI doesn't get called over the case of a deceased janitor unless something bigger is going on. So, that brings us back here." Olivia pointed to the middle card where she'd drawn a picture of a diamond. At least, tried to. It looked more like the doodle of a bored student trying to draw a mushroom cloud during a lecture, but hey. She tried. "So, let's talk about this diamond for a bit. What do we know about it so far?"

"We know that there weren't any scratches, scuff marks, or any signs of vandalism on the display case," Brock got up and moved toward the wall where he pointed to the diamond in the middle of Olivia's tree of evidence. "Which indicates that someone with access got to it. We know that there was sulfuric acid found on the scarf lining the bottom of the display case and that someone tampered with the footage and snuck in the back door on October 5th."

"So we're looking at someone with direct access. Someone with the keys to the display. Which eliminates," Olivia started pointing to each of the names taped up on her wall, "Skylar, Toby, Tessa, Nick, Dorian, and Darren. Darren's fingerprints were found on the case, but he helps push the displays back; he doesn't have the keys to it. Simon puts it away every night, and he also has keys to access it. So does Graham, and he knows what chemicals restore, so it's safe to say that he knows what chemicals can age a diamond up. So the possibility is there, too."

"What if it's not Graham at all?" Brock shrugged. "Someone could be trying to frame him. We've already established that the display case wasn't tampered with, so he wouldn't need that crown molding lifter. Maybe someone wanted the diamond for themselves, so they took it and then planted evidence in his locker. We don't know if he uses any of the chemicals needed to age the diamond, like the sulfuric acid. Besides, where would he get access to that stuff?"

"You need water and sulfur dioxide." Olivia sighed. "Which isn't something you can buy at your local supermarket."

"Exactly," Brock said.

"I suppose someone may be trying to frame him. But then again, who would that *someone* be? If we keep going at it like this, we'll have nothing but an infinite regress."

"Well, it's not infinite. *Someone* had to do it." Brock looked up at the wall display again and sighed. "You know what's terrible?"

"Hm?"

"Everyone on this wall has something against them."

Olivia knew about Simon and Graham. Even Elliot. Darren, with his access. "What about Ivy?"

"We don't know enough about her, other than she's the exhibit designer with direct access at all times." Brock settled back and turned to look at her. "She has an assistant with a record of petty theft and hacking. So it's not impossible for them to both be in on it."

"Good point. As for the rest, though, the staff of the front of house doesn't have access to the diamond. So while we can't rule them out, at least we can narrow things down to the most likely." At this point, Olivia felt like she was going around in circles and circling back to nowhere. She'd talked the evidence over with Brock... but she didn't feel like it amounted to anything this time.

"So, where do we go from here?" Brock's quiet voice burst into her thoughts. "Has your little wall of evidence helped you out in any way, shape, or form?"

Olivia sighed and bit her lower lip. Absentmindedly, she twisted her engagement ring on her left finger. Something about feeling the diamond spinning around her finger gave her a sense of grounding. Or was she just doing it idly while her thoughts did the same? She wasn't sure. Had any of this helped? Brock had asked her that, hadn't he? What could she say? No? Normally, her evidence tree helped her piece things together that she couldn't otherwise figure out. Sometimes it helped her visualize something she was missing. Not this time. This time, she had more questions than answers, and with a museum full of people who could have lifted the jewel at any time, she wasn't sure who to turn to first.

"Brock." She sighed. "I wasn't expecting this case to be this hard. And while I'm thrilled at the amount of information we have... I can't say I know what to do with it. I almost feel like it's too much information, because how do we work our way through the maze and get to the truth when there are just too many leads to follow? Too many hunches, too many possibilities!"

Brock pulled a move she wasn't expecting. He slipped his arms around her waist and drew her against him. "Will this help a bit?"

He breathed against her neck, and the warmth of his embrace sent her senses spiraling. "Well…" Her voice trailed off. "It's helping to distract me."

"Good." Brock waited for a few moments, then gently spun her around to face him. He gazed down into her eyes and smiled, all the contentment in the world shining from his face. "Sometimes you need to stop thinking about one thing and think about something else entirely. That's usually when the answer comes to you."

"Really?" Olivia lifted her chin to meet his gaze. "What would you suggest? You know I can't turn my brain off when it's working on something."

"I know." Brock grinned at her. Slowly, he leaned forward and touched his lips to hers. She savored the feel of his kiss for a few moments before he gently pulled back. "But the museum's not going anywhere. Nor are the suspects."

"You don't know that," Olivia countered. "The jewel could be halfway across the world in some trafficking distribution ring right now, and another employee could wind up dead…"

Brock placed another kiss on her lips, sealing off any words from bubbling to the surface. When he pulled back, his eyes danced with delight. "And you picking this thing to pieces won't stop any of that from happening, especially if we're as in the dark as we are now. So why not take my suggestion and think about something else for a while?"

Olivia fought the urge to sigh. The exhale died on her tongue as she gazed into his eyes and realized that no matter what, they were together. This was the love of her life; he was working with her to solve a case, and this time, they weren't working shoulder-to-shoulder like they normally did. Brock was usually off in a different part of the museum, and she was off in hers. She interacted with more people than she normally did in a natural setting. While she wasn't thrilled about it, it did give her something to think about.

"You know, the good thing about all of this?"

"What's that?" He planted a kiss on her jawline.

"We don't work together every single day, and it just reminds me how grateful I am to come back to you every night. Nothing compares to this."

His eyes lit up as he studied her. A slow series of nods began. "I feel the same way."

What was he thinking? He locked her into a gaze, the depths of his eyes indicating that he was pondering something harder than she'd been pondering the case. "You're stressed."

"What makes you think that?"

"You were twisting your ring earlier. I notice you always do that when you're stressed."

Olivia released an exhale harder than she intended to. "It's not that I'm afraid of running out of time or anything."

"Then what is it?" His fingertips gently touched the underside of her chin and drew her gaze up to meet his once more. She couldn't hide anything from him. He knew her so well.

Olivia didn't want to move. She felt it would shatter the way this made her feel. Putting the case aside, even for a few stolen glances in his eyes, helped her remember what was important. "I don't know."

He was quiet for a long time. There was something healing about his silence. When he spoke again, his voice was gentle, resonant. "I have an idea."

"We have work tomorrow!" Olivia protested as Brock pulled away from their hotel and turned the car up one of the side streets.

"I'm aware of that." Brock nodded as he drove quietly along.

"When I agreed to whatever your idea was, spending an all-nighter outside was not in the cards!" Olivia wasn't sure if she was joking or if she really was protesting her lack of sleep.

"Since when have you let a sleepless night stop you from taking on the world?"

Olivia clamped her jaw shut. "Touché."

"That's what I thought. This will only take as long as you want it to. Trust me, Olivia."

Olivia sat back in her seat and huffed a sigh. "Fine, fine."

Brock chuckled. "You act like you don't trust my ideas."

She had to laugh. At least, a little bit. Why was she being testy, anyway, when he'd been nothing but sweet to her? "Well. Some of them can get a little radical. Forgive me for being," she hesitated, searching for the right word, "apprehensive."

"You'll like this one. At least, I hope you will. If you don't, I'm turning in my badge tomorrow and becoming a hermit in the woods."

"Wow." Olivia breathed a laugh through her nose. "So dramatic…"

The city lights dimmed, and darkness grew around them. Under the cover of a waning gibbous, the world seemed darker, but somehow, more inviting. "So, where exactly are we going?"

Brock turned onto a road that noted something about a scenic route. That was all well and good… if it was light enough to see what was on the scenic route, itself! "You'll see."

"You keep saying that."

"Because you keep asking me," Brock grinned. "Just relax and you'll see in a little bit!"

He drove along the route a little bit. Olivia felt the car lift in elevation after a few curves until Brock finally pulled to the side. He killed the engine and switched off his lights. Then, casually unbuckled his seatbelt. "Watch your step."

He opened his door and stepped out.

Olivia blinked. "So he takes me out in the middle of nowhere at nearly midnight, and then leaves, like it's an everyday thing." Sometimes she loved him. Correction: she always loved him.

Sometimes she was just reminded of why.

She stepped out of the car and looked up, catching her breath before she could lower her other foot to the ground.

Brock came around beside her and slipped an arm around her shoulders. "Beautiful, isn't it?"

Olivia looked up at the blanket of stars coating the night sky in a milky hue. Gentle starlight seemed to suck all the noise and distractions from her mind and cast it away somewhere else in the galaxy, leaving her only with a peace that hummed in her ears in the form of a gentle wind blowing. "It is."

"My dad and I used to come out and look at the stars sometimes when I was a kid," Brock explained softly. "I was always fascinated by it. It still gives me a sense of peace coming out to the middle of nowhere like this and just… watching the wonder of nature."

"You could have told me that this is where we were going, you know."

Brock chuckled. "How could I between all your incessant questions? It would've ruined the surprise."

"Thanks for that." Olivia laughed quietly. Anything louder would shatter the stillness of the night.

"So?" Brock tucked her against him, tighter. "Was it worth it?"

"Worth it?" Olivia turned to look at him. Could he see the gratitude in her eyes, or was her face a shadowy blur as the stars made up for the light? "I'm sorry I ever complained."

"I figured you needed some quiet. Your brain can be so loud sometimes, Olivia." Brock smoothed his free hand over her forehead and through her hair, releasing whatever leftover tension the stars had not dissolved.

"You know me so well." The only thing that would make this moment better?

This.

She leaned on his chest and looked up at the sky, trusting him to hold her upright and not let anything happen to her. For once, she didn't have to be Special Agent Olivia Knight. She could be Olivia. A girl who loved the man standing behind her, arms folded around her as she listened to the beating of his golden heart through his chest. They'd been through so much together. Moments like this were cherished treasures. They weren't getting shot at, teased, lured into a trap, solving a murder, wounded, held hostage... they were just existing and soaking in a beautiful night sky. Relishing in each other's warmth.

Olivia never wanted to leave.

After a while, Brock's voice hummed inside his chest. "I love you, Olivia."

"I love you, Brock."

"I know this was last minute, but..." he pulled away. She felt his fingertips under her chin again as she searched for his face in the starlight. "I wanted to remind us both of something."

"Hmm?" She hummed her approval. She loved it when they needed a reminder, if it led to something like this.

"We're going to be getting married someday. We have a future ahead of us that's separate from the FBI. Sure, it'll always be our job, but there's a part of our lives that's just ours. Just you, just me. We're buying a house together someday soon. Getting married. Starting our lives." His gentle fingers brushed her hair over her ear. "Sometimes I think we can both let our job—or whatever case we're working—get in the way. But we always find our way back to one another. We need to remember that."

Olivia felt chills running up and down her spine the way he spoke of their *future*. What more could she want? So what, this case was making her go a little crazy from all the leads she had to follow? She had Brock. Like he said, she always had him to come back to. Not only that, but by her side, supporting her as he had throughout their relationship. Olivia was more than happy to give back when he needed her to, as well.

"Thank you," she finally murmured up at him. "I needed that. And I needed this."

"So did I." He leaned forward and once more, kissed her under the starlight. His lips on hers felt so much more tender even than they did back at the hotel room. Was it the starlight that brought out the tenderness, or the fact that he'd brought her back to what mattered most? Their love, their story.

Olivia let him break the kiss when he wanted to, and his fingers traced along her jawline. "Sometimes I just look at you and I can't help myself but fall in love all over again," he said to her gently.

Words escaped Olivia. At least, she scrambled for something to say in response to that. "I always wanted someone who I could fall in love with every day. Who would do things like this to deepen that love. I'm just…" She slipped her arms around him and pressed herself to his chest. "I just need you. And love you. That's it. That's all I have to say."

Brock let the starlight speak for both of them as he folded her close, imparting some of his warmth to her as the October air threatened to steal their comfort. Together, they stood looking up at the Milky Way galaxy and the tiny specks of the satellites that traced their way across the midnight sky.

CHAPTER
TWENTY-THREE

O LIVIA WASN'T READY FOR WORK THE NEXT DAY. THE moment she'd shared with Brock the night before had brought both a sense of calm and contentment that had lingered even as she woke the next morning. He was already up, throwing some coffee together in the Keurig, but Olivia selfishly chose to take five minutes for herself, not to snooze but to replay her night with Brock over and over in her head. She longed for his touch and would have spent all day in that moment, but of course, she and Brock had a job to do.

Even as they went about getting ready and driving to the museum, Olivia held onto the feeling. She even felt calmer as she approached the front door of the museum at less than her usual brisk pace. "Um," she turned to him as they neared the stairs, and looked into his eyes. Rather than in the usual rush to start the day, she clung there for a few moments before letting a smile radiate. "I really don't want to say goodbye for the rest of the day."

"I'll be around." He winked at her.

"Yeah, but," she laughed, "I feel like a teenager, again, who doesn't want to say goodbye to her boyfriend before going to class or something."

"Well, then make sure that you have a ton of things to talk to me about tonight." Brock gently touched her fingertips and gave them a squeeze. Then he released her hand. "I love you."

"I love you. See you later."

She wanted to kiss him as he walked away, but the cameras were watching. The last thing she needed was to give the employees something else to gossip about. Two security guards, falling for each other? Olivia would proclaim it with pride, but she and Brock had decided not to broadcast their engagement, not even to Selena and Levi. Levi was intuitive; he probably already suspected that there were far more than sparks flying between them. But no one else needed to know.

Olivia took her time climbing the steps and entering the museum. The environment hummed with the usual noise for the day, and just like that, the moment from beneath the blanket of stars ebbed away. The peace she'd found still lingered, but was now joined by a sense of duty.

Tessa looked up from her desk as Olivia entered. "Good morning!" she greeted cheerfully. "You know you can go in the back door, right? You don't always have to come around front."

"I enjoy the walk." Olivia smiled as she walked up to her. "The trees are so beautiful this time of year."

"Aren't they?" Tessa grinned. "Well, it's whatever you want! I was just thinking it would save you a few steps."

"Thank you, but I think I'm okay. I walk around the museum all day, anyway. But I appreciate your concern."

Toby chose that moment to pop up from where he was behind the desk. "Fixed it! The switch was just turned off."

"Ugh." Tessa facepalmed and Toby laughed, looking toward Olivia to explain. "Tessa's computer wouldn't turn on. She had it plugged in and everything, but the switch to the power strip was off."

"Yeah, yeah, yeah." Tessa laughed.

"I've done that," Olivia said as she walked away. "Happens to the best of us!"

She paused briefly to wave at Skylar who stood in the doorway of the gift shop. "Hi, Olivia!"

"Morning, Skylar! How ya doing?"

"Much better, thanks to you!" Skylar gave her a thumbs-up.

"Glad to hear it!"

As she took the old familiar route to clock in, Olivia pondered how easy it was to see that the staff at the History of Art Museum was just like a family. They weren't like the usual coworkers who clocked in with groggy voices and bad attitudes every day. Despite the fact that one of them was likely a thief, they all seemed to be pretty decent people. It wasn't every day that young adults like Tessa and Skylar got along with older people like Simon or Graham. And, of course, there was Nick thrown in there who could get along with any age group if he tried hard enough.

Olivia took the stairs in stride and paused briefly to look up the hall at Dorian's closet. Would it hurt if she paused just to peek inside? She looked up the hallway, seeing no one was watching her, and walked over to the closet. She flicked on the switch and let a sigh ripple through her. She surveyed every corner of the closet from where she stood. The chalk line and blood evidence had long been removed, the blood stain bleached as best as it could be. Levi had said something about replacing the floor just so that the reminder wasn't here anymore, but of course, they'd have to wait until Selena pulled through her coma to make any decisions. Levi was doing a fine job in her absence, but Olivia still wondered if the museum would survive without Selena. It also struck her as oddly ironic. The highest position and the lowest position of the museum—the curator and the janitor—were both the ones who were taken out. It was like parentheses surrounding the case that brought her and Brock here. She wondered if that meant something, some cruel, hidden message.

She turned off the light and left the closet, meeting Brock on his way out the back door. "Hey," he murmured to her and held up a pair of gloves in one hand, a trash bag in the other. "I'm going dumpster diving. Want me to see if I can find a burger or something in there for you for lunch?"

"Eww." She laughed. "After the nice, romantic night we had last night, you're going to ask me a thing like that?" She kept her voice low and cast a glance around the employee-only area.

Brock aimed a boyish grin at her and started walking away. "Gotta keep you guessing."

She huffed a sigh that buzzed her lips. "How delightful."

Brock snickered as he left the area, closing the door behind him. Olivia sighed and started toward the employee break room again, playfully rolling her eyes before assuming a more neutral face.

Graham was raiding the fridge and Simon sat at the break room table, going over something on a piece of paper in his hands. "Hey, guys," Olivia greeted cheerfully.

"What's going on, Knight?" Graham closed the door and poured himself some orange juice. "There's juice in here. Levi hit the reduced bin at the store last night. Keeping us stocked with healthy stuff to get us through, I guess."

"I'll take some!" An eager young voice called out behind Olivia as Elliot skipped into the room ahead of Ivy.

Olivia went to the machine and observed everyone as she worked to clock in. "I'm okay, Graham, but thank you."

"You're like me." Ivy smiled as she reached for a bottle of water. "I'd rather have something with a lid on it."

"That and I'm ready to get to work." Olivia finished clocking in and turned to Ivy. "Am I in your way?"

"No, I've been here since eight. I'm just taking my lunch with Elliot." She rolled her eyes, but a hint of a smile played on her thin red lips. "I'm not getting anything done in the classroom, but that's okay. Winter break is coming up in December."

"Oh, you're a teacher?" Olivia already knew, but she didn't want Ivy to catch onto that.

Ivy nodded. "Chemistry."

"And the best teacher around, eh, Miss Landon?" Elliot looked over at Olivia. The shy boy only spoke up when it came to something he was familiar with. "Miss Landon was my high school chemistry teacher, and she got me the job here as her assistant. I didn't know what to do with my life after I graduated, so she helped me with that."

Olivia hesitated for a moment. "Hey, Graham, do you have any of that orange juice left? I realized I'm feeling a little shaky." She faked a laugh. "Must've been the pastries I ate this morning."

"Sure thing, honey." Graham poured her a solo cup and handed it to her. Olivia took the time to ponder what Elliot had said. Ivy had gotten Elliot the job at the museum? Did she know about his record? Surely there wasn't something... else going on between teacher and student, was there? Memories of the case she and Brock worked in South Carolina flashed across her mind.

"Thanks." She thanked Graham and took her juice. "Well, that's awesome, Elliot. Are you thinking you want to stay in the museum world forever?"

"I don't know yet." Elliot shook his head. "I didn't do so well in school, but Miss Landon said that she can help me get a good job. So she's training me to be her assistant."

"Elliot's the best assistant I could've asked for." Ivy sent him a smile as she sipped her water. "He's learned so much since he started working with me."

Elliot looked down as his sudden burst of courage slowly dissolved in the face of Ivy's compliment.

"How long have you been juggling two jobs?" Olivia asked Ivy.

Ivy's eyes searched the ceiling. "I've been a teacher since I was twenty-four. I started working here when I was twenty-six, so going on seven years, now."

"What made you decide to do both?" Olivia kept her conversation natural.

"For many reasons, actually." Ivy's voice always remained calm no matter what they were talking about. "One is obviously for financial stability. Selena and I go way back after we worked on a project together. She reached out to me asking a few chemistry questions. That, and I've always been good at organizing and being an event planner. I tried it, it clicked, so I decided to do that in addition to teaching, both here and at a few other local museums. I need something quiet after being in the classroom all day, you know?"

"I understand perfectly." Olivia smiled as she sipped her drink.

Nick chose that moment to come bursting into the room, all smiles as always. "There's our honorary Nancy Drew!"

Olivia stopped sipping her drink slowly and took her time setting her cup down. "Nancy Drew?"

"Why, yes! I hear that you're doing some looking into things, on top of all your guard duties!"

Olivia froze. While she was using that as her cover, she didn't exactly want it broadcast, either. "How did you hear about that?"

"Word travels fast."

"Nancy Drew?" Ivy looked at Olivia with confusion.

Nick answered for her. "Olivia here, is wondering if she can solve the case of the missing Ratnashree diamond!"

Wow, Darren, thanks for keeping my confidence. Olivia decided to own up to it, rather than acting guilty. "What can I say? I'm like you, Ivy. I like to do two things at once. Besides, being a security guard is only my first step. I was hoping to break out of this," she swept her hand down the length of her side, "uniform and try to be something more."

Ivy studied her for a few moments with an unreadable expression, then lowered her eyes to her bottle of water. "I wish you luck. Sadly, that diamond is probably long gone by now. You don't just steal something and keep it around."

Her proclamation brought the mood down severely. Uncomfortable in the face of the sudden silence, Ivy shook her head and waved her hand. "But don't listen to me. Chemistry is yes and no, black and white. Life rarely operates like that, but I will admit that it's turned me into something of a cynic. Don't mind me." She grabbed a Sharpie off the counter and uncapped it, scribbling her name to label her water bottle. Something, Olivia had noticed, she'd done with every bottle she'd grabbed.

"We don't mind you, Ivy." Nick grinned at her. "You're the best exhibit designer in the world! How can we be upset with you? You do such amazing work, we're lucky to have you. And you, too, Elliot."

Elliot smiled, tight-lipped.

Nick clocked out for his lunch and flung himself down at the table. "So, Lady Knight. I can't say *Sir* Knight, you know." He beamed up at her. "Discovered any clues yet?"

"No, unfortunately, not yet." Olivia finished her juice and tossed the cup. Brock entered the room with a disgusted look on his face and headed straight for the faucet to wash his hands. Olivia itched to ask if he discovered anything. "But if you hear anything of use, let me know, would you? Just don't tell Levi! I don't want him thinking I'm shirking my duties in my quest for grandeur!" She added a laugh that brought the mood up as Graham and Nick joined her.

Nick slapped an open palm on the table. "Of course! I love this stuff. I can't believe this is happening in our own museum! This is just like the Star of India jewel heist from 1964!"

Whoa. Olivia paused, wondering if the world had stopped or if Nick's statement had been so startling that it felt like it did. She noticed Brock pause in washing his hands, tuning an ever-attentive ear to what Nick was saying. "You know about the Star of India heist?" Olivia admitted she needed to brush up on the details, but it was one of the greatest American jewel heists in history. If not, the greatest.

"Of course I do!" Nick adjusted himself at the table, cleared his throat, and began. "So it was October 29th, right? These three beach boys from Miami, Roger Clark, Allan Dale Kuhn, and Jack Roland Murphy, also known as," he made air quotes, "'Murph the Surf,' head over to the Museum of Natural History in New York. While they're there scoping out the place, they realize that security is basically non-existent! The alarms don't work, the museum isn't well guarded, and the windows are always open. So they can't help themselves, right? So they have a lookout driving a white Caddy around town while they hop a fence and sneak through the fire exit. They use the fire exit to get to a rope, which they use to hook onto a pillar by an open window on the fourth floor."

Olivia cast a look toward Brock, who was in the process of drying his hands, his back to Nick. The way he tilted his head told Olivia that he was listening with as much intensity as she was. "Clever," she murmured. For once, she was grateful for the history lesson.

"They used duct tape and a glass cutter to breach the cases. They snatched three great jewels, including," Nick dropped his voice for dramatic effect, "*The Star of India*. It was the world's biggest sapphire. After the heist, they were worried they'd set off a silent alarm, so they went back the same way they got in and took separate getaway cars." He clapped his hands once with a flourish. "And that was the heist of 1964."

Nick told the story like he'd studied it more than anything else he spouted off. "Were they ever caught?" Olivia knew the basic details but was curious to see what Nick said about it.

"The authorities received a tip which said that there were guys in one of the rooms at a hotel near the museum who were spending money like they had a machine making it. The authorities found a book on precious gems and some marijuana and get this: a floor plan of the Museum of Natural History..."

"Fascinating," Olivia mused. She'd found a book on precious gems in Skylar's locker... coincidence?

"Nick," Graham held a warning note in his voice. He looked up at the young redhead with weary eyes. "Can you wrap this up a bit? Not all of us are on lunch and some of us have things we have to do."

"Right, right, right." Nick settled back. "Listen, I'll tell you what happened some other time. This whole investigation, it's amazing. The stuff movies are made of."

"It sure sounds like it." Olivia didn't bother to look at Brock, though she wanted to. She'd give anything to read his facial expression. Nick had basically laid out the *how, why,* and *when* of something that sounded eerily similar to their own jewel heist, with a few differences. The jewels were both from India. A book of precious gems found, in both cases. And they were both lifted during the month of October.

"Well, I need to go grab some lunch. Anyone want anything from Cruizers down the street?"

"No, thank you. I need to get to work." Olivia started toward the locker room to retrieve her badge and nightstick. Brock kept his back to her, only to send a small glance at her over his shoulder. Olivia caught his meaning as she left the room.

"Oh, you know what, I forgot my badge, too. I swear if my head wasn't screwed on."

Good. She itched to talk to him. Olivia took her time getting her things together and waited until Brock joined her in the room. "Nick sure seems to know a lot about that jewel heist from 1964." He kept his voice low, barely audible for Olivia to hear.

She slipped her badge over her neck. "I know. Unnervingly so." She adjusted the nightstick on her belt. "Do you think that we're dealing with a copycat here?"

"I was wondering that same thing." Brock slipped his badge over his neck and sprang from the room. "But our heist was clean. There was no glass cutting or broken display cases involved."

"But he knew how they got in." Olivia threw a glance out the door. Her mind buzzed. What if someone had used a fire escape? Climbed through a window that the security cameras may not have reached? It would explain why they never saw anyone re-enter the museum. The mild conversation gave Olivia food for thought, and let the sweet nothings of last night slip away.

"We can't talk here," Brock's voice was still low. "Meet me in the security room tonight. We'll go over all this there. We have some things to look for now."

"Be safe out there." Olivia adjusted her badge and left the room. She glanced one more time at Nick in the break room. Should she be keeping a closer eye on him? Did he have access to the cameras? Did he use a fire escape?

Was he a copycat?

Olivia reviewed everything she knew about him. How he monitored everything that went on in the museum, down to the habits of every employee. This was proven when he'd come to Olivia about Skylar.

She hasn't been eating much.

How else would he know that? He hadn't given her an entirely satisfactory answer when she asked why he monitored the museum staff so intently. Sure, it was his work family, but not even Selena watched that closely.

Olivia went about her day, eager for the time that everyone went home so she and Brock could piece this thing together.

When the day finally drew to a close, Olivia practically ran up to the security room and plopped down next to Brock who – not surprisingly – was already at the monitors. "Find anything?"

"Just Nick being Nick. Wandering around the morning of October 5th, talking to patrons and doing most of his work in the afternoon."

"I think if we are dealing with Nick as our suspect, we're not going to catch him on camera." Olivia pushed her hand through her hair. "He knows the inner workings of this museum better than Selena does. And he also knows a lot about a certain jewel heist, too. So, tell me." A grin worked its way onto her face. "Do you remember where the fire escapes are?"

"Darren showed us that as part of the tour. We have two." Brock pointed to each of the cameras. "The one where the camera angle is pointed at the wall in the employee-only area, right by the janitor's closet."

"M-hm." Olivia leaned back. "And the door did open and close the night of the diamond theft. But whoever was sneaking around would have a hard time getting upstairs and across the museum floor without triggering the laser alarms."

"Exactly. So the other one," Brock pointed to the screen, "is off the wall from the Hall of Vases."

Olivia chewed on her lower lip in thought. "Have we ever looked at that one?"

"Just during the tour."

Olivia took a moment to think. What if that's where Nick— or whoever the thief was— entered the museum? Was it even possible to get to the museum from there? Olivia decided her questions would be better answered if she saw it in person. She straightened to her feet. "I want to take a trip to the Hall of Vases. Care to join me?"

"Sure." Brock stood and followed her. Olivia strode with purpose toward the hall and quietly entered. She scanned the room before spying a door marked *Emergency Exit Only*. The door was tucked back behind the pathway that led through the vases, near the back of the room. Olivia examined it, sweeping the ground for any signs of someone being there, but any evidence would have been long gone by now.

"I know what you're thinking," Brock said. "If the thief used this fire exit, they would have had a hard time getting past the alarm. The one downstairs doesn't have any alarms rigged to it because it's just an exit, but this one does. The laser system goes across the hall and there are cameras in this room. So it would be impossible to sneak in through the fire exit here just by opening the door alone."

Brock was right. Olivia nodded in thought as she took slow steps toward the "Hey, Brock? I have an idea. Can you disable the fire alarm on this door from the security room?"

"I should be able to."

Olivia pulled her radio out and held it up for him to see. "Let's communicate like this. I'm going to take a peek and see what it looks like outside. I've only been out there once."

Brock nodded. "You got it." He turned and headed back toward the security room.

Olivia looked the door up and down, curious where it would turn out. After what felt like an hour went by, her radio finally crackled. "Breaker, breaker, testing one-two, sending copy, do you read me, over?"

Olivia held it to her mouth. "I don't think that's what they say, Brock."

He made fake static sounds with his mouth and triggered the call button several times. "Breaker copy to blue forty-two, open hailing frequencies. All systems go for launch, over."

She couldn't help but laugh. "Seriously, Brock. English."

"Try the door, I disabled the alarm."

Olivia nodded and pushed the door open. She stepped out, her foot landing on a metal landing. She stepped all the way out, then looked as the fire escape zigzagged up the side of the museum in a zipper pattern. The landing where she stood had a set of stairs that led down to the ground below. The stairs that led up the side of the building, however, were connected to the landing only by an extendable ladder. Olivia examined the unit as a blast of chilly autumn air hit her. She held her radio to her mouth. "Can you see me on camera?"

"Yes," Brock confirmed.

Olivia's eyes traced the fire escape to the top floor. Each time there was a landing, it had to lead to somewhere, right? "Hold on a second." She clipped the radio to her belt, then reached for the ladder on the level above her head. With a rusty creak, the ladder groaned in protest as she lowered it down far enough for her to climb.

"What are you doing?" She heard Brock's voice on the radio and ignored him. She turned, testing the durability of the ladder before starting to climb it to the second level.

"Olivia, what are you doing?" Brock called to her on the radio. "If you fall ..."

He didn't have to finish the warning sentence. Olivia was determined not to fall. *Here goes nothing.*

"This isn't part of the job description, Olivia."

Olivia climbed up the ladder until her head poked above the landing on the next level. She flattened her palm against the landing and pushed herself to her feet.

"Hey, what's going on? I'm not joking!" Brock still tried to get her attention on the radio. "Are you okay?"

Olivia clutched the rail with one hand and picked up her radio with the other. "I'm okay. I'm assuming that means you can't see me?"

"No, I can't. Where are you?"

"Second level of the fire escape." Olivia looked up. "I'm standing next to a brick wall right now, but I'm going to go up a few levels and see where this leads."

Silence on the other end. Did he disapprove? "Just be careful. This thing is probably older than half the stuff in this museum."

Olivia managed a laugh as she started to climb the stairs to the next level. "I doubt that. Not unless it was made in the first century."

"I don't like this, Olivia."

"Don't worry about me!" She laughed. "I'll be fine."

"Sure you will."

She clipped the radio to her belt and clung to the handrail as she went up. She moved with ease up the staircase, turning around twice to climb to the second level until she got to one a little higher than where she was at first. The landing sat right next to a window.

"Hey, Brock?" She dug out her radio again. "Can you see me at all?"

More static, but his answer was quick. "No, I can't. Where are you?"

"I'm in front of a window. I didn't go up very far. Can you find which one?"

"I'm on my way."

"I'm standing right outside of it. You can't miss me."

Olivia waited for a few minutes until Brock's face appeared in the window, stricken with worry and maybe some slight annoyance. He raised the window without any trouble and leaned out. "Are you out of your mind? You could have fallen and gotten hurt, or killed."

Olivia grinned at him. "Brock. That was easy. All it took was climbing some stairs. Now. Where are you right now?"

Brock sighed and rolled his eyes. He muttered something about "crazy woman" before looking around. "Selena's office."

Olivia's eyes rounded. The escape led them to the curator's office? No wonder she wasn't on camera. "No. Really?"

"Really. Oh, and get this." Brock leaned forward. "Her window was open. It wasn't locked."

Olivia stood on the landing for a long time. She glanced down at the maze of stairs that twisted up the side of the building. "I guess I hadn't realized her office was up so high."

"I noticed the floor that leads to her office is something of a ramp. It took us up a second floor, I guess."

Olivia chewed her lip in thought. "So. Selena has a jungle gym outside her window that any brave soul can get to via her fire escape. All they'd need to do was grab a ladder and climb to the level that I did, and they wouldn't be on camera. You lost me when I got to the first level, right?"

Brock nodded. "As you were climbing the ladder."

"An open window with no cameras. Selena's office leads to the front of house, where you can get to the security room without tripping the alarm system. Brock... I think I found out how our thief got inside. It wasn't the downstairs door. It was here."

Brock's annoyance with her little climb faded into deep thought. "Nick would think to use the fire escape."

"And just a random thought, but he knows a lot about Skylar. A few days after the museum opened after Dorian's death, Nick came to me and said she wasn't eating." Olivia bit her lip. "How would he notice a little detail like that? Maybe he was singling her out, especially for the purpose of either framing her or working together? We found a book on precious gems in her locker."

"Just like in the story." Brock looked around once more, then returned his gaze to her. "What if Nick is a copycat? The only difference is, the thieves in 1964 took advantage of a security error."

"What if the security error is one *they* made?" Olivia shrugged. "The display cases in 1964 had no alarms. Nick could have disabled the alarms himself."

"But does he have the know-how to do *that*?" Brock asked aloud. He and Olivia both stood in silence for a few moments until he sighed. "You're onto something. Even if you risked your life to get here."

"Thanks." Olivia grinned, winningly. "Now, can you help me through the window so I don't have to climb back down?"

"Oh, no." Brock shook his head and laughed. "You got yourself into this mess." He reached up to close Selena's window. "You can get yourself out."

"What? No! Brock, I..."

He shut the window.

"Brock!"

He cracked the window again. "Oh, I'm sorry, did you say something?"

Olivia playfully glared at him through slits in her eyes. "Jerk."

CHAPTER
TWENTY-FOUR

F OR A SUNDAY, THE MUSEUM HUMMED AND BUZZED WITH regular weekday chaos as it came alive with the preparation for the Pompeiian exhibit. The crew kicked the work into full gear, calling in some extra help. Darren, Olivia, and Brock mostly kept to the main exhibit hall. Elliot had learned to drive the crane—which certainly drew a nervous crowd— and was working to move it from the back of the upstairs vault to the main exhibit hall.

Olivia learned that near the end of October, the staff took an extra Sunday to move everything into place. It was better to do it when the museum was closed, so the staff didn't have to work around the patrons who usually crowded the exhibit hall.

Simon and Graham were even there, working to help put the murals they'd received from Victor Sterling and also from a few other local areas on display. Ivy and Selena were right. There was something hauntingly inspiring about the art discovered at Pompeii. As Graham and Simon occupied the bucket of the crane, they worked to hang the mural on loan to them by Victor Sterling. Olivia studied it. It was a long rectangle that looked like it could occupy the main hallway of a villa somewhere. The people it depicted were all dressed, thank goodness. Olivia knew that some of the murals in that era might not be socially acceptable to display these days.

The mural showcased a table, filled on one side with people draped in togas and tunics. One man faced a woman whose hair was done up in an elegant braid and a sweeping bun at the back of her head. Her arm was angled upward, the veil of her toga falling off her upper arm in a graceful position and her fingers curled in feminine grace. Her face was even gentle as she gazed upon the face of the man she was conversing with, who pulsed strength and intelligence in his gaze. But, sadly, some of the bottom was stained by about two inches and the edges and corners were eroded away. The gentle woman and strong-looking man remained untouched by whatever age or chemical had damaged the bottom of the mural, but Olivia bemoaned the fact that it had been damaged at all.

"It has never ceased to amaze me." Ivy came up beside Olivia, joining her to gaze at the artwork. Her gentle face took in every single detail, eyes probably examining every brush stroke of the artist. "How the painters and artists back then were so good at depicting a person's character. Look how intelligent he looks."

"I know it," Olivia remarked, slowly nodding. "Some actors today can't even pull off those facial expressions if they haven't spent their lives studying like these men did."

"And with intelligence, character. It's like they had a snapshot camera."

Nick shouldered up beside Olivia and she caught herself glancing at him. He also studied the painting with awe and delight. Now Olivia had to wonder if there was something else behind his studying, as well. *"The Wedding of Caecillius,"* he announced, pronouncing the name like a true Latin speaker with hard *k* sounds for the *c*s and a long *e* for the *i*. "Painted in AD 68 by Areleus Lucius as a gift for his son Caecillius on his wedding day."

"Who was the bride?" Olivia asked. Somehow she figured Nick would know.

Of course he did. Off the top of his head as if his brain were an encyclopedia rather than high-functioning grey matter. "Her name was Lucretia. Caecillius wrote her poetry, describing her as the fairest maiden in Pompeii. She was the daughter of a vineyard owner."

"A vineyard owner, eh?" Simon called down from the crane's bucket. "I bet they had a heck of a wedding, then."

"I'm sure they did." Nick laughed. "The painting was excavated in, what, 1840, Ivy?"

"Correct." Ivy nodded. "Graham, I think we need to center it more." She called out.

Graham nodded, then returned to his work, assisted by Simon to help him center it.

"What happened to it?" Brock asked as he passed by.

Ivy drew in a breath through her nose. "Caecillius had a *horto…*"

"Oh!" Nick interrupted with a raised hand jutted into the air. "That's Latin for *garden.*"

Ivy closed her eyes. A small sigh escaped her nose as her lips pressed together in a half smile. Olivia wasn't sure if she was more annoyed at Nick's classic interruptions, or the fact that she was mixing Latin with English out of habit. "Right. Garden. Caecillius had a garden inside his atrium which was all open and exposed to the elements. He had the mural of his wedding painted on the side of the garden leading into the villa so his guests could see it and he could remember every time he walked into the villa from the garden. Well, with a roof that was all exposed to the elements, when Vesuvius erupted, the atrium had no protection from the eruption or the acid rain. However, when everything crumbled, it was sealed almost airtight under all the rubble. So the rest of the mural was practically perfectly preserved."

Olivia nodded along as Ivy spoke until something snagged her attention. "Acid rain did this?"

Acid rain. Sulfuric acid. The same thing they'd found on the silk under the diamond? This time, she actually did exchange a glance with Brock.

Ivy nodded.

"How does that work?" Brock asked.

"Sulfuric acid is just what it sounds like – acid. When a volcano erupts, it releases a mixture of gasses, mostly water vapor H_2O and CO_2. But also sulfur dioxide, SO_2. That SO_2 rises up into the atmosphere and reacts with water vapor to form sulfuric acid. Once that forms in the clouds, gravity pulls it back down to earth, producing acid rain."

Ivy gestured to the mural. "It's not like the comic book kind of acid that eats through steel, but it does react with the minerals and pigments of the paint. Over time it erodes them, causing chemical breakdown or fading. And because this mural was in an open atrium, it had no protection from that kind of exposure. Especially the bottom half."

"That's so sad," Was all Olivia could think to say in the face of an entire chemistry lesson. Which she should have expected from a chem teacher. "This painting was probably his pride and joy, only to be ruined by the great disaster."

"What's even sadder is that Lucretia died in the eruption," Nick piped up.

Well, this turned heavy. Olivia shook her head. "The whole thing was a disaster."

"No one saw it coming," Graham sing-songed as he worked to put up a display rack on the wall for a different mural found in one of the bathhouses.

161

Brock nodded, staring at the mural. "Can you fix it?" He nodded to it, probably testing out Graham's knowledge of the chemicals in question.

Graham shook his head. "Not without damaging it further. It's like washing a quilt that's already coming apart. The whole thing could unravel. Best just to leave it alone."

Olivia was bursting at the seams by the time the displays were going up. Now that the fake diamond was nicely tucked away out of public view, the Pompeii exhibit became the focus of everyone's attention. Especially Olivia's.

"Did you hear the way Ivy was going on about sulfuric acid?" She asked rapid-fire to Brock once they were back in the hotel.

He nodded as he plopped down on the bed. "I did."

"You don't think …" Olivia's voice trailed off. "Ivy's a chemistry teacher, she knows about chemicals and she knew all about acid rain. The same components we found in the glass display case near the diamond."

"And Elliot has been known to hack," Brock added.

Olivia sat on the edge of the chair she'd claimed by the window, her laptop open, ready to do more research on Ivy and Nick, but too excited to tell Brock what she'd learned. "I was talking with Ivy and Elliot over their lunch the other day. Remember how I mentioned that they seemed to have some kind of special relationship going on or something? That Ivy got him this job?"

"Yes."

"What if she got him the job because she's been planning this all along? She may have had Elliot hack the system while she swiped the jewel. She's the exhibit designer. If anyone has access to the artifacts, it's her!"

"She could have also used Nick's knowledge of history and the employees to aid in her theft." Brock pointed out. "It's just a theory—just because a chemistry teacher knows about sulfuric acid doesn't prove that she stole a jewel—but if Nick is constantly watching people like you mentioned he is, then that could mean that he's the perfect pawn for her to use."

"Or maybe they're all in on it." Olivia sat back. "Maybe we've been looking in the wrong place. Of course Simon and Darren's fingerprints are going to be on the display case; they push it back into place every night. Graham's crown mold lifter we found is hardly a clue of any kind. He's a conservator, so naturally, he's going to have some tools. Who's to say he doesn't need that one? But Ivy, though. Ivy has both the opportunity and knowledge to pull something like this off. If it wasn't for that sulfuric acid drop we found on the cloth, I wouldn't even think twice about it. But Brock, I've mentioned this before. Sulfuric acid does not belong in a display case for an international diamond at a museum."

"Here's what we do." Brock leaned forward. "We can't blow our cover. Not yet. This is all just theory and a major coincidence. But we watch the footage of both Dorian's date of death and the day the jewel went missing after hours tomorrow. We pay attention to Ivy and Elliot, and throw Nick in there, too. Remember how I said that the clue we need might be in the security footage, and we just have to know where to look for it?" He sat back. "This is that clue. We watch those three from the moment they arrive till the moment they leave. You know what? Let's grab those tapes and take them back here rather than watching them at the museum."

"We could have a movie night you and I, and watch nothing but museum footage with popcorn and jammies," Olivia joked. She felt the light come back into her eyes now that they were so close to figuring this out.

"I'd rather watch a thriller, but you know what, that works for me." Brock grinned. "Well, my love. Are you as stressed as you were a few nights ago?"

"No." Olivia leaned forward, affection in her eyes. "But it's not because of any of this."

"What is it, then?" Brock slipped his fingers through hers and traced her knuckles with his thumb.

She relished in his touch and let it show through her smile. "The love of my life helped a lot with that."

CHAPTER
TWENTY-FIVE

"I'M GETTING TO BE VERY FAMILIAR WITH THIS ROOM," Brock said as he plopped down in front of one of the monitors in the security room. In his hand, he clutched a cup of decaf coffee. Olivia had giggled when he said he was telling himself it was caffeinated to give him the jolt he needed to work late again.

"Hey." Olivia shrugged, taking her usual place beside him. "It gives us time to be alone and work on the case together. That should count for something, right?"

"Sure." Brock grinned at her over the rim of his coffee cup. He set it down and clicked the monitors to life. "So, let's see. Ivy."

Olivia nodded. "Ivy."

"The chemistry teacher who knows all about sulfuric acid and sulfur dioxide. Where was she the day that the jewel came up missing?"

"Let's find out." Olivia set down her own cup and watched the screen. "Along with everyone else who's said a few things that sounds like they might know too much."

Brock pulled up the footage from late afternoon on October 5th. "Let's start with the evening and see what she was up to."

The footage showed Ivy wandering around the museum without Elliot in tow. Now that the Ratnashree diamond display was up and running, it appeared that she was only polishing a few things for the jewel display and wasn't quite needed other than to make sure it was in good shape. After they secured it in the vault for the night, Ivy poked her head in the back room for a few minutes.

"I could be reading too much into this," Olivia said. "But the jewel had been on display for more than five days at this point. What is she doing here at the museum, since the next exhibit wasn't originally supposed to be around for another couple of weeks?"

"Maybe managing it? She's the designer, but also the installer, so maybe she was fixing something?" Brock shrugged. "Or, maybe, she was scoping out a good time to steal it." Brock moved the footage along toward the end of the day. Shortly after the museum's closing time, the cameras showed Ivy going downstairs. Brock followed along with the monitors to show her clocking out at 5:20, then leaving the museum and disappearing off camera around 5:25 p.m.

"Nothing overly suspicious. She works here; she could have been here for any reason, whether her job was done or not." Brock sat back in his chair.

"She could have been figuring out a way to use the sulfuric acid to age it up a bit before she pulled off the heist," Olivia suggested. "But do you think she could have used any other chemical to do so? Is sulfuric acid really the best option?"

"It might be what she had access to at the time." Brock reached forward to sweep a small particle of dust off the screen. "Who knows what all is in her chemistry lab at the school."

Brock pulled up the footage from October 6th. Beginning with the morning, he scrutinized it with sharp eyes. Olivia looked over his shoulder. "I'm not seeing her at all," Brock pointed out. "But you know what?"

"What's that?"

Brock rolled over to another computer and typed something in. "I can look at the employee log and see when she got here."

Olivia settled back and reached for her coffee, letting Brock do the heavy work this time. "That sounds a lot easier than watching for her."

Brock pulled up the employee logs of when each member clocked in and out. "Ivy clocked in at 3:17 on October 6th."

Olivia set her coffee down and took hold of the mouse, scrolling as she did to the footage that showed when Ivy arrived. "Ivy got busy almost immediately after clocking in," she called over to Brock. She watched Selena, hastening to meet Ivy in the downstairs break room. After a brief conversation Olivia wished she could hear, the two of them went straight to Selena's office where Ivy wasn't seen until about an hour later, coming out and looking closely at the display case, showing off the fake diamond. Olivia couldn't tell any emotions from the footage very well, but Ivy seemed just as distressed as Selena was. She put her phone to her ear and paced the length of the exhibit room, running her fingers through her hair.

"She has all the symptoms of being stressed," Olivia narrated, wondering why Brock was still looking at the employee's clocking-in log. "Either she had no idea, or she was worried about being caught."

Olivia wasn't sure who to believe anymore. She took notice of everyone on camera the day the jewel was discovered missing. Nick looked beside himself, as did Simon and Graham any time they hovered over the display case. Olivia watched the behavior of each of the employees as they examined the display case. Simon and Graham stood there a long time once the museum had closed. Simon ran his fingers along the side of the glass case, his shoulders stooped and worry lining his face. Ivy came up to them after a while and shared a tense conversation before they each departed downstairs. Even Darren seemed to watch everyone more closely.

"So I did some digging on some other things." Brock rolled back over to her in his chair.

"What's that?" Olivia set her chin in her palm, looking lazily over at Brock.

"I didn't just look at Ivy's log. I looked at a few others as well. Doesn't it strike you as odd that no security guards were present the night of October 5th?"

Olivia's eyebrows lifted. "You're right... the museum was empty, wasn't it? Except for whoever was running around, messing with the cameras."

"So I viewed Darren's history." Brock listed off his notes. "He always works nights, except twice a week. Wednesday nights and Friday nights."

"You're kidding." Olivia straightened her posture. "So Darren is always off on Friday night? What about the other part-time security guards?"

"For some reason, they weren't scheduled that night. It was put into the system that they both requested the night off." Brock stared at Olivia, seriousness in his tone.

Olivia glanced back at the monitor. "No security," she repeated. "That's one more parallel to the Star of India heist. Do you think the thief knew that there would be no security guards that night?"

"They'd have to. They picked the perfect time to do it," Brock answered. "But they still would need help shutting down the system and there are only a few select people who know how to do that."

Silence hummed around them for a few minutes as Olivia processed what this meant. "Let's watch the footage from October 13th. The day Dorian was killed. Can we pull that up?" she asked.

"Sure." Brock took over, switching out the current footage and finding Dorian's. "By the way, let's not forget to take these sets of tapes back to the hotel with us so we don't have to constantly be up here in this room after hours at the museum. We could be doing other things, and doing this when we're not here."

"Now who's getting too wrapped up in the case?" Olivia's lip creased with laughter.

"I learned from the best." Brock shot her a grin out of the corner of his eyes. He grew serious as the footage from that busy day at the museum began. Olivia watched for their three—or four because she wasn't throwing Darren out—main suspects like a game of I Spy. Ivy and Elliot showed up together and both clocked in around nine. Elliot trailed Ivy upstairs to do whatever they were doing. Nick didn't talk to as many people that day, as he seemed busy with his tasks. That left Ivy to be the one to mingle with the crowd, not talking to people as much as Nick did, but blending in, nonetheless. Olivia watched her until she stole away downstairs into the employee's area.

Suddenly, Olivia had a thought. "Hey, Brock. Can you pull up Ivy's usual hours when she's here?"

"Sure." Brock rolled back over to do as Olivia requested from the log across the room.

"It looks like she has a few full days every other week," Brock said. "So probably when she is designing and installing exhibits. The last week of September has Ivy here four days out of six. She's putting in eight-hour days, sometimes more. Other than that, her hours are basically a handful of hours in the evening and sometimes after closing."

"So she works during the night, mostly." Olivia turned to look at Brock. "Because she's a schoolteacher, she comes after hours. So why was she here at nine in the morning during a school day when she wasn't planning an exhibit? Shouldn't she be teaching?"

"This was after we had the meeting about the Pompeii exhibit." Brock rolled back over to Olivia's side. "She could have been prepping for that."

"But at nine in the morning?" Olivia shook her head. "Something seems off about that. Especially since there were so many tours that she barely had room to look around in the exhibit hall and plan for her next one."

"Good point." Brock creased his lip and returned to watching the footage. Olivia checked the time. Sometime around 9:50, Ivy was seen going out the back door.

Olivia exchanged a glance with Brock. "She went outside. When does she come back?"

Brock rolled the footage through. "10:40."

"Plenty of time for her to sneak in and then back out again if she keeps close to the wall. Do you think she killed Dorian?" Olivia sat back, steeling Brock with a stare.

"What motive would she have to kill him, though?" Brock worked on the answer mentally for a few minutes. "Maybe to cause a distraction? She and Simon would be the most obvious candidates for the thief since they have direct and unquestioned access to the jewel at all times. Maybe she knew this and was trying to distract us from looking at her as the thief?"

"Not us, per se. She doesn't know we're FBI. So any potential law enforcement looking into the case?" Olivia asked.

"Right." Brock nodded to the monitor. "The only thing is, I never saw the door reopen until 10:40 when she came back in."

"I wish they had better cameras around the janitor's closet," Olivia growled, leaning forward to study the footage from below. Other than the three cameras that pointed to the vault, one down the hall near the stairs, and one pointing at a terrible angle near the back door, the employee area wasn't very well-recorded.

"Me, too. It would have answered a lot of questions. Especially with the employees coming and going throughout the day."

"That day was so busy, anyone could have slipped in and done it if they were in the employees' area."

Olivia and Brock fell silent, watching the footage play out before their eyes. After a while, Olivia's eye caught on a flutter of movement toward the stairs. Tessa scampered down the stairs, looking right and left before sneaking off toward where the janitor's closet was. Olivia studied her as she disappeared off camera, but never went out the back door. She glanced at the time, seeing it was around eleven, but still. Why was she going to the janitor's closet?

"That girl is always sneaking around in places a receptionist shouldn't be," Olivia remarked.

Brock nodded. "She is. And she always acts guilty about it, too."

Whatever the case, fifteen minutes later, Tessa reemerged back onto the stairs and took them, two at a time until she reappeared on camera in the exhibit room. She looked around again, then straightened her shirt, then walked back to the front like nothing was wrong.

Olivia bit her lip. Something nagged at her, something she couldn't quite place. "We've got to be missing something. I have a feeling that whatever we're missing is so obvious that when it comes to light, we're both going to feel like newbies."

Brock chuckled. "Oh, I hope not. You think whatever we're missing is hiding in plain sight?"

"Possibly." Olivia thought for a few more minutes, wishing she could put her finger on exactly what was bothering her. "Anyway, I'm sure it'll come around eventually. I'll grab the footage."

Brock stood to his feet and stretched. "We need something more solid. Something that colors in the lines. Everyone seems to have something against them, but how do we connect those dots?"

"Simple." Olivia wished it were simple. Her tone of voice was as clipped as Brock's, as irritated as he was about continuously coming up short. "We keep trying."

CHAPTER
TWENTY-SIX

OLIVIA DIDN'T STAY UP LATE WATCHING THE FOOTAGE. She could memorize the position of every employee on the recorded security footage, but in the end, she realized that whoever had the knowledge to steal the jewel also had the knowledge to avoid all the cameras, erase the footage, and somehow slip past the security system. So anything beyond what they'd found already was worthless information. At this point, she wondered if it was any one person who stole it or all of them. Olivia wouldn't put it past Simon, Graham, Nick, Darren, Ivy, and Elliot to bring what knowledge they had to the table and use it to pull off a jewel heist. Maybe they were secretly upset with Selena about something that no one was talking about. Maybe it was one person's idea, and they all would receive a cut. Or maybe it was just one person, working alone.

Maybe it wasn't even an employee.

Maybe it was a patron who frequented the museum or maybe someone had seen Nick's Facebook post and wanted the jewel for themselves.

Maybe, maybe, maybe.

Olivia tossed the answers in her head like a salad as she did her rounds the next day. She was almost getting tired of doing the same thing, yet at the same time, she was so close. She had that sense, that feeling that there was something they were missing. Was it going to be so obvious that both she and Brock would facepalm and question their status as FBI agents?

Should she take a step back? Let it go for a day, exist in the museum and go with the flow?

"Tanner, Knight, Steele, code 3, please?" Skylar's voice on the radio crackled into Olivia's reflectiveness.

Code 3? Possible shoplifter? Olivia held the radio to her mouth. "This is Knight, Code 3 responding." She clipped the radio back onto her belt and started off in the direction of the gift shop.

She pushed through the doors that led to the front of house. She walked past the empty reception desk and into the gift shop. There were only two parents, their child, and a young teenage boy, looking a little too hard at some of the items. Olivia's gaze collided with Skylar's behind the counter and she sent an inconspicuous nod in the direction of the teenage boy.

Olivia moved closer to the counter, observing the teen out of the corner of her eye. Skylar was right to peg him. The way he looked around the sides of his hoodie to scope out the shop was as suspicious as his hovering was. Olivia distinctly saw his hand come out of his jacket pocket, reaching toward a magnet that said *Virginia Museum of Art History* on a cartoonish picture of a Monet painting. Then the magnet disappeared, and the teen's hand buried itself in his pocket.

Olivia approached until she was standing right beside him. "Good afternoon, sir."

The teen jumped, uttering a small grunt through his teeth and pivoted around to face her. "Oh, sorry, ma'am, you scared me."

Sure she did. Guilty consciences were easily startled. She nodded to his pocket. "I see what you're doing."

"What I'm doing?" He tried and failed miserably at innocence.

Olivia nodded. "I'm going to give you a chance to either put that back or pay for it up at the counter, over there." She nodded backward to the counter where Skylar was perched, watching the whole thing come down.

The teen's jaw hovered up and down and his eyes went big, behind a flushed crimson face. Then, he tried for another lie. "Oh-oh, you mean this?" He pulled the magnet, along with a small snow globe, out of his pocket. "Nah, I wasn't stealing, I was using it as a basket."

"That's fine." Olivia smiled knowingly at him, authority slanting her eyebrows. "Then you wouldn't mind if I took those to the counter for you while you finish your shopping?"

"Actually you know what?" His tight grin told her the truth. "I forgot my wallet, so I'm going to just leave them here with you."

"You can put them back," Olivia suggested. "Along with anything else in your pockets."

"There's nothing else in my pockets, I swear." The teen emptied the pockets of his hoodie, only a piece of gum falling out. Olivia wasn't going to ask if it was paid for, either. "So, uh…uh…" Eloquently, he looked around and then snatched up the items. He stuffed them back onto the shelf, then ran out of the gift shop.

Olivia breathed a laugh, smiling after him and shook her head. "That boy is trouble." She walked up to the counter. "You okay, Skylar?"

"Yes, ma'am." Skylar smiled up at her, gratefully. "He came in with the group of teens, but he's been hovering around here."

"You were very observant to point him out. Great job," Olivia smiled, applauding Skylar for her intuitiveness.

"Thank you so much! And thanks for your help."

"That's what I'm here for." Olivia's gaze drifted down to the book on Skylar's lap. Beside her on the counter sat the same receipt that Olivia had spied in her locker, set aside like it was a bookmark. She glanced up at Skylar, gently knocking on the door for conversation. "How have you been doing after we talked?"

"Oh, much better." Skylar's smile was genuine, this time. "I tried your advice and I've been able to handle it better, now. Thank you. I couldn't have done it without you."

"It's my pleasure." Olivia smiled and nodded to the book. "Whatcha reading?"

"Oh, this." Skylar looked down at the book as if it wasn't that important. She flipped the cover closed and showed it to Olivia. "I really enjoy reading up on the artifacts that we have showcased as our main exhibits. Since this time was the Rat... you know what, I can't even pronounce it."

Olivia laughed. "Me neither. The diamond from India?"

"Yeah, that." Skylar giggled. "I was reading up on diamonds and the history of India. Like the Gupta Empire and all that stuff since the jewel was from back then. I like to talk to the guests as they come through the gift shop about cool facts from history. I know I got stuck in the gift shop, but I kinda want to do more than that, you know?"

"I get that all the way." Olivia nodded, eagerly. That was part of her cover story, so she leaned into it. "So you've been reading up on diamonds? Learn any cool facts?"

Skylar shrugged. "Not really about diamonds themselves as much as the history of the Gupta Empire. I learned that they form deep in the earth, but they can be brought to the surface during a volcanic eruption. Which is really cool considering that Pompeii is our next exhibit. I'm super excited about that one! I'm going to be checking out a book on Pompeii, next."

"That's really something." Olivia's eyes drifted down to the counter where the receipt from Miller's Pawn Shop faced up at her. Surely Skylar wouldn't have something so obvious out in the open, right? Granted, the total was rubbed off where no one could see what it actually was, but still. "So, let me guess?" Olivia grinned like she was trying to be a teenager again and nodded to the receipt. "Is that so you can buy more books?"

"No." Skylar laughed and drew the receipt closer to her. She studied it for a few moments before her quiet voice hinted at a change in subject. Or at least a change in how she felt about it. "Remember how I said that my mom and I don't have the best relationship?"

Olivia nodded. She didn't see how that was related to any of this, but she bought it for now.

"Well, she wanted me to learn to play the flute. She got me one, put me in band, everything. I never had an interest in music, so after I graduated, it just sat in my room forever. And, well," her eyes shimmered with something else like she was about to reveal a huge secret. "Can I tell you a secret?"

"I love secrets!" Olivia leaned closer, practically drooling for whatever the secret could be.

Skylar shot a look out the door, then leaned toward Olivia and whispered eagerly. "I really like Toby. Me, him, and Tessa all went to school together and would sometimes hang out and stuff. But I'm kinda shy and quiet, you know?"

Olivia would never have gotten that from Skylar. But then again, she might be great at customer service and not so great at personal relations. "I get that."

"So I really like him, but he's always been super into Tessa because she's more flirtatious and outgoing than I am. So I thought, why not try to catch his eye in a more meaningful way than a belly button stud?"

Was that animosity Olivia detected in Skylar's tone or just jealousy?

"So I know Toby really likes to play the electric guitar and his broke last year." Olivia looked out at the reception desk again, then looked back at Olivia. "So I pawned my flute and am using the money to save up to get him a new guitar. I've pawned stuff at Tom Miller's before, so he knows me real well. He set back an electric guitar for me. I'm going to get it for Toby out of my next paycheck."

The story made sense, but Olivia wondered if it was too easy. Skylar seemed terrified—understandably so—after seeing Dorian dead, and had a convincing story about the pawn shop receipt. Not to mention, she didn't have access to the diamond at all. The book on precious gems, although something of a reminder of the Star of India heist, could be nothing more than a good coincidence, and it sounded like it was. Olivia shelved her suspicions about Skylar for now, keeping the idea that she might be lying in the back of her mind. "I think that's a great idea."

"Do you?" Skylar blushed. "I don't know. I hope it's not too forward."

"Anything's worth a try." Olivia grinned. "Don't worry. Your secret is safe with me." *From the staff at the museum, that is.* She was telling Brock everything later.

Movement stirred at the front desk, drawing the attention of both Olivia and Skylar. "Oh, hang on." Skylar huffed a sigh and slid out from under her desk. She put her book upside-down on the counter and jogged toward the front desk. "Hi, welcome to the Virginia Museum of Art History!"

Her voice was cheerful now, but Olivia hadn't missed the annoyance that hissed through her teeth before she left the gift shop. She slowly followed Skylar to the front desk, wondering why Skylar was taking the money and letting the two guests through the doors to the exhibit hall, rather than Tessa or Toby. Both of whom were still missing. When Skylar started back in her direction, Olivia tilted her head. "Where are Toby and Tessa?"

Huffing a sigh, Skylar rolled her eyes and clamped her arms over her stomach. "Tessa usually takes her break when we're not busy, and Toby has been in the restroom for fifteen minutes! They do this to me all the time!"

"They leave you to babysit the front desk?" Olivia asked.

"Yes! It's getting annoying."

"Why haven't you brought it up to management?"

"What are they gonna do? They can't exactly tell Toby not to use the bathroom when he has to, and Tessa's trying to be the responsible receptionist by picking a time for her break that's not busy. It's not like they mean to do it; it's just annoying."

Curious, Olivia thought. "Well, let me see if I can find Toby for you. Maybe he went somewhere else?"

"I doubt it, but if you want to, I appreciate it." Skylar glanced over her shoulder at the gift shop. "It's not like I can watch both the gift shop and the front! That's why they hired two receptionists."

"I understand. Let me see if I can track Toby down for you," Olivia reassured her. But before she could walk through the doors in search of Toby, the doors burst open. Both Tessa and Toby stumbled through, side-by-side. Olivia examined them in a quick glance. Some of her curiosity melted into concern. Something was wrong. Both were completely out of breath as if they'd run around the museum three times. Their faces bore the same shade of pallor, glistening with a little sweat. Olivia stopped, urgency lining her features. "Are you guys okay? Where've you been?"

Tessa's hand clutched at her chest as she struggled for breath. "I... I was running back from my break."

"I went to go take mine. Thought we could switch." Toby gasped air as Tessa did. "Then I realized she was down there and no one was watching the front, so I ran upstairs with her to get to the front desk."

Sounded about as likely as Nick claiming to despise history class. "That right?"

"I'm sorry, I didn't realize I was gone a little past my time." Tessa swayed on her feet and leaned against the desk as if the floor rippled beneath her. What was going on? She and Toby both looked nervous, like Olivia would somehow have the authority to write them up for neglecting the front. But something else showed fear through Tessa's eyes. Something that went deeper than trying to talk her way out of coming back from break late.

"Tessa, are you okay?" Olivia asked in a voice sterner than before. She approached her and leaned over the girl, who snapped up to meet her with frightened eyes. As if she knew she'd been caught doing something wrong. Olivia would worry about their obvious white lies later. Right now, it appeared as if they had some kind of medical emergency. "What's going on? Why are you breathing so hard?"

"I'm a little dizzy." Tessa dropped into her chair and put her hand to her head. She reached under her desk and pulled out her bottle of water. Shaking hands unscrewed the cap. "I guess I haven't had enough water today."

"If that's the case, then why is Toby the same way?" Olivia glanced up at Toby, who was also panting for breath.

"I guess something's in the air. We both suddenly started feeling it," Toby said. Olivia wasn't sure if he was lying, or slowly starting to admit something else.

"Short of breath?" she asked him.

"A little dizzy, but I'm sure we'll be okay. This museum needs to air out once in a while, you know?"

Tessa rubbed her head, cringing as if it hurt.

Olivia studied her for a few minutes. They might try to brush this off as something non-important. "I'm going to get Levi out here. We need to see if you're having a medical issue."

"Oh, no, don't! Please don't call Levi!" Tessa looked up, her eyes wide and begging Olivia not to take that next step. "He's... he's busy and he might be upset with us for neglecting the front desk."

"I was watching it," Skylar said from her place behind Olivia. "He won't be mad, he'll be concerned. Listen to Olivia, she's right. Something's wrong with you guys."

Tessa stared at Olivia. Her face twisted as if she wanted to plead for her life, but then, she slowly nodded. "Okay."

Olivia nodded, then held the radio to her mouth. "Levi, Code 2 up front please, Levi?"

"I'm coming." Even on the radio, Levi sounded calm.

Olivia lowered the radio, lowering her voice authoritatively. "Tessa. Why are you afraid? Levi's not going to be mad. Is there something else you need to tell me?"

Tessa's chest heaved. Her face blushed bright red, spreading all the way to the tops of her ears. Her mouth hung agape. Olivia looked up at Toby, about to ask him the same question. What was going on? Olivia didn't believe their story for a minute, but if something had happened to cause them both to be short of breath, she needed to know.

Suddenly, a high-pitched shriek pierced the air.

Beep! Beep! Beep!

Was that a fire alarm? Tessa and Toby both jumped and looked behind them. Tessa stopped breathing altogether for a few seconds as she focused on the door to the exhibit hall, before slowly looking up at Toby. Skylar stiffened and gasped from her place behind Olivia and looked toward the front door.

"What was that?" Skylar asked, breathlessly.

"Sounds like a fire alarm." Olivia was torn between making sure Tessa wasn't going to pass out and investigating. "Toby, get Tessa outside and stay with her. Make sure she takes a few good breaths. Skylar, stay near the door for a minute. I need you to calmly direct the guests toward the exit, okay? Can you do that for me?"

"Yes, ma'am." Toby nodded, more obedient than usual.

Skylar, however, looked at Olivia with wide eyes.

"Skylar?" Olivia raised an eyebrow.

"Yes, ma'am, I can."

Out of the corner of her eye, she caught Levi hastening down the hall. His own wide eyes held the same concern that Olivia felt. "What's going on?"

"I don't know. I'm about to go check. Toby can tell you why I originally called you." Olivia pushed through the door into the exhibit hall where the shrill beeping made her eardrums twitch and cower. Her gaze swept the exhibit hall where patrons had frozen in their steps and looked around timidly and fearfully. She expected to see smoke rising to the ceiling or pouring in from the downstairs area, but there was nothing. Not even the smell of smoke in the air. What was going on? She walked further into the room, driven with purpose.

Darren burst into the room from one of the exhibit halls, calling in an authoritative voice,

"Ladies and gentlemen, I'm going to need everyone to move to the front of the museum in an orderly fashion. Do not panic, but we need everyone toward the front as soon as possible. I need you to form two single lines and go through the front exit, in an orderly fashion."

His voice was strong and trained to hold no fear, only a sense of control like everything was fine. Olivia wondered what was really behind the calm facade he put on. What did he know that no one else did?

To her right, Brock thundered down the stairs from the security room. He spied Olivia and rushed up to her, speaking in rapid tones low enough for her to hear before the guests arrived at the door.

"CO_2 alarm."

CO_2? Olivia held her breath. She feared in some ways that was worse than a fire. A fire you could see. Smell. Taste even, but invisible gas with no odor was the silent killer. Her mind flashed back to Tessa and Toby both being out of breath and suddenly it all made sense. How long had these people been breathing it?

"We gotta get these people out of here." She sprang into action, propping the doors open for the patrons of the museum to go through. She stepped through the door, looking around for Levi, and paused only long enough to fill him in. "CO_2 alarm."

"Are you kidding me?" He breathed through his lips and shook his head.

"We need to evacuate now. Tessa and Toby are showing signs of CO_2 poisoning. You call the fire department—I'll handle the floor." Olivia spoke rapidly, not caring that she sounded very much like the FBI agent she was in that moment. At least Levi knew.

"I'm on it. Skylar, do as Olivia said and help me direct guests to the front." Levi jogged toward the front doors to prop them open with one hand while digging his cell phone out with the other.

Trusting Levi to follow through, Olivia turned back to the stampede of panicked people heading her way. She stood on one side of the door, directing them toward the exit. Despite how Darren repeated the phrase *orderly fashion*, they threw that to the wind. One lady dropped her purse in the path of an oncoming teenage girl, whose foot collided with it and she went down. Brock raced toward her to help her up, speaking calmly as he did. One child started screaming as the mother took him into her arms. Two guys near the front elbowed their way through the crowd as if somehow they deserved to be first.

Olivia stepped forward to usher them through the door, raising her voice over the din of frightened people and the shrill beeping of the alarm. "Ladies and gentlemen, we have this under control." For all she knew it was completely out of control, but they didn't need to know that. She just needed to get them through the door without a repeat of the sinking Titanic's evacuation. "I need everyone to form into two lines and exit the building in an orderly fashion."

CHAPTER
TWENTY-SEVEN

T HE ALARM CONTINUED TO ECHO THROUGH THE MUSEUM, nearly deafening her. Olivia stood her ground, helping patrons exit the building. The words *orderly fashion* were more like a gentle suggestion at this point as guests tried to cram themselves through the door, possibly trampling others in the process. "Two at a time, guys, two at a time," Olivia called with no fear of being in authority. She was well used to situations like this. A woman ran by with a baby on her hip. "What's going on?"

"Keep moving forward, ma'am." Olivia urged her through, only to be stopped by another teen on his way through.

"Is there a fire?"

"Keep the line moving, ladies and gentlemen – all the way out," Olivia called. "Others need to evacuate."

The exhibit hall emptied itself of patrons. As the last two stragglers made it through the door, Darren strode forward with more urgency than Olivia had ever seen him exhibit. "Tanner, check the Hall of Vases, I've got the museum room. Knight, get everyone outside, check the front. Meet in the middle!" Darren fired off.

Brock didn't need to be told twice as he disappeared into the Hall of Vases. Shortly after he disappeared, a couple of patrons emptied out of the hall and ran toward the front entrance. At least it wasn't a stampede this time. Olivia's heart hammered in her chest. Now that most of the evacuation was over, her mind buzzed with the need for answers. What was going on? Where was the CO_2 leak coming from? What was happening at this museum?

She followed Darren's direction. She wasn't used to taking orders from someone lower in rank, but she didn't mind it. It was better to follow along so that everyone knew what they were doing, rather than holding unknown rank over Darren's head. Olivia burst through the door, noting Skylar and Levi still nearby. Levi was speaking calmly into the phone. His dark brown eyes flashed her way as she hurried toward the ladies' bathroom first. "We've almost got everyone," she assured him as she burst through the doors.

"Is anyone in here? You gotta evacuate." Her voice echoed in the empty bathroom.

When she didn't receive a reply, she dropped low, doing a quick look under the stalls. After assuring herself they were empty, she left the ladies' bathroom behind, hurrying as fast as she could. She knocked on the men's door before swinging the door open. "Anyone in here?"

Met with the same silence, she did another swoop, seeing no one was inside. She closed the door behind her, charging up the hall toward where Selena and Levi's offices were, among others. She knocked on each of the doors before swinging them open, determined not to leave anyone behind. Checking the offices took longer than she wanted, especially since no one was back there, but it was better to be safe than sorry.

Leaving the front of house, she walked briskly back into the exhibit hall to find both Brock and Darren racing toward the stairs where Graham came stumbling up. Olivia didn't slow her pace, but her heart rate kicked up a notch. Graham didn't look good at all. He clung to the rail, hunched forward, and heaved for breath as if the staircase had been Mount Vesuvius to climb.

Brock reached out to stabilize the conservator who swayed on his feet the same way Tessa had.

"You okay, there, man?" Darren asked.

Graham wheezed out a cough and it nearly sent him backwards downstairs. Brock lunged forward, catching the back of his shoulder blades. "Whoa. Let's get you away from the stairs, shall we?"

"Yeah..." Graham hobbled forward a step and looked up at Brock, Darren, and Olivia.

"Are you the only one down there?" Brock asked, knowing they'd still have to verify anyway.

Graham shook his head. "No... Nick went down there." He rolled his eyes. "He went back for that stupid tapestry that he's obsessed with and Simon went to go get him. He won't come."

Olivia sighed. "We'll handle it. Let's get you to the front."

"I'll take him." Concerned, Darren reached for Graham to help stabilize him. Brock came up beside him as Darren spoke quickly. "You guys go get anyone else who might be down there. There are emergency masks in the supply closet. Grab those. I'll close the main vault door when I get back inside."

"Copy." Brock nodded.

Olivia didn't want to take the time to stop and grab the masks, but she knew if there was a CO_2 leak, she wouldn't do much good if she couldn't breathe either. Even though she and Brock rushed toward the closet Graham spoke of, the hallway felt like it stretched longer with every step. Brock yanked the closet door open and seized two compact, bright-orange hoods sealed in vacuum packs. Emergency escape respirators. He tore them open fast and handed one to her before taking off again, not bothering to close the closet door. "Just like old times, huh?"

"You mean everyday times?" Olivia muttered, sliding the hood over her head and pulling the neck seal into place as they moved. She followed Brock at a clipped pace. By the time Brock was descending the stairs, his mask was securely fastened. The transparent visor was slightly fogged from his breath, his voice muffled beneath the air filter.

Olivia stepped off the last step, casting a look in both directions. Except for the chaos of the shrieking alarm all around the museum, the downstairs area looked calm as usual. Brock led her toward the locker room, calling out Simon and Nick's names through the muffled filter. Olivia stayed close behind him, knowing that whoever was down here would probably need help getting upstairs. The patrons upstairs seemed unaffected, except for their panic. Anyone who came from downstairs exhibited symptoms, which told her the leak was somewhere down here.

There was no way this many incidents kept happening without being intentional. For all she knew, whoever killed Dorian was also trying to sabotage the museum.

"Brock, I'm calling for backup," Olivia dug her cell phone out of her pocket.

"You do that," Brock said to her, before calling out full volume. "Hello, anyone down here? You gotta evacuate!" He slipped into the locker room while she paused outside.

Olivia speed-dialed the number and put the phone to her ear. "This is Special Agent Olivia Knight. I'm on site at the Virginia Museum of Art History. We've got a CO_2 alarm going off – possible sabotage. Requesting immediate backup and medical assistance."

After receiving a confirmation that they were on their way, Olivia called to Brock. "Wait up."

He popped out of the locker room. "No one in here or the break room!"

"Hello?" A weak man's voice called from the janitor's closet. What was he doing over there?

Brock's attention snapped toward the voice and he pointed. "There."

Olivia pivoted to see Simon limping out of the janitor's closet. What in the world was he doing in there? The weakness and lethargy that haunted his sluggish footsteps were far worse than Graham's symptoms.

Olivia and Brock hurried up to Simon. Olivia reached him first and stretched out her hand to help him. "Simon, there's a CO_2 leak somewhere in the museum, we gotta get you out of here, okay?"

"My head," he said, weakly, reaching up to rub his forehead.

"Don't worry, we're going to get that taken care of." Brock reached out to take his arm.

"S-sorry, I thought that was the door." Simon looked back at the closet, confused.

"That's okay," Brock said, reassuringly. "We'll get you out. Simon, where's Nick? Where's Nick at?"

Simon weakly pointed up the hall. "He's... in there."

"In where, buddy?"

Simon stumbled forward and Brock caught him. Olivia glanced up at Brock, her eyes wide. "We'll find him. He can't have gone far. We need to get Simon out of here ASAP."

Brock took one of Simon's arms while Olivia claimed the other. Together, they started walking him toward the rear door. "You doing okay, man?" Brock knew he wasn't but he kept talking to him, nonetheless.

"Oh... sure. Just peachy, man." Simon's voice rasped. He moved too slowly for the situation. Olivia wanted to usher him to the door as fast as she could, but Simon moved too slowly for that.

Step. Step. Step.

Come on, come on, Olivia urged. They crawled at a snail's pace past the janitor's closet.

Step. Step. Step.

CHAPTER TWENTY-EIGHT

INALLY. THERE WAS THE BACK DOOR.

Brock swung the door open, allowing light and fresh air to rush in, replacing the dangerous leak that somehow permeated the lower level. "Okay, out you go. You're going to be okay."

Olivia helped Simon through the other side of the door and tugged her radio up to her mouth. Calling as loudly as she could through the mask, she spoke clearly. "This is Knight, we need help at the rear emergency door. One guy still inside, the other needs medical help immediately. Do you copy?"

A few seconds later, Levi appeared around the corner, phone stuck to his ear. At the sight of Simon, his eyebrows shot to his hairline and he jogged forward. Despite the calamity, he spoke calmly into the phone. "They found another one." He pulled the phone down, mouthing, "911's on the way. Anyone else inside?"

"Nick is." Brock nodded to Simon. "Can you take him to the front and get him to medical help?"

Levi nodded and reached for his old comrade. He pulled the phone down from his ear. "Skylar? Skylar, come here!"

Simon glanced back over his shoulder at Olivia and Brock as he passed. "Thank you."

"Sure thing." Olivia smiled, replying cheerfully even though she felt far from happy. As soon as Levi was leading Simon away, she and Brock turned back inside. She checked the janitor's closet first since that's where Simon had been. "Nick!" she called. "Nick, where are you? Can you hear me?"

The janitor's closet was empty, so she moved her search to the HVAC room, Brock on her heels. "Nick!" he called, voice muffled, but loud enough to be heard through the mask.

Olivia was about to leave the HVAC room when something snagged her attention. She stopped, looking back again as her mind raced to make sense of what she saw. Right next to one of the giant gray ducts lay a massive CO_2 cylinder with a busted valve, leaking gas right into the air conditioning system, and spreading it throughout the entire museum.

"Found it!" Olivia called through her mask and rushed into the room.

"Who, Nick?"

"No. The leak!" Olivia would tease him about *it* versus *him* later. She scrambled into the room to the container. She reached for the valve and tried to turn it, only to realize that it was broken completely. There was no time to stop the leak, but she could at least keep it from doing more damage to the air conditioning system. She lifted the container upright and moved it a few feet away, far from the air duct. "This isn't good. Someone is trying to sabotage the museum."

Brock ducked back out the door. "Nick?"

Olivia grabbed her phone and dialed while she left the HVAC room. "This is Knight. Leak located in the HVAC room. Broken valve on a CO_2 container. Leak is active. Still searching for one individual inside. Requesting immediate backup and medical support."

She hung up the phone and called again through her mask, "Nick!"

Brock paused for a moment, then raced toward the vault. "He's probably in here. He went back for an artifact, remember?"

Oh, great. Trapped in a room with no ventilation was even worse than being trapped down here at all. Olivia hurried behind Brock's heels as he raced to the vault. His shoulders visibly relaxed. When he moved out of the way, he revealed Nick, standing at one of the shelves. "Nick, buddy, we gotta get you out of here, there's an emergency."

Olivia glanced around the room. A vent hovered just above Nick's head. Probably used for climate control in the vault. Also, a perfect channel for CO_2, blowing directly into the room. Nick was getting the poisoning firsthand.

"There's... there's a fire." Nick turned around, his voice low. His eyes refused to focus on Brock, as if he were drunk, or high. Olivia's pulse drove up a few notches. She stepped forward, side-by-side with Brock, and carefully reached for him. "Nick, Nick, listen to me. Leave the tapestry, it's going to be all right, you need to come with us."

Nick's numb fingers grasped a tapestry, probably the Norwegian one he'd been obsessed with. Sweat glistened on his pale face as he took shallow breaths. In that moment, Olivia didn't care if he was the thief or not. He was not going to die like this, and he was not going to have permanent brain damage.

"Come on, Nick, let's get you out..." Brock reached for his upper arm, but Nick fell forward to his hands and knees, knocking Brock out of the way to nearly stumble against the shelf.

Olivia was at Nick's side in an instant. "Brock, he's not responding."

"Fire…" Nick asked, questioningly, looking up at Brock. His arms and legs buckled like his muscles had been replaced with water and he crumpled to the floor, his eyes closed.

"Nick!" Olivia gently shook him. "He's unconscious."

"We've got to drag him." Brock crouched beside him, taking his arm. Olivia did the same, taking his other arm in her hand.

"Together, on three," Brock instructed. Olivia nodded. "One… two…three!"

She grunted as both she and Brock rose to their feet, carrying Nick between them. They started for the vault door.

The unthinkable happened.

With a creak and scrape, the vault door began to slide closed, sealing off their only escape. Olivia's heart hammered in her chest. "No!"

She gently lowered Nick to the ground, then raced forward as if she could somehow open the vault door. "No!"

The vault door slammed closed with a deafening *bang*, sealing Brock, Olivia, and Nick inside in a tomb of CO_2, darkness, and silence.

Brock gently set Nick down and looked into the corner where a red dot alerted him where the camera was. "Hey!" he yelled, even though he knew he couldn't be heard. "Darren! Darren, we're down here!"

"We're in here!" Olivia waved her hands, madly. She dug her radio out of her pocket. "Darren, do you copy, we're in the vault! Repeat, we're in the vault!"

Nothing but quiet in response, as if her battery was dead. Only silence greeted them.

CHAPTER
TWENTY-NINE

"THIS IS NOT GOOD."

Olivia looked around frantically, wishing her heart wasn't hammering so hard. She should be accustomed to these types of situations, having to work against the clock. It wasn't her or Brock she was worried about. They had enough oxygen in their respirators to last them a while. But Nick didn't. He was already lethargic by the time Olivia and Brock had arrived, and now he was unconscious. Olivia knew the stakes. Brain damage could set in after about four minutes, and death shortly after that. There was no time.

She looked around the room.

"Let me try calling Darren." Brock whipped out his cell phone, having added Darren to his contacts earlier. He pushed the call button and held the phone to his ear. He counted the rings while Olivia counted the seconds. She cast another look at Nick, dread hitting her like a tidal wave. *Don't you die on me, Nick.*

"No signal." Brock lowered his cell phone. "There's too much steel around here. We're trapped."

"We need to think of a way out." Olivia reached for her cell phone and clicked the light on, shining it around the room to see what they had to work with. *Oh. A painting of a knight receiving the dub on his shoulder. That's exactly what I need. A samurai sword? Perfect.* There had to be something useful around here!

Brock tried the radio. "Darren, do you copy? We're trapped in the vault." He didn't even have the courtesy of static this time. "Darren, this is Brock Tanner, we need you to open the vault door, do you copy?"

"It's no use." Olivia breathed hard, reminding herself to breathe more gently, so she didn't use up all the oxygen in her mask. "There's no signal and if we don't do something, Nick is gonna die."

"Not only that?" Olivia heard the warning tone in Brock's voice even through his mask. "Our oxygen supply isn't going to last forever, Olivia. These things aren't from the fire department."

Fire department. Olivia had told them where the leak was. Could they hear them calling through the vault? No, that was useless. They needed a way out. *Now.*

The clock was ticking.

Then it hit her. The ticking clock. Suddenly, she was back in the training room, vaulted in by walls of steel and the hammering of her own heart.

"I'm going to try and manually override the system."

Brock's eyes widened beneath his mask's visor. "Olivia?"

Was that doubt in his voice? Or hesitation? Either way, it caused her to tilt her head in annoyance, non-verbally challenging him to complete his sentence.

"It's not that I don't believe you can do it. I do." Brock pointed to the panel. "But if you short-circuit that thing, it'll fry the entire system and there will be no getting anyone out of here without an entire team higher than we're getting paid."

Olivia didn't need the reminder. She already knew it. It just added pressure she didn't need. "I have to at least try. Nick has four minutes. Tops." She shined the light toward the panel and shot toward it. "I'm not going to just stand around and let him suffocate."

Brock knelt beside Nick. He turned him over onto his back. Whatever he did from there, Olivia didn't bother to stop and see. All she cared about was getting out of there. The walls were closing in on her. Not that she was claustrophobic, but the suspense was killing her.

She shined the light around until she found the wall where the panel was located, a few feet from the door. She dropped to her knees, examining the panel.

You've got ninety seconds...

The voice from her training echoed in her head, sending her an unnecessary reminder that time was crucial. Only this time, the consequence wouldn't be a red, blaring alarm that announced her failure to the training office. It would be one life she could've saved.

Olivia set everything aside. She switched to a robotic manner of thinking just so she could concentrate. Forget Nick. Brock was handling him. She needed to focus.

Phone first. That's how it started before.

Eighty-five seconds...

She opened her list of apps, finding the one she'd downloaded for museum security systems. While Darren was the only one with exclusive authority to open the door from his phone, she could use it for manual overrides, given the proper know-how. Using the code Darren had given her, she typed it into the system on her phone. Her device vibrated in her hand and suddenly, she was in.

The diagram unhelpfully showed her the guts of the Vanguard Core system. But of course, it didn't show her an easy 1-2-3 step to override it. She had to re-learn all of that from memory.

She typed in a code. It let her access the system. But now, how to manually override it?

Eighty seconds…

No, she needed to stop counting. That was her issue before. The brainpower it took for her to count everything down was brainpower she could be using to hack the system.

Focus, Olivia.

"Nick, stay with me, buddy," Brock spoke calmly to the archivist behind her, voice muffled in his mask. "We're gonna get you out of here."

Olivia found the screen and typed in the code again. Once again, the screen lit up with a warning red that doused her face in the alarming color. As she was last time, she was close to triggering the anti-hack system.

Olivia hated Vanguard Core. It was designed so that no one could hack it easily, and if someone was even remotely trying – emergency or not – it would shut down and it would take a miracle to get it undone. If she triggered the system fully, that door was staying locked until someone – maybe Darren or Levi – realized it. But when they didn't show up, would anyone think to look in the vault? Probably not right away.

She carefully X-ed out of the screen, trying not to bump anything that would trigger the alarm. She pushed a hand through her hair, smearing sweat just above her temple.

"How are we doing?" Brock's voice sounded too clear. Olivia's head whipped around. Her alarm spiked when she saw that he'd removed his mask. "Brock Tanner, what are you doing?"

"Sharing some air with him. Don't worry, not all of it." Brock looked worried but settled the mask securely over Nick's head.

"You're going to…"

"So is he," Brock cut her off and pinned her with a stare. "Come on, honey. Get us out of here. I believe in you."

Olivia whipped back around, her fingers fumbling madly. Her heart stampeded in her chest. She had to figure this out. One more time. She typed in the code one more time.

The red faded to green.

Olivia breathed a sigh of relief. The anti-hack system wasn't flashing a warning at her anymore. She was in. She carefully scrolled through the diagram, spotting what she needed right away.

The yellow wire. The one that controlled the lock was yellow.

Olivia shined her light at the panel. The next step was getting that thing open. She jumped to her feet, swinging the light around the vault. "Brock, help me look for a screwdriver, anything sharp. I need to get the panel off."

Brock gently lowered Nick's head to the ground, leaving the mask on him before using his own phone as a flashlight to look around. Olivia took as much care as she could not to damage any artifacts, but paintings and swords were of no use to her. She needed something small.

A toolbox! There on the top shelf. She reached for it but glanced over as Brock put a hand to his chest as if trying to get a deep breath. "Brock!"

"I'm okay..." His voice sounded breathless. He waved her off with his other hand. "Whatcha need?"

Olivia frowned. "Get your mask back on, get some breaths, I've got the toolbox."

"Yeah..." He nodded. "I'm fine, just a little light-headed."

Light-headed nothing. "Share your air, Brock, don't give it all to him or you're both gonna die."

The toolbox was just out of her reach. Was there a ladder nearby? She didn't have time for a ladder! She glanced around, spotting a box that looked sturdy enough to hold her weight. She shot toward the box, dragging it under the shelf where the toolbox lay. "Who puts a toolbox on the top shelf?"

No answer.

"Brock, you okay?"

"Fine." His voice was muffled, meaning he had the mask back on. Good.

Olivia tested her weight on the box before hopping up on top of it. She reached for the toolbox. Her fingers barely brushed the underside of it, but it was still out of reach.

"Now that you're not suffocating to death, can you reach this toolbox for me?"

Brock hustled over to her, breathing through his mask. "'Go breathe some air. Put your mask back on. Help me reach the toolbox.' Anything else on your honey-do list?"

For once, Olivia wasn't in the mood for his jokes. Couldn't it wait? "Can you just get the box down for me?"

Brock stretched to his limit, scooting the box out with ease. He brought it down and handed it to her.

"Thank you." Olivia rolled her eyes playfully.

"You're welcome, Your Highness." Brock chuckled, returning to Nick's side.

"What's so funny?" Olivia barked as she knelt back down in front of the panel.

"I'm trying to keep it light." Brock settled beside Nick, removing his mask once again. "We're already tense enough. We're going to get out of this, Olivia. It's okay."

Olivia rifled through the toolbox until she spotted a Phillips screwdriver. How much time had that little adventure cost her? Thirty seconds?

Stop counting, Olivia.

Twenty seconds?

Olivia shook her head and jammed the screwdriver into the front of the panel before ripping it off. Inside were the neatly arranged wires of the system. Now. Which one was the yellow wire?

Olivia lifted her flashlight again, slowing down to examine this. All she had to do was pull the yellow wire and the door should open from a command on her app. *Come on, come on, which one is it?*

Oh, yeah. There it was. Buried behind the red, blue, and green-striped wires.

Of course.

Olivia sighed. She reached her hand back into the panel, moving the cords aside as she did. Using the feel of her fingertips, she fumbled around until she found where the wire plugged into the panel.

"Gotcha."

She pulled, but not all the way. Following a startling *buzzing* sound, sparks flew, blinding her for a few seconds as a shock zapped her hand.

"*Ahhh!*" Olivia cried in shock and a little pain, falling backward in a heap.

"Olivia!" Brock shouted. He left Nick's side and hurried over to her. "Oh, crap, it's on fire."

CHAPTER THIRTY

F IRE. PAIN. AND A POSSIBLE SHORT-CIRCUIT.

Brock got to his feet behind her. Something crashed on the shelf. Olivia held her shaking hand, angry at the blisters forming there. She was *not* getting taken down by a blister, but that burn mark on the side of her wrist might do the trick.

Brock was at her side, glancing around frantically. And, of course, no mask. He spied something near the door and sprang up. In a flash, he broke some glass from a container next to the vault door and ripped a large fire blanket from the container on the wall. Thinking quickly, he approached the fire and threw the blanket over the panel, dousing the flames in seconds. But it was too late.

A low wail pierced the air, an alarm that sounded outside the vault and buzzed on Olivia's phone. She looked back down at the app, seeing the screen blinking red again, this time with an alert. The system had sensed the fire.

Olivia cursed under her breath and got to her knees again.

"Are you okay?" Brock asked.

"It doesn't matter if I am or not," Olivia bit out, angry at herself. "I was pulling the wire, but I must have accidentally pulled another one up with it and crossed them." Probably short-circuited it. Either that or triggered a heavier lockdown.

She carefully lifted her phone into her hand. Her mind raced. Darren was sure to be getting the same alert on his phone, considering the app alerted them any time there was movement or something messing with the panel, like a fire. That was hopeful. But Nick was down to less than two minutes. She was sure of it. And Brock wasn't helping by running around without a mask.

Shaking fingers dismissed the alarm. "Good. It didn't trigger a lockdown. Yet." Next time, it would.

She ripped the fire blanket off the panel. She shined her flashlight back inside, sighing at what she saw. A mess of melted, plastic wires, more copper than plastic. Meaning the colors had melted away, too, and she'd have to look harder for that yellow one. "Great."

"What is it?" Brock sounded out of breath. He reached up, leaning against the wall.

"I don't know which one is which, now." Olivia sighed.

"Oh, great." Brock ran his hand through his hair. "Listen... maybe we should..."

"No." Olivia shook her head. She remembered where it was. Not how it looked, but where it was. There was no more fire. She could do this. "Nick is dying. I'm hoping it's not too late, already. We need to get out of here. You and he both need medical attention. You know what?" She ripped off her mask and shoved it at him. "Wear this."

"No!" Brock shoved it back at her. "I'm not giving this up so you can..."

"I'm working!" Olivia reached back into the panel with the hand that hadn't gotten burned. Her fingers fumbled for the wire, where she remembered.

Was that the wire?

Or was it close to the original wire?

"Olivia!"

"Put the mask on, Brock. We won't be in here long." Olivia wanted to scream and pound on the door, but she forced her voice to be calm. Her burn throbbed, distracting her. Her body tensed, expecting another scare of sparks flying out of the box. She wasn't falling for that, this time.

Her fingers found the wire. She looked harder, tracing it down to see where a small bit of plastic remained. Her eyes adjusted to the thin yellow stripe running along the side. She closed her eyes.

Ten seconds?

Probably not. That stupid alarm in training would have gone off by now.

This wasn't about the alarm. Or impressing anyone. This was about survival. Now that they'd all breathed their fair share of CO_2, it was time to get where there was oxygen.

Olivia pinched the wire between her fingertips. Prayed it was the right one and that her eyes weren't deceiving her.

I know it is.

Pulled.

No sparks. She gasped and reached for her phone.

"You did it?" Brock only held the mask to his mouth but didn't put it on. Stubbornly, he reached forward and settled the mask over her nose and mouth. Olivia breathed. She would never again take fresh air for granted.

She didn't answer. She didn't need to. Once the code was typed into her phone, the heavy clunk of the door to the vault sliding open was all the answer she needed.

Brock gasped. "You did it."

"We gotta get Nick and you out of here." Olivia scrambled to her feet.

"Hey. Mask."

Olivia looked over at him and smiled for a moment before taking the mask and slipping it over her face. Brock retrieved his mask from Nick, doing the same and securing it at the back of his head before he reached down.

And, here we go again.

Olivia slipped Nick's arm over her shoulders and rose to her feet, Nick between them. They sprinted for the door. Olivia almost half-expected it to close on them again, but they slipped through the door and back into the hallway. They were fine. They were safe. Thank goodness.

"Back door, back door!" Brock nodded to the back door.

Footsteps thundered down the stairs. Voices of firemen and HAZMAT called to them. Where were they five minutes ago when they needed them?

Olivia ignored them. Nick needed fresh air, he needed to get out of this box of suffocation that was once a museum.

Brock jammed his shoulder against the door. He must not have latched it securely earlier, as the door opened with ease. Beautiful sunlight spilled into the open doorway. Olivia and Brock hurried out into the fresh air where quite a crowd had gathered near the front of the museum.

"*There they are!*" Skylar screamed. She took off running toward them, followed by Levi and several firemen. Tailing them was Darren. Worry completely overtook his face. Was that even a hint of relief that flashed in his eyes? His shoulders dropped with a sigh.

Olivia gulped in some oxygen, feeling lightheaded herself. She lowered Nick to the ground between her and Brock, then ripped off her mask. Instantly, they were surrounded by first responders.

Brock took off his mask. "Nick was down there too long, we're afraid. He's been unconscious for close to four minutes. I was timing him." He held up his phone. "And he was lethargic before that. He was trapped in a room with no ventilation."

The EMTs began talking among themselves, barking orders and calling for a gurney and oxygen. Levi's posture was stiff and his voice tight as he approached. "What happened to you? Where have you been?"

Olivia looked up at him, her chest heaving in and out with rescue breaths and welcome oxygen, chilled by the late October breeze. "Simon said he went back to get that Norwegian tapestry or something? Anyway, he was in the vault and when we found him, he passed out. Then the door closed and we couldn't get out."

Horror struck Darren's face and he clapped a hand to his mouth, curling it around his chin before speaking over the top of his fingers. "You were in the vault?"

"We were." Brock's irritation was cradled in his voice by a question. "Did you check the cameras?"

"I was in too much of a hurry. I knew you had gone down to get Nick, but I didn't think you were in the vault. I just was going through standard operation procedure and closed the vault's door. I didn't know you were in there!"

His voice rose, and panic lined his features. Brock's irritation died and he put out a hand. "We're okay, man. Everything's fine now. We handled it. Mistakes happen."

"I could have…" Darren raked a hand through his hair and turned his back on Brock.

Levi reached back to console him. "Hey, man, they're okay now. Everyone's okay."

They loaded Nick onto the gurney as Skylar stared at Olivia with enormous eyes. "How did you get out?"

Darren paused, then turned around, the questions on his face dissolving his earlier panic. Levi pinned her with a knowing stare.

Olivia squirmed under their attention. But after an incident like this, there was no going back. They couldn't keep moving forward like they were, so who needed a convincing story, anymore? She wasn't ready to blurt out her status as an FBI agent, but she wasn't going to lie about anything, either.

"I know a thing or two about manually overriding security locks."

"But... but this is Vanguard Core!" Darren exclaimed, breathlessly. "You don't just hack the panel when it's VanCore, there's steps you gotta go through."

"And Olivia knew the steps." Brock gave her a side glance and winked at her. "Whatever the case, she saved our lives. At least, we hope Nick is going to be okay."

CHAPTER
THIRTY-ONE

THE HOSPITAL STAFF CRAWLED LIKE ANTS FROM AN ANTHILL that was kicked over. Olivia didn't like being in a separate room from Brock, but since her exposure was less severe than his, she knew she'd be released in a few hours.

After enduring the pokes and prods of the necessary blood work to clear her, Olivia breathed in some straight oxygen until her doctor came in with her test results. While waiting for him, she lay back on her pillows, trying to process everything that happened. So much chaos was packed into so little time that she was certain she had forgotten something in the process. She replayed the scene over and over again in her mind. Tessa and Toby running up from downstairs, breathless. A CO_2 container leaking into the HVAC system, overwhelming the air conditioning with chemicals to make people pass out. Who knew how many people inhaled it?

Now that the museum was closed again—wasn't this the second time this month?—Olivia itched to go back. Since most of the staff were already hospitalized, she and Brock could work in relative peace. But she knew that there was no chance of going back today. Not with the incident report she knew she'd have to send in and the doctor's orders to "rest."

As the curtain pulled back, her doctor appeared, holding a clipboard. "Agent Knight, you're all clear. We're just getting your discharge papers together."

"And my fiancé?" Olivia asked.

"He's down the hall. You can see him when we get your discharge papers if you like."

Olivia smiled. "Yes. I'd like to."

She waited for another half hour before she was finally released. Rather than heading for the exit, she found Brock's room and knocked on the door. "Hey, handsome."

Brock looked up at her and beamed when she entered. The sight of an oxygen mask on his face unnerved her at first. How much had he breathed?

Obviously not enough. He pulled the mask down around his chin as she came in. "There's my beautiful Olivia."

Olivia snorted and sat down beside him. "What did they say?"

Indignation shadowed Brock's face. "They're keeping me for observation for the next six hours. Six hours, Olivia! I didn't even have that many symptoms, just lightheadedness and difficulty breathing, but I was fine when I got back outside."

Olivia grinned. "They just want to be sure you're okay."

"I'm fine." Brock sighed. "How come they let you go so early?"

"Because." She lightly punched his arm. "Unlike *somebody*, I kept my mask on most of the time and didn't take it off for longer than a few seconds."

"Not entirely true," Brock countered with a grin. "And, hey. Would you rather I let him suffocate?"

Olivia softened into a smile. "No. Which is another reason I love you." She leaned forward and brushed a kiss against his lips. It felt good to show affection in public again, rather than staying under the guise of two undercover security guards going through the motions in life. "Now. Speaking of putting your mask back on?"

"Yeah, yeah, I know." Brock rolled his eyes and slipped his mask back over his mouth.

Olivia sat back down. "You know I'm going to have to call this in, right?"

"You make the call." Brock nodded to her. "I have a mask on and can't really speak that well."

"You jerk." Olivia laughed and pulled out her cell phone, dialing Calvin's number. After filling him in, she waited for his answer.

He was quiet for a few minutes before asking. "What do you mean a CO_2 leak? Are you both all right? What happened?"

For once, Olivia was grateful that Calvin showed much more emotion than their previous supervisor. She heard the concern in his voice through the phone, even though he kept his tone professional. "We're still figuring out where it came from," she explained. "But Brock and I are still at the hospital. Brock's being held for observation and we probably won't be able to get back over there until tomorrow."

"I'll get in touch with the local police and let them know to communicate fully with you," Calvin said. Olivia thought she heard him chuckle a bit. "But more importantly, are you two okay?"

"We both had minimal exposure." Olivia filled in the details of how Brock had shared some of his air with Nick and how she had hacked the Vanguard Core system. She braced herself for a reprimand, seeing as how she hadn't been able to pass a single test before now.

"And you effectively hacked the system?"

Olivia nodded, smiling despite herself. "I did."

"After failing the test?"

Yeah, she knew that was coming. She felt her chest tighten up again, almost like receiving a reprimand from her supervisor was as nerve-wracking as being in the vault all over again. "I did, sir. But at the time, I was more concerned with saving a life than protocol. I'll sign whatever you need me to, but I don't regret what I did."

Another long pause preceded his answer. When he replied, his voice had warmed a notch or two, almost like he hadn't wanted to have this conversation in the first place. "You saved a life. That counts for something. Good work, Knight."

Olivia released a breath she didn't realize she was holding. "Thank you, sir."

"Now, you and Brock take the rest of the day off. We'll be in contact tomorrow morning and see where we're at if you're able to continue the investigation tomorrow. I'll call first thing."

"We will be waiting. Thanks, again." Olivia hung up and swooped her hair out of her face. Brock stared at her expectantly over the top of his mask. "That sounded tense."

"I didn't exactly have clearance to hack the security system." Olivia shrugged.

"But?" Brock raised his head, a smile creasing his lips under the mask. "You saved all our skins down there. Let 'em try to reprimand you for that. I told you you'd master that thing, yet."

"Thank you." Olivia felt her face warm and she glanced down. "I'm just glad I didn't fail when it mattered most."

"You're going to ace that test next time you do it." Brock tugged her tighter. "And I'll even brew up some old nasty instant coffee for you when you do."

Olivia snorted a laugh. "I'm going to need more than instant coffee when I pass that test, Brock. Maybe a bottle of merlot or something stronger?"

"What?" Brock dramatically set a hand to his chest. "You're turning down a cup of your favorite battery acid?" He reached forward and put a hand to her forehead. "Are you sure they checked you for CO_2 poisoning?"

"Oh," Olivia slapped his upper arm and laughed. "Get your head in the game. We've got work to do."

Brock was finally released late that night, but by the time they got to the hotel, it was past midnight. Even despite how late they were getting in, Olivia could hardly sleep. She didn't want the local police to be the first eyes on the scene, even though she knew there was no other choice. She and Brock had been on the inside; they were more acquainted with the case than anyone. So rather than working it at the scene, she turned it over in her head.

There was no way these things just kept happening. The jewel heist, followed by Dorian's death, followed by Selena's car accident, followed by the CO^2 leak were just too much. Some of it—if not, *all*— had to be related.

Olivia was ready to throw off the cover of a security guard and put on the full-blown FBI agent who would take control and charge of this case. She was ready to get to the bottom of whatever was happening.

After talking with Calvin the next morning and ensuring that they were both fine for light work, Olivia drove toward the museum with Brock by her side. It felt good to be back in a business suit rather than the uniform of a security guard.

"Are you sure you're feeling all right?" Olivia asked as she closed her car door behind her.

"Just fine. They really didn't need to keep me that long yesterday. I feel back to my normal self," Brock assured her, falling into line beside her.

"Remember. Both Calvin *and* the doctors said no strenuous work for at least 24 hours."

Brock side-eyed her as they approached the stairs to the museum. "Define strenuous, again?"

Olivia laughed. "Our job. But we're not going to tell anyone that. We're just here to, you know." She shrugged. "Collect fingerprints, examine the HVAC room, you know. Nothing too hard."

"Right. Exactly."

Side by side with Brock, she strode up the stairs to the museum. She showed her badge to the officer in charge. "I'm Special Agent Knight, this is Special Agent Tanner, we're working this case."

The officer gave them a bright smile. Definitely not the world-weary big-city cop that the prior detective of Dorian's homicide had been. "Detective Jill Bryant. Come on in."

Professional and courteous. Olivia liked her already.

They followed Detective Bryant into the museum. As they did, Olivia was suddenly hit with a wave of melancholy at the emptiness. She didn't dare admit out loud that she was starting to get attached to the staff here. Tessa, Toby, and Skylar, who greeted her every morning, and Levi, who always gave her a secretive smile as she and Brock passed him in the hallway. Dare she even say that she missed Nick in all his glory and ill-timed historical facts? The museum seemed so sadly empty without them all; she just wanted to solve this thing so that they could return to normal.

"When we got here, it was a mess. The fire department had their hands full with the air ducts, but they gave it the all clear, now." Bryant tossed occasional glances over her shoulder as she walked.

"By the time we were allowed in here, we didn't touch anything but left it for you guys. They said you were working the case."

"We are," Brock said as he followed her downstairs.

"Good luck with that," Bryant said as she led them to the left.

Olivia stepped into the HVAC room where police were gathering what little evidence and photos they could. "Thanks, guys, we'll take it from here," she called to them.

Nodding their acquiescence, they dispersed from the room.

"Thanks for your help," Brock said.

"No problem. We'll just be upstairs if you need me," Bryant assured them before stepping from the room. Olivia surveyed the HVAC room from where she stood in the doorway. "Okay. While we were in here before, all we could see was what showed up on the surface."

"Meaning," Brock followed up her train of thought. "We can actually take our time and look at everything here."

"Exactly." Olivia stepped toward the canister of CO_2 she'd moved yesterday. "This was leaking right into the air vents. Do you think someone set it off?"

"Tessa and Toby weren't where they were supposed to be, first off," Brock pointed out.

"They probably know a thing or two. You can learn anything on the internet, these days." Olivia crouched down, taking a picture of the CO_2 tank before turning the valve with her gloved hands so she could examine it. Her attention was drawn to the scuff marks lining the side in white scratches, along with an obvious dent. Olivia also noticed that the valve was not intact and that a piece of it was missing.

"Brock, take a look at this." She beckoned him closer.

He crouched beside her. "What is it?"

"Does this look intentional to you?" Olivia turned the canister so he could see it better.

Brock examined the dent and the scuff marks, along with the broken valve. "It's hard to say. Maybe it was battered around and damaged to look like an accident?"

Olivia looked up and around the room. Among the heating and AC ducts that bulged into the small space, some metal shelves lined the areas that weren't occupied by air passages, making the room a maze of dismal gray. What items were on the shelves, though? Olivia wondered out of curiosity. She set the container down and examined each of the shelves. Cleaning supplies, power tools and other items filled the shelves, but the one toward the front contained something else. Some other tanks, about the same large size as the CO_2 container occupied one of the lower shelves near the front. Olivia approached the shelf, curious. "We've got more CO_2 here."

"My question?" Brock stood and began pacing the outline of the room, weaving between the maze of shelves and air ducts. "Why do you need so many containers of CO_2? What could they possibly be used for?"

"Don't know." Olivia shook her head. "Oxygen, I can understand for some intents and purposes, but carbon dioxide? Do they use it to maintain the exhibits or something?"

"That's a Graham question," Brock called to her from behind one of the shelves. His silence felt suddenly heavy. Olivia was about to call out to him until his voice drifted from between the shelves. "Hey, Olivia? You're going to want to come take a look at this."

Olivia left the shelf she was examining and headed over to where Brock stood behind the shelves. "What is it?" As soon as her eyes fell upon it, she knew she didn't need to ask.

Spread out on two sawhorses that made a makeshift table was a mural that looked very familiar. The *Wedding of Caecillius* faced upward, as if ready to be worked on. Surrounding the mural were small egg-shaped containers with chemicals and what looked like test tubes.

"What in the world?" Olivia stepped forward. "I thought we hung this in the exhibit hall."

"We did. And it was still there." Brock eyed her. "I noticed it before we came downstairs. It's still hanging in the exhibit hall."

"Then what…" Olivia's voice trailed off as she looked behind her. Brock raised an eyebrow and approached the side where she wasn't. After snapping some pictures, his gloved hands plucked one of the containers as he held it up to what little light they had and examined it. "What do you suppose this stuff is?"

"Deadly, probably. Don't drink it." Olivia joked.

"Oh, so probably some of that instant coffee junk you drink?"

Olivia laughed and rolled her eyes. "Bro-ock," she said in a warning tone before reaching for one of the vats herself. She held it to her nose, nearly gagging at the sulfur cocktail. "Definitely not my coffee. I'm taking some of this back to the lab to confirm what I already think it is"

"What's that?" Brock set the container down, then started to examine the painting more closely.

"Sulfur dioxide mixed with water. Maybe some other stuff."

Brock nodded. He studied the mural intently, then cranked his head to look at it better. "Hey, Olivia?"

"Yeah?" She stepped up next to him.

He pointed. "Can you tell me what's wrong with this painting?"

Olivia studied it. The woman pictured was standing in the same pose as the one upstairs, the man still looking at her adoringly with the same character that she and Ivy had admired…

Then, she saw it. "There's no damage. The painting is in perfect condition." She stepped back, numbed by the realization for a moment. She looked back down at the chemicals lining the painting about to be destroyed and glanced back at Brock. "We need to get these back to the lab. I wonder if that's why there's so much CO_2 hanging around."

Brock nodded back to the shelf Olivia had been studying. "Why don't you dust that for fingerprints while I collect some samples?"

Olivia nodded. "You got it." She returned to the shelf, reaching into her kit to grab her fingerprint powder.

"Why do you think these containers are related to the painting?" Brock called to her.

"Think about it. Ivy was just saying what the main gasses are during a volcanic eruption. She specifically mentioned CO_2, water, and sulfuric acid. Well, sulfur dioxide. Then she gave us an entire lesson we didn't pay her for on how sulfur dioxide becomes acid rain."

"Hey, we got paid to listen." Brock chuckled. "I'm cool with that, either way. But it doesn't make sense at the same time."

Olivia took up the brush and reached for the containers... when suddenly the shelf startled her by tipping backward a bit. She let out a yelp reflexively as the shelf moved back, then rocked forward again.

"Are you okay?" Brock charged around the corner. After yesterday, they both seemed to have more heightened senses of what was going on around them.

Olivia nodded. "Yeah." She put her hand up on the shelf to see what had caused it. Holding onto the gray bar that ran up the side, she rocked it back, then forth again. "The bottom of the shelf is uneven. Easily topples forward and backward."

As she rocked it back into place, one of the containers of CO_2 began to slide toward the floor. Not wanting a repeat of yesterday, Olivia lurched forward to catch it. Her eye caught on the warped shelf like someone had stepped on it or tried to use it as a ladder. "This isn't the best place for these containers."

"I'll say." Brock approached the shelf, testing the teeter-totter it made for himself. His eyes traced the ground, then traced a pattern to the HVAC system. "Just a thought. Do you think that it was intentionally sabotaged, or *could* it have been an accident? What do you think?"

"I'm not thinking anything right now." Olivia avoided brushing against the shelf as she dusted the containers for fingerprints. Seeing a few, she took out her tape. "I won't know more until we can get to the bottom of certain things with our suspects. See what the tapes say. Who was down here right before the chaos erupted? What was everyone doing? How long had it been going on?"

"I'll grab the new set of tapes on the way out," Brock promised. "We need that movie night, remember?"

"Oh, I'm so excited." Olivia rolled her eyes and lifted the fingerprints. "How about a movie night at the lab, instead, while I run some things through?"

Olivia settled down in her chair once again at the lab, glad it wasn't so late at night. Her eyes usually worked better when they weren't droopy and her hands didn't fumble as much when her body wasn't running off a system hoping to sleep soon. The late afternoon sun faded in the windows outside as she worked to run the fingerprints she'd lifted through IAFIS and test the chemicals in the containers.

"Thank goodness the museum wasn't as busy that day," Brock said as he scrolled through. "It's easier to see who came and went when there isn't a large crowd of people standing around the exhibit floor."

Olivia sent the results to the printer, then rolled over to see what Brock was talking about. "Who are we looking at?"

"Well, this is about thirty minutes before the incident." Brock pointed to the screen. "Ivy was there. She was one of the first to get out. She and Elliot went out the back door downstairs, and went around to the front about the time Levi and Graham came outside."

"Interesting," Olivia nodded. "She came from the break room?"

"It appears that way." Brock scrolled the footage a little more. "But here's who went down there fifteen minutes before. Check this out. Remember what Skylar said?"

"About what, exactly?" Olivia rubbed her temples. "Remember we don't share a brain."

Brock chuckled. "Sorry. I'm getting ahead of myself. When we asked where Tessa and Toby both were, she said Tessa was on break and Toby was in the bathroom?"

"Oh, right." Olivia nodded.

"Watch this." Brock set the time to about fifteen minutes before Tessa came running back upstairs. Tessa indeed left the front desk to look around, then headed down to the break room. A minute after she left, Toby got up and poked his head into the gift shop. Probably told Skylar where he was going and asked her to watch the front. Then, he approached the bathrooms but never went in. He looked back toward the gift shop, then scurried out of the front of house.

"What does he think he's doing?" Olivia hummed, leaning forward and watching.

Brock switched the monitors to the exhibit hall to see Toby run past and disappear downstairs.

"He and Tessa both turned left at the bottom of the stairs. You know that blind spot where the cameras are around the janitor's closet and HVAC room?"

"Yeah." Olivia's eyebrows rose and she sat back. "You're not saying he was there..."

"They both went into the blind spot. They were there for fifteen minutes before, this." Brock clicked to the next footage to show both Tessa and Toby, running full tilt toward the stairs, then up the stairs. The camera followed them running through the exhibit hall – rather unprofessional, Olivia added – then bursting up front seconds before the alarms went off. She remembered the rest from there.

"What were they doing down there?" Olivia chewed her lower lip in thought.

"I think it's time we conduct some interviews." Brock sat back in the chair and folded his arms over his chest. "Because I don't think the museum will be reopening any time soon. This kind of stuff can't go on." He gestured toward the monitors.

Olivia shook her head. "No. The entire staff will wind up dead at this rate."

"We have several leads. Tessa and Toby were definitely downstairs at the time of the leak."

The printer beeped as Brock was talking. Nodding to show she was listening, Olivia scooted back and snatched the paper with the results of her chemical test. "And, we have one other with probable cause."

"Let me guess." Brock raised an eyebrow. "Ivy?"

"Yep." Olivia turned the paper around. "The chemicals we found around the forged mural downstairs? Sulfuric acid. Something she knows a lot about."

Brock studied the paper. "Sounds like she was trying to imitate the damage with the same chemicals that damaged the original. Same stuff we found on the silk scarf underneath the Ratnashree diamond."

"You're right, Brock." Olivia slapped her paper down on the table. "It's time that these people come clean."

Brock picked up a phone. "I have to make some calls. We need to talk to a few people as early as tomorrow."

"Me, too." Olivia picked up her own. "We're gonna have a full day."

"Fine with me," Brock grinned. "At least we're finally getting somewhere."

CHAPTER
THIRTY-TWO

O LIVIA TICKED OFF HER TO-DO LIST FOR THE DAY ONE
item at a time from the time she got out of bed to when
she and Brock pulled into the field office around 9:00.
She had so many people to interview, and couldn't wait to get
to the bottom of everything that was happening.

"So I heard from the hospital this morning. Forgot to tell
you." Brock held the door open for her as she passed through.

"What's that?" Had Selena pulled through her coma? Olivia
thought of her daily, hoping she'd make it through.

"Nick's going to be okay. We cut it awfully close, but they told
me he's going to pull through."

Well, she wasn't disappointed to hear it, but she was eager for the day when the same could be said about Selena. Still, her heart rejoiced at the thought that Nick was out of danger. "Really?"

"Really." Brock followed her into the field office. "He has a few lingering effects, so they're going to keep him for a couple days but he is up and talking as usual."

"Spouting off historical facts about the first hospital and Florence Nightingale, no doubt." Olivia laughed.

Brock echoed her laughter. "I know I'll probably regret saying this, but I've missed his little thirty-second history lessons."

"Those history lessons proved to be something that pointed us in the right direction." Olivia looked over her shoulder at Brock as she walked with confidence through the halls. "Whether he did it or not, I'm sure he gave the thief the same information he gave us, about that heist of 1964."

After they both grabbed some coffee from the break room, Olivia and Brock made their way toward the center of the office, away from the lab where they had discovered the sulfuric acid last night. They were met by one of the agents near the interview room. "Ivy Landon's here. She's in room 3."

"Thank you," Olivia said as she and Brock started in that direction. Olivia paused at the window and looked through the glass at the chemistry teacher who sat at a table, drinking something from a paper cup with trembling hands. She seemed calm given the situation, but the little behavioral changes gave her away. Her shaking hands, her gaze shifting around the room from time to time as Olivia watched her.

"Do you think she'll confess to everything?" Brock asked.

Olivia shook her head. "Difficult to tell. She seems good at hiding a lot of things. Her emotions, the truth, you name it."

"Let's get to the bottom of this." Brock glanced around, then gently brushed his fingers against Olivia's. "Are you ready for this?"

"Absolutely." She smiled up at him for a few moments. With him beside her, she was ready for anything.

Brock opened the door first and stepped inside, followed by Olivia, who clutched a notebook in plain sight. Ivy glanced up to see who she'd be talking to and surprise doused her face. Her eyebrows raised and her mouth hung open slightly. "Knight? Tanner?"

"That would be us." Olivia gave her a knowing smile.

Ivy studied her for a few moments, barely moving as Olivia and Brock moved to sit down in front of her with their notes. "I should've known," she said, once they were seated across from her. "Security guards don't poke around like you do."

"We just have a few questions for you," Olivia leaned forward at the table. "Thanks for coming in today."

Ivy studied her, then nodded, slowly. "You're welcome." Her voice sounded hesitant as if she had a boatload of questions to ask but wasn't sure if she should. "Is this about what happened at the museum on Thursday?"

Brock shook his head. "Not exactly. There are a few other things we'd like to discuss with you first."

Olivia let him take the reins with the conversation at first. He was always better at talking to people, so she opted to sit quietly and let him steer.

"Miss Landon, before we continue, I need to inform you of your rights. You're not under arrest, but you do have the right to an attorney. If at any point you'd like one present, you can stop the conversation and request legal counsel. Do you understand this, and are you okay speaking with us without an attorney right now?"

Concern once again lifted Ivy's brows. "An attorney? Do I need one?"

"That's entirely up to you," Brock stated. "We're just here to ask a few questions. You can choose to have an attorney present, or you can speak with us now. If at any point you change your mind, we'll stop until you have legal representation."

Ivy looked between them for a few moments, her posture visibly tensing. Her shoulders squared, but she managed to maintain her calm facade. She took a long sip of her drink, then set it down with the same poise as would make Selena proud. "I don't need an attorney. I haven't done anything wrong, so go ahead. Fire away." She didn't fold her arms but kept them crossed over her lap.

Brock nodded. "Okay." He opened his folder, reading over what he had written down. "Miss Landon, where were you on October 5th?"

"October 5th?" Ivy glanced down as if she couldn't remember. "I don't remember day by day what was happening. What was that, a Friday?"

Brock nodded, his face giving no indication of what he was thinking. "Yes."

Recognition dawned on Ivy's features and she nodded. "Ah. I see. The jewel was discovered missing the next day, wasn't it?"

"You remember that?" Brock asked.

Ivy nodded. "I do remember, because Selena called me into her office, horrified about what happened. It happened the first weekend in October, so it was hard to forget. Not a good way to start the month."

"Can you tell us what you remember from the day you realized the Ratnashree diamond came up missing?" Brock settled back, open to listening to what she had to say.

"The details are kinda blurry, but I remember most of what happened," Ivy said before she searched the ceiling for answers. "I came by to check on a few things for the exhibit as I usually do on Saturday, especially after the first week of it being on display. Before I could even finish clocking in, Selena found me in the break room and urgently asked me to her office. So I put my stuff away and went up to her office where she closed the door and told me that the diamond we had on display was a fake. She asked if I knew anything about it, and of course I said 'no.'"

"So you didn't know that the diamond was a fake?" Brock confirmed. Olivia watched Ivy's reaction.

"No!" The word shot from Ivy's mouth as what looked like genuine horror haunted her eyes. "When I put the display together, it was real. We made sure everything looked good on October first when we first put it on display. Levi checked it out, as did Simon, Graham, and myself. We all had eyes on it, and everything looked good, so we displayed it. I have no idea how it was switched with a fake."

"Do you know anything about diamonds?" Olivia decided to ask her first question. "Such as how to spot a fake, or maybe how someone could age up a fake diamond to make it look like the real thing?"

Ivy pinned Olivia with a stare, looking her right in the eye. "I design exhibits, Agent Knight." She didn't bark the words, but they were no less definitive. "I know a little bit, as much as anyone. I know that soaking paper in tea overnight can make a paper look like it's from 1770, I know that money is fake if it doesn't have a hidden image of Ben Franklin's face, but when it comes to spotting real and fake diamonds, I don't have the kind of confidence that Levi does. My first ring was a cubic zirconia and I thought it was a real diamond."

Olivia glanced down at her hand to see Ivy's currently empty finger. She didn't remember seeing anything in the records about Ivy being married. "Engagement ring?"

Ivy drew her hands under the table. "Yeah. We never made it to the altar. Hard to marry a man who's cheated on you the whole time you've been together."

If anyone understood breaking off an engagement, it was Olivia. "I'm sorry." She nodded empathetically before Brock got everyone back on track.

"What about chemical reactions to artifacts?" he asked. "Can you tell us a little about that?"

"I know about chemical reactions. I'm a chemistry teacher," Ivy admitted with no shame.

Brock leveled another stare at her. "What can you tell us about sulfur dioxide and sulfuric acid's effect on a diamond, fake or not?"

Ivy blinked. Her face didn't move from the icy facade she carried with her, nor did she act uncomfortable. "Well, if it's a real diamond, sulfuric acid won't do anything. Diamond is pure carbon and sulfuric acid can't touch it. But if it's a fake like glass or cubic zirconia, you might see a reaction over time. It wouldn't dissolve, but the surface might get cloudy. Maybe etched." She cast a suspicious glance between Olivia and Brock. "Why? Did someone tamper with the diamond? If they did, they should have used something other than sulfuric acid."

There was enough acid in her tone to dissolve a real diamond, no matter what she said. "Such as what?" Olivia asked.

"Hydrofluoric acid, maybe." Ivy shrugged one shoulder. "If they were trying to fake the sparkle of a counterfeit diamond, that is. But not even that would make a fake diamond look real; it would make it look like someone smudged it clumsily while cleaning it. It's not a good idea to mess with the surface of a diamond at all, because any chemical reaction is going to draw attention to it. Whether it makes it dull or smudged, someone will notice that it's not sparkling like it should. If anyone wants to make a diamond look real, it's better to forget using chemicals altogether."

Brock nodded as he jotted it down. "Let's talk about something other than diamonds for a moment. What about the effect of sulfuric acid on the mural from Pompeii, the *Wedding of Caecillius*." He glanced back up at Ivy. "We talked about it recently."

Ivy nodded, confused. "Where is all of this going?"

Olivia pushed one of the pictures she'd taken of the forgery across the table at Ivy. "While we were working the scene of the CO_2 leak, we came across this setup downstairs in the HVAC room."

Ivy took the picture in her hands and studied it. After a while, her eyebrows lifted again in what seemed to be surprise. "Is this the mural?"

"It's a forgery of the *Wedding of Caecillius*." Brock settled back in his chair. "We found containers of sulfuric acid on the same table near the painting. The painting was behind a shelf with containers of CO_2. Both chemicals were present at the time of the Vesuvius eruption and both had an effect on the original mural."

Olivia wasn't sure if Ivy was playing stupid or if, perhaps, she didn't know. When she looked up from the picture, her eyes snapped and she looked more affronted than anything. "What, are you saying *I* did this?" She flipped the picture down on the table and set her elbows on either side. She buried her fingers through her hair, letting her head sink into her hands. A sigh blew from her lips. "Oh, boy."

"You look a little stressed there, Ivy." Brock leaned forward. "You okay?"

"Not entirely. It's just that," Ivy plucked her head from her hands and nailed them both with a stare. "I don't know anything about this forgery downstairs. But I know that's not a good enough answer for you people."

"Well, maybe we can get to the bottom of it together." Brock kept any antagonizing tone out of his voice as he changed directions. "We'll get back to this mural in a moment. There's something else I'd like to know."

"What?" Distress leaked into her voice, like a teenager having to take out her earbuds to answer whether or not she did her chores.

"We noticed that on October 13th, you were at the museum in the morning when you should've been in your classroom. We have footage putting you there early on a Friday when you don't normally come in until the afternoon. Can you tell us why that day of all days, you were there early?"

Ivy sighed. "Dorian." She licked her lower lip and raised her eyes to the ceiling. "That day was cursed from the start." She leaned forward, begging them both to believe her through the urgency in her pale eyes. "I had a substitute teacher take over for me that day. The day before, Selena came to my classroom before class was in session. She asked me to come in that following morning to discuss the possibility of putting together a bigger and better exhibit. While we were in the classroom, just her and me, she confessed to me that the museum wasn't doing as well as it should financially. It could do much better, and she was worried about that. The theft of the Ratnashree diamond certainly didn't help anything, either. Selena was worried that it would put the museum in financial ruin, so she asked me to come in so we could talk about what would be a great exhibit. Then, that night, we had the staff meeting and we decided on Pompeii. But I'd already had the substitute teacher covering my classroom, so I came in that day to do some early prep on the Pompeiian exhibit."

Olivia took careful notes, although her mind screamed louder than her pencil could write. The museum wasn't doing well? She had noticed a decrease in guests and how empty it was most of the time. The weekends hummed with enough business to keep the doors open to compensate for the dwindling crowds during the week, but was it really in such dire straits as Selena mentioned?

Now that was something to look into.

"Was anything unusual about Selena stopping by your classroom?" Brock asked. Olivia wondered where he was going with the train of thought. She glanced up at him, wondering why he chose to ask that question when they weren't looking at Selena. "Maybe," he went on, "she was feeling nervous that day, or it was out of the ordinary?"

"Selena's always welcome in my classroom," Ivy stated. "In fact, she comes by every once in a while to have lunch if I'm not going to be coming into the museum. She uses the time to talk museum business just to get away for a while."

Brock nodded and made a note of that.

"Miss Landon." Olivia looked up and leaned across the table. "Do you know how long the museum has been struggling financially?"

Ivy puffed a small breath through her lips. Her voice sagged into something more somber. "I've had my suspicions for a long time. I started noticing things this last year. Ever realize how we operate on a skeleton crew? Three front of house members who work for minimum wage, one full-time security guard and three part-time rent-a-cops who don't know any more about guarding old artifacts than they do about the Gupta Empire?" She put out a hand. "Not talking about you two. You aren't security guards, I know that now. I'm talking about the young ones who just like the look of being in uniform."

Olivia had noticed them a time or two on the busier days but had hardly said a word. She'd never even spoken to them. They were off in their own little worlds. They were the ones she and Brock had almost entirely ruled out from the start.

"She was cutting corners in other ways, too," Ivy went on. "Not as much complimentary pizza for the staff, not as many creature comforts like a new vending machine when the old one was spitting out nothing but Dasani when customers would select soda, things like that. I really started to figure it out around the beginning of October. Selena and I were sharing lunch and she brought up that she was worried about the last quarter of the year. She mentioned maybe trying to squeeze in another exciting exhibit in addition to the Ratnashree diamond that might draw a crowd during the holidays. She said the numbers were looking slightly more concerning than they had last year, and she was hoping to boost something so next year's books didn't look so bad."

"Do you think someone knew about this and was trying to take advantage of it?" Olivia asked.

Ivy shrugged. "I don't really know, Agent Knight. We were all family at the Museum of Art History."

So she'd seen. And heard from everyone there. "But someone has to be the black sheep."

Ivy cupped her drink and ran her thumb around the rim of her paper cup. "Every family has one."

Her tone indicated that she may have been that black sheep. Olivia let that settle for a moment before Ivy glanced up at them both. "So am I in trouble?"

"Don't go anywhere, we'll have more questions for you," Brock told her. "But you're not under arrest."

Ivy nodded. "Look, for what it's worth? I don't know who stole the real diamond and replaced it with a fake. I also don't know anything about the mural downstairs. I promise you, I had nothing to do with that."

"Can you explain the chemicals that we found?" Olivia asked.

Ivy pondered for a moment, then shook her head. "I can't."

Ivy looked defeated as she left, but they didn't have any probable cause to hold her – yet. So what if she knew about chemicals? They hadn't officially tied her to the scene, yet.

Olivia hadn't missed the defensive way she reacted to their questions. Some might mistake it as being fired up over what happened at the museum, but it seemed to Olivia that she was more upset about being accused. Alone with her thoughts in her office, she did a more detailed background check on Ivy as best as she could. What of her personal life, her family life?

A few pictures popped up and she scrolled through them. Ivy's old Instagram which she hadn't updated in years popped up for Olivia to explore. She ran across one picture of Ivy looking stunning in a mermaid-style sequin gown and an oversized corsage to match. Another picture of her showcasing that cubic zirconia ring that she had mentioned during interrogation. Olivia studied the picture, recognizing the decomposing happiness in her eyes. The smile, as fake as the diamond on her finger. Olivia had felt that same unhappiness, once. Her mind flashed back to Tom, ancient history, when he had proposed to her and she'd thought herself to be in love, blurting out the word *yes* before putting the brakes on and thinking of her future. How far she'd come since then.

She glanced down at the new engagement ring that decked her finger with joy and happiness and studied it for a few moments. The case she worked now was more exciting than life-threatening, and it gave her and Brock more stable hours to themselves, rather than racking their brains trying to figure out how to survive the next stunt some crazy criminal wanted to throw at them. The quiet time was much needed to reflect on life, and how deeply happy she was. Her first engagement had been happiness from the outside, trying to work its way in, but her engagement to Brock was overflowing joy, bursting out from the inside out.

Why was she letting herself get distracted? She had a case to conduct.

Smiling, she flattened her hand against her desk and scrolled some more. Ivy had abandoned her Instagram shortly after her engagement, so there weren't any more photos of her at the museum, in the classroom, or anything more of her life.

Olivia tapped her finger in thought. Even though Ivy denied having anything to do with the theft of the Ratnashree diamond, she had to be involved somehow. She had ties; she had knowledge. Maybe she was too smart for anyone's good and was just as good at lying as Claude was in their last case. Claude, an overt narcissist who had looked Olivia in the eye and told her how much he missed the woman he'd killed and had nothing to do with her death.

Olivia didn't believe anyone anymore.

"Olivia?"

She looked up as Brock stood in the doorway, watching her. "Oh, hey. Sorry, was looking a little bit into Ivy's background."

"Find anything?" Brock leaned against the door.

Olivia shook her head. "Nothing more than what she told us."

"Well," Brock jabbed his thumb backward. "Are you ready for the next interview? Tessa and Toby are both here."

This should be good. Grinning, Olivia got to her feet. "Let's do this."

CHAPTER THIRTY-THREE

O LIVIA WOULD HAVE PREFERRED SPEAKING WITH TESSA privately in one room while Brock grilled Toby in another. But the two young adults were together in the same interrogation room, their wide eyes conveying that they thought they were in trouble. Olivia paused at the window to look inside, seeing Tessa mouth the words *FBI* to Toby. Toby shrugged, but the bewildered look on his face indicated that he was probably at a loss for words. Indeed, Olivia figured that they probably never imagined that they would ever be called into something as high-level as an FBI investigation.

"Are you ready for this?" Brock grinned at Olivia. "Since you do *so* well with teenagers and young people."

"Not like we haven't had enough of them in the past year or so." Olivia laughed a bit. "I'm ready. Let's go easy on them. I think they're probably more scared of us than anything. For all we know, they could just be mischievous youth getting into trouble at the museum."

"Very true." Brock sighed in mock annoyance. "Man, I was looking forward to doing the Good-Cop, Bad-Cop approach."

"Let's try just being ourselves and letting them paint themselves into a corner," Olivia teased. She and Brock exchanged a smile before she pushed through the door into the room.

Tessa's posture snapped upright as did Toby's. They both looked ready to confess everything, including stealing their seventh-grade classmate's lunch money, until they saw who was walking through the door.

"Olivia?" Tessa gasped. "Brock?"

"That's us." Olivia gave her a smile that held authority, but still offered room for friendliness.

"What are you guys doing here?" Toby shifted uncomfortably in his seat and looked around. "They told us that the FBI wanted to talk to us. The *FBI!* We aren't any terrorists or anything."

Well, that escalated quickly in his mind. Maybe this would be easier than Olivia thought. "We didn't call you guys in for a terror threat," Olivia assured them as she sat down next to Brock. "We just need to ask you a few questions about some things that have been going on around the museum lately."

Again, both kids shuffled in their seats. Toby moved side to side as if unsticking himself from the chair and Tessa's fingers twisted into knots on the table as she kept looking over at him.

"Okay." Toby took the lead. "What kinda questions?"

"This is about the fire alarm, isn't it?" Tessa asked, breathlessly.

Brock put out a hand. "Let's take it slow. We'll ask the questions and we'll get to everything in time, okay?"

Tessa nodded, eagerly. "Okay, okay."

"Before we go any further," Brock opened his notes stored in a folder. "I just want to make sure you both know, you have the right to speak to an attorney. You don't have to answer any questions if you're not comfortable."

Tessa's eyes went wide. "An attorney?"

"We're not here to accuse you of anything," Olivia reassured her, taking a gentler approach than she did with Ivy. "But if either of you wants to pause and get legal counsel, that's completely your call."

"I don't think we need an attorney." Toby swallowed. "We... we were just there at the museum yesterday."

"Yeah, we're here to answer anything you need, right Toby?" Tessa elbowed him in the ribs. "We're fine."

Brock's eyebrows raised slightly before he gently cleared his throat. "Okay, then." He glanced over his notes. "First of all, let's start with this. Where were you guys really, when the CO_2 alarm started to go off?"

Tessa and Toby froze, their faces paling as if they were reliving that moment all over again. "It was a CO_2 alarm?" Toby asked, nervously.

Brock nodded. "Yes. Regardless, where were you both right before it went off?"

Tessa cleared her throat and refused to meet their gaze. "I was still on break. Like Toby said..."

"We know what Toby said," Olivia interrupted, "but you were both exhibiting signs of CO_2 exposure."

"The doctor checked us out," Toby mentioned. "Said we were fine to be released this morning."

"But you did have exposure?" Olivia confirmed, knowing full well what the answer was. When Tessa glanced at Toby with guilt, Olivia went on. "The leak was downstairs. Toby mentioned that he went to the break room when your fifteen minutes were up and when he realized you were still down there, you both ran back up to the front desk. The issue is, you both were showing the same symptoms. If Toby had only been down there for a few seconds, you wouldn't have reacted at the same time, or to the same degree."

"You see," Brock leaned forward. "CO_2 poisoning builds gradually. It's not instant, especially in a wide open space like you were in. People don't look like they're about to pass out from walking into it and turning around. If you were both affected like you were, then Toby, that means you were down there for longer than a minute or two."

"Okay, five minutes, I wasn't really paying attention." Toby tried to back out, his eyes darting to the left before looking back up at Brock and Olivia.

Brock clamped his jaw shut, remaining silent, a tactic he enjoyed using. Someone who was lying could not stand silence. Toby squirmed. Tessa looked down. Finally, Tessa's voice rose, quietly from where she aimed it at her lap.

"Okay. Okay. We were both down there during the whole fifteen-minute break. Toby didn't have to use the restroom. He said he did, but he was really sneaking down after me."

Now they were getting somewhere. Olivia nodded, noticing Tessa's face flush hot red.

"I really was on break." Tessa looked up. "So was Toby. We've... we've been doing that."

"Doing what?" Olivia asked. "Taking your break together?"

"Not exactly. Not all the time. Sometimes we still take breaks separate from one another." Toby sighed. "Me and Tessa are kinda a thing. We haven't told Selena or Levi or anyone there because we didn't want them putting us on separate shifts or making a big deal out of it. But when we take our breaks, sometimes we sneak around and meet up with one another during our breaks to, you know. Make out and stuff."

Classic young adult behavior. Leftover from their high school glory days. Olivia nodded, understanding Tessa's bright red face and Toby's shifty behavior. Brock's head slowly moved up and down. "I see. Was this what you were doing when the CO_2 alarm went off?"

"It was an accident, I swear!" The words burst from Tessa's mouth, a stark contrast to Toby's calm confession.

"What was an accident?" Olivia asked.

Tessa's hands continued to twist in her lap. "Me and Toby have been sneaking around for a long time. We used to go to the security room since no one's usually up there during the day. That's why I burst in on you guys that one time. We knew that no one would think to look for two receptionists in the security room. But when we saw you guys in there, we needed to find a different hiding spot."

"We knew that the janitor was dead," Toby explained. "So no one would be in his closet or the HVAC room next to it."

What a way to have respect for the dead, Olivia thought.

"I didn't want to be where a dead guy was, so we've been hanging out in the HVAC room. Plus, it's dark all the time," Tessa blurted out. "I didn't mean to tip the shelf over."

"You didn't knock the shelf over," Toby countered. "Just something on the shelf."

Their story was starting to make sense, aligning with a few things Olivia and Brock had found. "What happened exactly from the time you entered the HVAC room to the time you left?" Brock asked in a low tone.

Olivia couldn't imagine how uncomfortable it was to admit the details of their secret little affair. But she couldn't care less about what the two young adults did on their break and more about what happened.

Tessa sighed. "Me and Toby were making out and getting into it. He pushed me against one of the shelves in the HVAC room. I sort of lost my balance and tripped and bumped into the shelf. One of the thingies that was on the bottom shelf?"

"The giant fire-extinguisher-looking things," Toby explained, helpfully.

"Right, those." Tessa agreed. "A whole bunch of them got knocked over and one fell and started hissing. It rolled away from us. Toby and I picked up a few before we went back to, you know. Doing stuff. Well after about fifteen minutes, I started feeling really dizzy and lightheaded and so did Toby."

"So I rushed over to grab the container and noticed that it was leaking," Toby said. "There was a hissing sound or something. So, we panicked. We weren't sure how long it was leaking into the room, but I realized that it was probably oxygen or something and that we'd get in trouble not only for being down there but for messing with something like oxygen. We don't usually have it around, so how were we to know what it was?"

"You don't always have containers of CO_2 or other gasses downstairs?" Olivia narrowed a stare at them.

"The canisters weren't there before." Tessa shook her head. "They just recently showed up."

"How recent?" Brock asked.

"After we started using the closet as our hiding place." Toby shrugged.

"Which was after Dorian died?"

Both Tessa and Toby nodded. "We figured they had something to do with that Pompeii exhibit or extra security or something." Tessa blew a wisp of hair out of her face. "Especially since Selena hasn't been buying a lot of new stuff for the museum, lately. We've been needing to get updates in our system, like, forever, and she doesn't have the money to do that, but she'll buy these random containers we don't need."

Olivia leaned back in her seat, musing over what Tessa had said. The CO_2 containers had showed up around the time of the Pompeiian mural, which was being vandalized by the same chemical composition of a volcanic eruption. Her mind flashed back to what Ivy had said in the exhibit room that day.

The main gasses present at a volcanic eruption are H_2O and CO_2. But there are other gasses present, as well.

She was trying to recreate the events that led to the damage of the mural, wasn't she? Using the same gasses that damaged the original to make it look like it was damaged during the eruption of Vesuvius.

"Why didn't you just pick up the container and tell someone what happened?" Brock asked.

"I didn't want to get in trouble. Neither did Tessa." Toby nodded to her. "We just panicked and ran."

"We had no idea it would cause that much craziness at the museum." Tessa shook her head. "Honestly."

Brock, of course, chose this as a moment to point out a life lesson. He was always good, that way. "Sometimes we don't see the consequences of our actions until it's too late. That's why it's so important to be future-minded, and aware of our surroundings."

CHAPTER
THIRTY-FOUR

66 **I** THINK IT'S SAFE TO SAY THAT TESSA AND TOBY ARE
guilty," Brock said over the cheeseburger he'd ordered
for lunch, delivered to the field office, "of tipping over
some containers and causing a HAZMAT issue at the museum.
Everything else?" He waved his hand. "Not so much."

Olivia picked at her salad. "I think you're probably right. They
were more scared about knocking over a canister and breaking it
than doing the right thing. Imagine if they'd actually stolen the
jewel, or killed Dorian."

"It doesn't entirely rule them out from accidents, though."
Brock pointed out.

"Dorian's death was not an accident." Olivia shook her head. "Whoever stabbed him did it with intention and precision, not something two young adults would know how to do. Especially ones who think that it's okay to break something and not tell anyone, hoping someone would find it. Did they not think it could be dangerous, whatever was in those containers?"

"Doesn't appear to be that way." Brock grabbed a napkin. "You know, I've been thinking about that. We're going off of who was there at the time of Dorian's death, but have we considered that anyone in that museum would have the knowledge to pull off such a clean death and get away with it, blood-free? I didn't even find any bloody raincoats in the trash can. I looked. Believe me."

"You looked thrilled when you went dumpster diving that day." Olivia laughed. "What *did* you find?"

"Nothing but a bunch of things I never want to see again." Brock glanced down at his lunch. "And certainly nothing I wanna talk about over lunch."

"Oh, come on, you've seen it all, a few banana peels aren't going to get you all queasy on me, are they?" Olivia teased.

He raised an eyebrow. "Olivia." A warning note sent her into silent laughter.

Brock's cell phone sharply cut into the conversation. He reached for it. "Oh, it's the hospital."

"Selena?" Olivia asked hopefully.

"Let's find out." Brock answered his phone. "Agent Tanner. Yes."

He carefully put the cheeseburger down, wiping his hands on the napkin as he listened to the party on the other end. A small smile played with his lips as he nodded. "Good. We'll be sure to stop in after a while. Thank you."

He didn't sound elated enough for the good news to be related to Selena. Olivia waited patiently as he hung up and reached for his lunch again. "Nick is awake. They say he's still recovering, but he's going to be okay."

Olivia breathed a sigh of relief. "What about brain damage?"

"They said we got to him just in time. I think the mask helped a bit, and since you moved the container away from the air duct, it helped to keep the room from just filling with nothing but CO_2."

"That and the heroics of a man who couldn't keep his mask on." Olivia grinned at him. "I'm still mad about that, by the way. Do you know what kind of a scare it gave me to turn around and see you without a mask?"

"What? I couldn't let you have all the glory!" Brock shrugged, taking another bite. "Wanna stop by and see him in a bit?"

"I'd love to." As much as Olivia didn't want to admit it, she missed Nick a little bit. She could use a dose of his lighthearted humor.

As long as he wasn't the one who lifted the jewel.

At 4:30 the daylight hours grew short as Olivia and Brock strode out of the elevator onto the hospital floor where Nick was being held. They quickly found his room and knocked.

"Come on in!" the doctor called through the door.

Brock opened the door, allowing Olivia to go first. Nick lay in the bed with oxygen tubes running all across his face. His face lit up when they walked in. "Lady Knight and Sir Tanner! From what I understand, my heroes!"

"Hey, Erickson-Stark." Olivia grinned back at him. "Descendant of one of the fiercest Vikings known to man."

"Actually, that would be Erik the Red. He was before my ancestors' time. But! I'll take the compliment." Nick sounded cheerful, even with a groggy voice and a tube stuck in his nose.

The doctor approached Olivia and Brock, nodding to them. "I'll leave you. He's stable, for now. If you have any questions, I'll be in the hall."

"Thank you, Doctor," Brock said. Once they were alone, he stood by Nick's hospital bed. Nick, of course, was the first to reignite the conversation.

"Darren was in here an hour or so ago. He feels so bad about what happened! Apparently, he's the one who locked me in the vault or something?" Nick's eyebrow creased. "So from what I hear, you two saved my life. You were in the vault with me and somehow cracked the code to the Vanguard Core system and got me out of there? That's what Darren said. Dude, I don't remember any of that!"

Olivia chuckled, modestly. "That's because you were taking a CO_2-induced nap while we were doing all the hard work."

Gratefulness flooded Nick's green eyes as he nodded to her. "Thank you. You really are a *knight*, you know that? Not just your last name, but you saved my life. Thank you."

"It was all part of the job, Nick. And you can't blame it all on me." Olivia nodded to Brock. "The Tanner's the one who shared his oxygen with you. You might not have made it out if he hadn't."

Nick looked over at Brock and the same gratitude filled his eyes. "I owe you one, man. Thank you."

"I guess the Tanner can actually be a hero, after all?" Brock winked at him.

Nick and Olivia shared in his laughter. "I guess so, man." Nick took a deep breath. Olivia imagined how good it must feel for him to be able to do that. "That sounds like a legend in the making, you know. Worthy of the *Chanston de Gestes*. The Tanner and the Knight, the unlikely pair that saved a kingdom. Who knew a lowly tanner could be a hero, right alongside a knight?"

Little did he know they weren't that unlikely at all. That they actually *were* a pair. Olivia wasn't getting into that. She and Brock acknowledged his little pun with a laugh.

"So I have to ask." Nick grew serious, again. "Darren kept going on and on about this. How *did* you hack the vault door? No one can hack that. It's made so that it can't be hacked." He looked between them. "There's rumors going around since the incident. Are you guys, like, CIA or something?"

He was the second one to reach for the dramatics. Olivia laughed and shook her head. "No, Nick."

Brock couldn't keep the grin off his face. "We're actually with the FBI.".

"The FBI!" Nick gasped. "Whoa, that is so cool! The FBI was looking around in *our* museum!"

Olivia wasn't entirely sure that was something to be excited about. But then again, it was Nick. He found excitement where he shouldn't, much of the time. Anything for a good story to be told as tomorrow's history.

"So, why were you guys there?" Nick settled back, understanding dawning on his features. His oxygen hissed, but he barely seemed to notice. "It's about the Ratnashree diamond, isn't it? Olivia was playing Nancy Drew, trying to figure it all out."

"We both were," Olivia answered. "And we still have a lot of questions."

She hated bringing this up now. Nick was so happy. If he was the thief, she was about to ruin his day. She hated that. She normally didn't let herself get attached to anyone during her investigation who could be a suspect. But this time, she hoped deep down that Nick was just an innocent bystander who happened to know too much without even realizing he did. "So, Nick. Think you could help us answer a few?"

"Help out the FBI who saved my life? I'll do anything!" He grinned. "What do you want to know?"

"You knew a lot about the Star of India Heist in 1964," Brock started out. He slowly sank into a chair next to Nick. "Did you happen to share that information with anybody? Maybe even… use some of it, yourself?"

Nick studied Brock. Olivia slowly sat down next to Brock as Nick shook his head. "I love the Virginia Museum of Art History, Tanner. Uh, Agent Tanner, sorry." He sniffed. "I would never do anything to sabotage it. I have a lot of respect for history and art and everything, man."

Brock nodded. "What are you trying to say?"

"I would never try to steal that diamond if that's what you're asking." Nick looked hurt that they'd even bring that up. "I was devastated when I heard it was missing when I came to work that day. I guess maybe I felt like it would be the museum's downfall."

Olivia stiffened. "What makes you say that?" Did he know about the financial difficulties?

Nick shook his head. "India's going to be ticked off when they get that thing back. Or a note, saying that we lost the original. We can't have that happen."

"Do you have any idea what could have happened to it?" Olivia couldn't help but wonder how he hadn't exactly looked *devastated,* to use his word, when he told her how this was just like the jewel heist of 1964. Excited was more the word.

Nick shook his head. "Anyone could have done it. Simon has direct access to it. No questions asked, he's the oldest member; but he's been around so long, he has the same respect for the museum that I do. Graham, he's always poking his head in exhibits to make sure they're all okay and everything, you know, conservators. But he's always been the kind to just do his job and leave, go home, just put in hours, you know? Darren is always wandering around but doesn't have direct access to it. Toby and Tessa, they're always sneaking around where they're not supposed to be. Especially since Toby was sneaking around downstairs right before the fire alarm or whatever went off." He nodded to Olivia and Brock as if the information was some sort of juicy gossip.

Olivia nodded. She wasn't about to tell him just why Toby was sneaking around.

"He was also there right before Dorian died." Nick shook his head. "I don't know, everyone has access. And those who don't are always sneaking around."

"What do you know about Ivy Landon?" Brock asked. "And her assistant, Elliot?"

"I don't like her," Nick blurted out. "I mean, I love everyone, but Ivy has no excitement, you know? This museum is just like a job to her. She's the only one – she and Elliot – who don't respect and adore the museum. Simon, Graham, Darren, me, we're all there for more than a paycheck but Ivy? She doesn't care. She's there to just build her exhibits, make sure they look good, get paid and leave. If you ask me, she should stick with chemistry where everything is straightforward. She has access at all times to the exhibits, and no one asks her why. She and Selena trust each other very much."

Olivia nodded in deep thought. "Have you noticed her or Elliot doing anything strange lately?"

"Not really." Nick shook his head. "They just kinda come and go as they please."

If Ivy didn't hold the museum in as high regard as everyone else seemed to, maybe Olivia would think twice about letting her go so easily. Sure, they didn't have any hard evidence against her. But maybe if they looked hard enough they could find some. "Nick, I have to ask you. Do you know if anyone in that museum has access to sulfuric acid, other than Ivy?"

"Sulfuric acid?" Nick asked as if Olivia had inquired what planet he was from. "Sure. We get it at the corner gas station all the time!"

Olivia and Brock had to force their laughter. Nick finally took it seriously and shook his head.

"Honestly, other than her, the only other person I can think of is Graham because he works with chemicals and stuff. I know I made a joke about it, but seriously, they don't just sell that stuff. Why do you ask?"

Olivia shook her head. "All part of the investigation."

"Well, if you're looking to tie in that stuff, I'm sure Ivy's got tons of containers lying around her school."

Olivia nodded. "Thank you."

"One other thing I wanna know, man." Brock leaned forward. "Why were *you* in the vault that day?"

A far-off look came into Nick's eye. "I was upstairs when I heard the alarm going off. It sounded like a fire alarm, so I thought there was a fire. All I could think about? That Norwegian tapestry that Selena isn't ready to put up yet. It was going to get burned up because Darren was busy with evacuations. I couldn't let that happen. That's my people's history, you know? So I went down to rescue it. Then I started feeling dizzy because I couldn't find it, and then I got worse and worse and I don't remember much after that."

Brock nodded, taking in the sight of him lying there. "Well, I'm awfully glad you made it out."

"Thank you." Nick looked back up at them. "If it wasn't for you guys, I wouldn't have made it out at all."

Olivia let Brock drive back to the hotel. They probably wouldn't be staying here much longer, she thought, as she drew her thoughts to a close. "Think Nick is right?"

"About not stealing the Ratnashree diamond?" Brock shrugged one shoulder, the other hand comfortable on the steering wheel. "We can't take anyone's word for anything, but I'm curious what he said about Ivy."

"Me too. And if anyone knows, it would be Nick. He watches that museum like a hawk." Olivia sighed and leaned her head against the headrest of the seat. "Why do you think Ivy would want to pull something like this off?"

"We can look into it," Brock said. "Maybe she has plans of leaving, or maybe she's been stealing all along and no one knows. It would strike me as odd if she hadn't been stealing all along, and now suddenly, she's lifted a diamond and forged a Pompeiian mural. From what it looks like."

"I don't care what anyone says," Olivia stated. "She can say all she wants that she knows nothing about it, but who else would think to have a duplicate of a mural sitting around with sulfuric acid and CO_2 about to deface it, like the original?"

"Someone who overheard her, maybe?" Brock asked. He was silent for a long time, turning it over in his head. "Do you think Ivy stole the diamond?"

Olivia thought back about what she knew about the woman. "She never seemed bothered by it being missing, other than the day we saw her on camera, going to check it out. When we were talking in the break room that day, she was more concerned that I was looking into the case than the fact that the diamond was gone." Olivia remembered the nonchalant way Ivy had shrugged it off.

It's probably long gone by now.

As if she didn't care. Everyone else sobered up and mourned the diamond's loss, except her. And then, she blamed it on chemistry teaching to make her so black-and-white about everything. "It has to be her. Who else could it be? She has direct access and the knowledge to make the painting look like it was damaged the same way the original *Wedding of Caecillius* was." Olivia shot straight up as an idea seized her. "Brock… Dorian was killed the day after we had the meeting about the Pompeiian exhibit."

"Right?" He nodded.

"Ivy was there when she could have been in her classroom."

"Right."

"What if she already had the forgery? The art collector who met with Simon that day showed up ready to present his collection to the museum. If she knew that the *Wedding of Caecillius* was among it, then maybe she was downstairs making the forgery somehow. Remember she went outside around the time of Dorian's time of death according to what little the cameras captured? What if the reason he wound up dead is because he caught her doing something she wasn't supposed to be doing?"

"Like forging a painting," Brock's voice rose with interest.

"And the only way to get him to be quiet about it was to kill him. No one would miss the janitor, right?"

"Exactly." Brock hummed as he thought. "The question is, how do we prove any of this?"

"We tear that place apart, tomorrow," Olivia said with determination. "There has to be something linking Ivy to the crime scene. There has to be. And if there is? We'll find it."

CHAPTER
THIRTY-FIVE

B ROCK'S COUGH AWAKENED OLIVIA AT 2:30 A.M.
She stirred, blinking her eyes open as her vision slowly
focused on the blurry red digits on her clock. She'd been
with Brock long enough to know his different coughs, and how
this one sounded like he was awake, rather than just choking on
lint in his sleep.

Frowning, she rolled over to see that she was right. Brock
lay on his back, arms folded under his head as she stared at the
popcorn ceiling. "Brock?" Olivia's voice was groggy. "Why are
you awake? Can't sleep?"

Brock shook his head, his lip pinched. "No."

Olivia turned over and propped her head up on her elbow. She stroked his shoulder with her free hand. "Do you need some tea or something?"

Brock shook his head. "It's not insomnia. I just... there's something that I can't seem to get out of my head."

Olivia glanced up at him. "What is it?"

Brock sighed; a heavy sound that told her he needed sleep. "CO_2 doesn't have the effect on murals and paintings that sulfuric acid does. Not in a time crunch. It can over time, but not to the damage extent that the mural needs. It wasn't liquid. If someone wanted to make it look like the original chemicals at the Pompeiian eruption, they didn't need CO_2; the sulfuric acid would have been enough."

Olivia nodded, blinking. What was he saying? "Okay?"

Brock turned to look at her, pinning her with a stare. "Being a chemistry teacher, Ivy should know that. So why did she need the CO_2 containers?"

Well, there would be no getting any sleep for either of them tonight. Olivia pondered this a moment before she slowly rose to a sitting position. "You think we're looking in the wrong place?" She reached over, clicking on the lamp by her bedside, flooding the room with light. She picked out the honesty in Brock's eyes, heavy with more than just fatigue.

Brock sat up and leaned against the headboard, shaking his head as he did. "I don't think we are. I think we're still missing something. I just can't get it out of my head that Ivy wouldn't need the CO_2 containers, and Tessa said they showed up after Dorian died, which is when we decided to do the Pompeii exhibit. That's why we assumed it was Ivy, who put them there for her little experiment."

Olivia swallowed. "You mean, *they* decided to put up the Pompeii exhibit." They weren't a part of the staff any more than Tessa was secretly a Knight Templar.

Brock nodded. "They decided. Right." He looked down, quiet for a moment. "Olivia? What if we're looking at the wrong person? We haven't found anything else that ties Ivy to anything, except for sulfuric acid on a forged mural downstairs in a room where there were also CO_2 containers. We didn't see her do it, so everything is circumstantial. Another thing? Anyone who has access to her classroom has access to her chemicals. All she has to do is step out and someone could swipe it."

"If they know what they're looking for," Olivia pointed out.

"Everything's labeled. It's Ivy. She labels every water bottle she drinks. She may not love her job at the museum as Nick accused, but she's the most organized one there, except for Selena. So she would have everything all nice and clear for whoever goes in her classroom to clearly see what they were taking."

"So, are you thinking it's been Elliot this whole time?" Olivia asked. "I know he's a troublemaker. He has a record."

"I don't think it's him." Brock shook his head. He was quiet for a long time, a heavy silence descending on the both of them before he asked. "Olivia?"

"Hmm?" The tone of his voice told her that he was thinking something possibly confrontational.

Brock sighed. He turned and looked at her, pinning her with an unblinking stare.

"Have we ever bothered to check Selena Vance's office?"

Olivia had somehow known he was going to land a bombshell of a question. She just wasn't expecting that one. Her head rang for a few minutes with the echo of his question which could turn the tide of this entire case. "Um." The admittance slowly sank in. Being in Selena's office didn't mean they'd looked around in there. "No. We haven't. She was helpful. She was the one who called us. She gave us permission to search everything and didn't hold anything back."

"Which doesn't make her innocent," Brock pointed out.

Olivia chewed her lip in thought. "So tomorrow when we go try to find the smoking gun that ties Ivy to the scene, are we really looking at Selena's office?"

"Selena gave us permission to search everywhere. Now that she's in a coma, it's a bit of a gray area, but I think I'm going to call Levi tomorrow and tell him we need to see Selena's office for some parts of the investigation. He's been honest and cooperative this whole time; he shouldn't give us any trouble." Brock's eyes searched the ceiling. "I'm thinking that we can't put this case to bed until we give Selena's office a look."

But it didn't make sense. The sulfuric acid... where did a sophisticated lady like Selena get her hands on that? "Would she have access to Ivy's classroom?"

"She was there!" Brock snapped his gaze down to Olivia's. "At least, according to Ivy. She stopped by Ivy's classroom and asked her to come in the day before Dorian died, remember?"

"That's right." Olivia snapped her fingers. She turned to look at Brock, her eyebrows raising. "Oh, boy. What if this whole time, it was..." She didn't even want to say it.

"Remember how you said we were probably missing something so obvious that it would be laughable?" Brock asked. "I think this is what we've been missing all along."

CHAPTER
THIRTY-SIX

F UELED BY TWO HIGHLY CAFFEINATED CUPS OF COFFEE
from a local coffee shop, Olivia and Brock made their last
run to the Virginia Museum of Art History. They both
sensed they were going to find exactly what they were looking
for, making this their last trip to the museum.

Olivia fought off the emotional attachment she'd made
with the place as she and Brock parked in the parking lot. They
closed the doors to the car, locked them, then started toward the
sidewalk. Halloween decorations littered the yards on either side
of the museum, reminding them how long they'd been here. Here
it was, almost Halloween and they were just now making headway
that actually made sense.

The museum stood achingly empty. A lonesome echo as the door closed, rather than the excited chatter of the staff and patrons. Olivia looked up one more time at the paintings that surrounded the rotunda above where Tessa and Toby usually sat. They said the museum would reopen by Friday, but it wouldn't be the same, especially after all this.

"How was Levi when you talked to him?" Olivia stared at the copy of the *Storm on the Sea of Galilee* that had drawn her attention before. This whole case felt like a storm, she thought. Was it about to be calmed? Or kicked up a few notches, based on what they found?

"He was fine. A little surprised when I said we wanted to see Selena's office, but he seemed understanding." Brock waited patiently as Olivia continued to stare at the paintings.

She nodded. Would their findings lead to Levi becoming the next curator of the museum? Would the museum even survive if they found out that Selena had been involved in some sort of fraud or criminal activity? She wasn't going to think about it. That wasn't her job. Her job was to find out who stole the Ratnashree diamond. The museum's fate was a concern she took on herself, and knew she'd have to leave behind.

"Well? Are you ready?" Brock asked after a while.

Olivia nodded. "Yep. Let's get started."

She stared down the hallway with Brock. Brock opened the office door and swung it wide. "No one's been in here since Selena's car accident, except for that one time you made me play hide-and-seek with you. You know, when you went up the fire escape?"

"That was fun." Olivia grinned.

"Easy for you to say. I was worried sick about you." Brock chuckled. "Where do you want to start?"

Olivia set her kit down. "I'll take the desk. You wanna take the computer and we'll go from there?"

Brock nodded. "Sounds good to me."

Olivia pulled out some gloves from her field kit and slipped them on. She started with the drawers while Brock settled in front of her computer and fired it up.

The first drawer contained nothing that an office shouldn't. Paperclips, pencil erasers, pens, pencils, some gum. All were neatly arranged, as was Selena's style. Even the pen caps all faced the same direction. So she was methodical as she was organized.

Interesting.

Find anything? Always her question whenever Olivia and Brock would come up to her office to discuss something. Was that the question of a guilty woman or a curious curator?

Olivia closed the top drawer and tried to open the second one. Something inside was jammed, making it difficult to open. That was odd. She didn't see Selena as the type to jam stuff in a drawer to the point where she couldn't get it open. Olivia pulled the top drawer open again and located a ruler. She slid the ruler between the drawer and its top, finding whatever was obstructing the opening, then pushed it down. The drawer slid open with ease, showing that it was stuffed full of envelopes and papers.

Olivia reached down, taking one of the envelopes in her hand. *Red Oak Assisted Living* read the return address. Curious, Olivia pulled the contents from the envelope and read them over.

Maria Vance. Same last name as Selena, so probably a relative? Mother, perhaps, or an aunt? Olivia went on to read the following numbers, with an insurmountable total near the bottom.

"I have a medical bill here for Maria Vance with a hefty monthly payment," Olivia said. "Looks like Selena got behind?"

"Ivy did say the museum wasn't doing well, financially," Brock said over his shoulder.

Olivia set the bill aside and opened another one. "This one's for Tim Vance." The numbers didn't look any better, either. Olivia combined the two numbers of a monthly payment from the assisted living and the hospital, both of which added up to between six and eight thousand dollars a month, depending on which month she looked at. Probably late fees, included.

Olivia dug through the drawer, finding more of the same. *Past due. Notice of foreclosure. Past due, Red Oaks Assisted Living. Collections notice, Richmond Medical Center.*

Olivia neatly stacked the bills, going through them one by one. "Chemo," she said aloud, reading the description in Maria's bill.

Could it be that both of Selena's parents had medical issues that forced them to stay in an assisted living? Olivia couldn't imagine the cost.

And the notice of foreclosure? Selena was just barely making ends meet to keep the museum alive. Ivy was telling the truth, according to the bills shoved in Selena's drawer. She didn't even take the time to organize them as was her style, just shoved them into her second drawer. That indicated she considered them a tomorrow problem. Something that she wouldn't do unless she was at the end of her rope.

"You're going to want to see this." Brock's voice was heavy as he leaned back in his chair and pointed to the screen. Olivia looked over his shoulder, seeing that he'd pulled up Selena's search history on the internet. Despite the fact that she was using a private browser, her history was still recorded in plain sight in a nice, neat little list.

Murals of Pompeii.

Most famous damaged murals of Pompeii.

What gasses are present at a volcanic eruption?

What are the effects of carbon dioxide on a mural from Pompeii?

Chemical reactions of CO_2 and sulfur dioxide on Pompeiian murals.

Acid rain.

Effects of acid rain on Pompeiian murals.

"She was sure doing a lot of research on these chemical reactions." Brock traced his finger down the list. "Notice the dates."

Olivia read them aloud. "October 9th, October 10th, 11t[h], 12th. We started our work here on the 10th, didn't we?"

"Yep." Brock nodded. "And the meeting was October 12th. So Ivy would have had no way of knowing they were doing a Pompeiian exhibit until they brought it up at the meeting. Meaning," his voice trailed off.

"Selena already knew." Olivia sat back. "She might have prompted Ivy to suggest it for whatever reason."

"I wonder why." Brock turned to look at her. "Because Ivy knows about murals and chemicals? Do you think they were working together?"

"They have a lasting friendship." Olivia held up the stack of Selena's bills. "Maybe Ivy was trying to help a friend out and it got away from her?"

Brock stared at the stack of bills and shook his head. The silence was shattered by his phone ringing again. Olivia looked back down at the stack of bills as Brock answered. After a few exchanged words, he hung up and turned to her, his expression heavy. "Selena is finally awake."

Olivia set the bills down on the desk and stared at Brock. The two exchanged a heavy silence before Olivia broke it. "Is she ready to talk?"

Brock nodded to the stack of bills in her hand. "I don't think she'll ever be ready to talk."

CHAPTER
THIRTY-SEVEN

B ROCK SLOWLY PULLED INTO THE HOSPITAL PARKING LOT
and turned the key. The engine stopped, throwing them
both into a meditative silence as they pondered where
this next step would take them. Brock sat next to Olivia for a
few minutes, gently breaking the silence with a question. "You
ready for this?"

"I'm ready to get to the bottom of it," Olivia replied. "So we
can put this case to bed."

It wasn't that she was tired of it. Olivia had enjoyed working
this case, more than several others due to the slow-paced nature
that didn't send her and Brock running for their lives or taking
weeks to come out of fight-or-flight mode. She loved the cozy

setting and everything about it, but it couldn't go on forever. Right now, she had a hunch. An assumption, based on what she and Brock found in Selena's office. High medical bills combined with collections and foreclosure notices didn't bode well hand-in-hand with a missing diamond that could be sold for enough to pay off all Selena's debts, maybe even having enough left over to buy another museum.

"So am I."

A gentle rain sprinkled the parking lot, enhancing the gloomy overall feel. It misted Olivia's hair and face as she and Brock strolled into the hospital. Halloween decorations draped over the receptionist's desk and hung from the walls in a paper-mâché attempt to lighten the mood of a hospital. Olivia found herself going through the motions like she always did. Counting down the time in her head. Finding Selena's new room. Riding the elevator to the top with Brock before the doors slid open with a ding.

Olivia and Brock walked with authority down the halls. Selena's door was open, but Olivia knocked on it, just in case. "Selena?"

"Come in."

Olivia stepped into the room, followed by Brock. She looked on the other side of the curtain at Selena who lay propped against some pillows. The coma had taken its toll on her, and the regal woman's voice was raspy, but she looked alert. "Olivia. Brock." She remembered their first names and dropped the formalities, Olivia noticed. "It's good to see you."

She wasn't going to be thinking that after this visit, Olivia thought. A faint smile flickered on her face before she let it fade. "It's good to see you, too. How are you feeling?"

"Still tired." Selena's voice was weary. "You'd think that after being asleep for a week or two, I would be alert and well-rested."

"I'm never alert when I oversleep," Brock attempted lightly, but it landed flat in the room.

"Have you found out who took the Ratnashree diamond yet?" Selena looked up at them both. Before, Olivia would have found her eyes to be eager, perhaps hoping that they had cracked the case and brought her good news. But now, given the new information they'd discovered, Olivia wondered if that hope was rather waiting with bated breath for them to say what they'd found. Maybe taking her chances, knowing there was a fifty-fifty chance that she was going to be found out.

Olivia exchanged a look with Brock. "We'd like to ask you a few questions if you're feeling up for it. We understand that you just came out of a coma, and –"

Selena held up her hand. "I want to know the fate of my museum, Agent Knight. I don't care how I feel, I'll…" She drew a breath. Held it. Released it, slowly, and looked up with dread. "I'll answer anything."

Olivia studied her. "Okay."

She and Brock moved to the edge of the bed. Olivia settled down in a chair near Selena's head to be eye level with her and pinned her with a heavy stare. "Before we go on, have you been in touch with Levi? Has he told you what's been going on since you've been here?"

"I've been in touch with him," Selena confirmed. "However, he told me that he'd rather wait until I get better before filling me in on what's been happening. I gathered from his hesitancy that whatever has been going on must be pretty bad."

"It isn't good news." Brock shook his head. "Do you remember Dorian dying?"

"I do remember." Selena's heavy gaze dropped to her coverlet. Her fingers traced invisible patterns and regret etched into her gaze.

Olivia nodded. At least she remembered well. "Dorian's death kicked off an investigation of its own. However, we are still chasing a trail on that one. When the museum reopened, the Pompeii exhibit was going up as planned. But there was an incident the other day. Two of your employees accidentally knocked over a container of CO_2 in the HVAC room, which led to a dangerous CO_2 leak and another shutdown of the museum."

"Oh." Selena put her hand to her forehead. Tears pricked her eyes. "I'm ruined."

Olivia exchanged a look with Brock. Maybe this wasn't the right time for this. Olivia was used to giving out bad news as part of her everyday job, but considering Selena's fragile state of mind… "If you like, we can come back another time…"

"No. Today. This ends today." Selena drew her hand away from her face with determination and pointed at a spot on her coverlet to emphasize her point.

"We can leave if you wish and talk another time…" Brock tried again.

Selena looked up at him desperately. "You don't understand, Agent Tanner. This will only get worse. We need to talk about this now."

What did she mean that it would only get worse? Perhaps she did know something they didn't, after all. Olivia scooted closer to her chair, looking empathetically down at Selena. "Very well. How well do you know your exhibit designer, Ivy?"

"We go way back," Selena said. Olivia noted the lack of surprise in her voice as if she knew all along that Ivy's name would eventually come up. Olivia figured that if she didn't know that Ivy was involved, she would have had a more questioning tone. *Why Ivy? Why are you singling her out, out of everyone who works there?* Yet there was nothing of the sort. Selena slowly turned her head, looking up at Olivia with sad and heavy eyes. "She and I worked on a chemistry project once, and she was so good at organizing that I made her my exhibit designer. She was looking for some extra work at the time, a quiet job where she could keep to herself but still do something of worth for the community."

"Do you trust her?" Brock asked.

"I don't trust anyone," Selena stated, emphatically. "Not even Ivy."

"Do you know anything about a mural we found downstairs? It was a duplicate of the *Wedding of Caecillius,* in perfect condition, but with some containers of chemicals nearby. We think that they are there to deface the painting, to make it look like the original."

"I don't know anything about that." Selena shook her head but kept her eyes on the footboard of her bed. Something in her tone was starting to hold back.

Olivia moved closer to the edge of her chair. She sank her elbows into her knees and folded her hands in front of her. "On a different note? You mentioned that you were ruined. Does that…" She closed her eyes. "Does that have anything to do with the financial state of the museum? Or, perhaps, your own?"

Selena stared ahead at the wall, her head slowly shaking from side to side. "I haven't talked about it, but the museum isn't doing as well as it should."

"I can imagine that affects your personal life as well." Brock sided with her. At least, his tone suggested it. Olivia knew he was remaining neutral until they knew for sure Selena could be trusted. "And with the medical bills and all that this," he waved his hand to her hospital bed, "is causing, I'm sure that it's put a further stress on you."

Selena closed her eyes, tears rolling down her face. She didn't say anything. He had that right, and Olivia knew it. But why wouldn't she look at them, anymore? She hadn't looked up since Olivia mentioned financial troubles.

"Selena," Olivia said. "Is there something you want to tell us? Is there more to the museum's financial ruin than just dwindling sales?"

"It was *me!*" Selena cried, the word bursting from her mouth amid a flow of tears. She tore her gaze from her toes and bolted it upon Olivia and Brock. Desperation clung to her expression, but something else was there, too. It almost looked like relief, as if a burden had been lifted.

No matter that Olivia had been expecting it, she still felt Selena's words hit her like gunfire. She stared at Selena, letting her talk.

"I stole the Ratnashree diamond!" Selena glanced down at her hands. Silence settled in the room like a heavy thunderstorm brewing. Olivia and Brock let it sit for a few beats. "It wasn't supposed to happen like this. I'm one of the best curators in the world. My reputation precedes me. I wasn't supposed to fall on hard times. Wasn't supposed to have any of this happen."

She adjusted her position in the hospital bed as if getting comfortable. She had a long story to tell. "Last year, my mother wound up with lung cancer. Her treatments have left staggering bills, through the roof. She is too weak, too sick to do anything. She was fighting it, tooth and nail, but I think now, she's all but given up and letting it run its course. My dad has gotten too forgetful to drive her to and from the hospital anymore. He almost set the house on fire several times because he forgot to turn the stove off. When he fell down the stairs and broke his hip, adding to the medical bills they already had, I knew that I had to put them both in assisted living. But of course, that's not covered by insurance. Not for the kind of care they need. It eats up their retirement and Social Security, but it's still not enough. So while my mom is living out the last of her days and my father doesn't even remember who I am, I'm stuck with not only her bills and his but a live-in cost of that nursing home."

Olivia closed her eyes. She knew the struggles that families had with care costs. It was wrong, so sickeningly unfair. Selena wounded her with every word, and Olivia wished with all her heart that she wasn't hearing this. That it wasn't Selena Vance, a broken woman, who had stolen the priceless diamond not because she was a criminal, but because she was in too deep for good reason. Taking care of her parents while trying to keep herself afloat, while trying to navigate the pain of losing them both before they were gone.

"Sales are dwindling." Selena went on to add highlights to the dismal mural of her life she was painting. "Have been for a while. No one knows about it but Levi and me, but the museum's almost had to foreclose several times. So when that diamond came through, worth millions, I saw an opportunity, and I took it."

"What did you do to try and resolve your situation?" Brock asked, softly, but with no less authority than a man about to make an arrest.

Selena was quiet for a few more minutes. Her tortured expression wavered as if admitting this out loud made her more of a monster than what she'd done. Finally, she lowered her voice, so that the beeping of her heart monitor was louder than her words. "There's a local crime ring in town. The Ashford Circle. They are miniature Mafia wannabes, but they aren't big enough to expand outside of Virginia. They're one of the most sophisticated bands of thieves around."

Olivia was almost certain she'd heard the name before. Something about an Ashford Circle being associated with a few notable historical artifacts that went missing.

"I found a way to get with the man in charge. I've known who he was all along. He comes by the museum all the time and we had a mutual understanding. I knew who he was and I didn't turn him in, and he respected my museum and didn't use it to scope out his next theft. I bargained with them to sell the Ratnashree diamond to him."

Selena took a breath, sadness in her tone. "It was perfect. No one would notice. So I thought. But the one thing that I hadn't factored in was Levi." She breathed an ironic laugh. "The reason I hired him was because he was honest and trustworthy. I even staged a little test with some forgeries back when I was looking for an assistant and his honesty proved to me that he could be trusted. Funny how the very reason that I hired him was the reason that my little crime didn't work out."

So it was Levi who threw a wrench into her plans. Olivia wondered why she hadn't thought of any of this, or put it together until now. Selena had perfect access to the diamond and answered to no one at the museum. No one would question her. She could sneak in through her window if she used the fire escape, knowing that it was well out of the camera's reach. She could open and close the basement door, knowing that the camera would catch the door opening, but not who came through, given the angle. She knew it would throw anyone off the trail of the fire escape that led to her office because they would be looking at who came through the back door. She could turn off the security system, erase the tapes and make off with a clean theft. Olivia wondered what might have happened if Levi hadn't noticed the fake diamond.

"When he brought the fake diamond to my attention, I knew that if I didn't do anything about it, it would raise a red flag," Selena went on. "So I decided that the best thing to do was be the perfect curator. Distressed that someone had broken my trust and compromised my exhibit. So I played it out, all the way. I got in touch with the local police who did a small investigation, but then they took it a step further and called in the FBI. I knew this, so all the while, I was planning another escape. I figured if I could make something subtle but obvious – something that you'd miss until you really thought about it – that it would take the focus off of me. So I did some investigating and tried to pin it on someone else."

"Ivy." Olivia guessed.

"Yes." Selena nodded. "I thought that I could plant some things and make it look like she did it. I knew the FBI was planning to send in some agents undercover, so I wanted to be one step ahead. When I was in Ivy's classroom, I secured a small dropper of sulfuric acid. I knew she was doing a class on it at the time. Then I used the dropper to plant the substance on the satin underneath the diamond's display, making it look like she used the chemical to alter the look of the fake piece. I mentioned the Pompeii exhibit to her shortly before you arrived at the museum, to get her thinking about it, hoping she'd bring it up. The leader of the Ashford Circle has an original mural, the *Wedding of Caecillius*. He also has a forgery of the same. So I asked if I could use that forgery along with putting the original on display. I planted the forgery in the basement and when I went to see Ivy the day before the meeting, I picked up more chemicals I knew were part of the original damage."

It wasn't that she knew. She'd been planning this all along. Olivia thought back on her search history, knowing that Selena had known what chemicals to go for.

"I figured that if I planted the sulfuric acid both on the diamond and around the forgery, eventually you would trace it back to Ivy's classroom and she wouldn't be able to dig her way out. In addition to that, I also sneaked in some containers of CO_2. That's why they were there. I had no idea they would be dangerous and cause such chaos. I was going to use the CO_2 and sulfuric acid to mix together and spread on the painting to imitate the damage, to make it look like Ivy was using it. I was trying to think like her."

Olivia nodded along as she listened but she felt her body grow tense. Selena had been trying to frame someone who trusted her completely. Ivy may not be the most enthusiastic employee, but she was innocent in all of this. Had they officially linked the sulfuric acid back to her classroom, compared with the footage of her in the HVAC area, they might have put away an innocent woman. Wrecked her life, and taken everything away from her, including her status as a teacher and the job she loved. Olivia fought back a rush of anger at the thought. How could Selena do something so uncaring? Olivia had thought her to be a wonderful curator, but it seemed that she really wasn't after all. Either that, or she was in too deep.

Olivia understood, to a certain point. As someone with a tumultuous relationship with her own parents, the situation with Selena's parents brought about an empathy she might not have for anyone else with the same story. A father with Alzheimer's and a mother with cancer, leaving her with nothing but a stack of bills she couldn't pay. It would drive even the sanest person crazy, after a while.

Selena sniffed. Her voice was heavy with her confession, but she kept going. "Unfortunately, the car accident happened before I could move the CO_2 containers out." She looked down and sighed. "So everything that happened – the disappearance of the Ratnashree diamond, the CO_2 leak and Dorian's unfortunate death, was all my fault."

Olivia frowned. "How was Dorian's death your fault?" Surely Selena hadn't stabbed the poor janitor, had she? Maybe she was responsible. Seeing as how no one had bothered to check her office, she could have hidden any bloodstained clothes or the murder weapon in her office until after hours. There could be blood evidence in there that they had missed.

Selena looked up at both Olivia and Brock, tears shimmering in her eyes. The guilt that weighed her down was tangible. "The day that I went to pick up the forged mural, I realized that I was in too deep. What was I doing? Trying to frame one of my best friends, while two very astute FBI agents were looking around? I knew I was going to be caught. So then I thought, what if I bought the diamond back? What if I gave them their money back, re-purchased the diamond and figured out another way to get myself out of debt? I thought that if I could replace the diamond with the real one eventually the investigation would die and it would go away. But that wasn't an option anymore.

"When I went to pick up the forgery, I asked if I could call the deal off and return the money in exchange for the diamond, which enraged the leader of the Ashford Circle. He made it clear that a deal was a deal and there was no going back. I either went forward with it and never spoke of it again, or bad things would happen. So I took the forged mural and my money, leaving the jewel with him. But the next day, Dorian wound up dead. It was a warning."

That explained why Dorian's wound was so precise. "So the leader of this crime ring, you think he did it?"

"He was there the day Dorian was killed," Selena admitted.

"What's his name?" Brock readied his pen.

Selena was quiet for a long time. Finally, a sigh rattled her. "I'm dead already. Might as well tell you. You know that rare art collector, Victor Sterling? I believe he mentioned he met Olivia that day, as a subtle reminder to me."

Olivia knew exactly who he was. "Yes. I do remember."

"He is the leader of the Ashford Circle. He runs it like he's the Mafia when all they do is steal or pull off heists of historical artifacts or valuable jewelry. But he also is a dangerous man. You don't want to get tied up with them... as I did." She hung her head.

Victor. Of course. Olivia remembered feeling uncomfortable when Victor repeated her name as if memorizing it for future reference and more than just a friendly hello. She hadn't seen him since that day. She remembered the footage showing him going down to Simon's office and not reappearing until after Dorian's time of death. Why hadn't she thought of him? He had managed to stay in the blind spots of the cameras all day.

"Your car accident." Brock waited until a few moments of silence passed. "Can you tell us what happened? Do you remember it?"

"I do, unfortunately. Which is why I said that I was dead already." Selena looked up at Olivia and Brock once more. "I was driving home. When I got to the bridge, there was a car coming toward me. I guess he pulled out from one of the driveways along the road like he was waiting for me. When I got to the bridge, he weaved into my lane, tried to run me off the road. I tried to swerve to avoid him, but I wound up going over the edge. I remember being terrified, thinking I was going to die. And I remember seeing the car that did it. Pretty sure it was Victor's car. Even though I went ahead with the deal, I think he suspected me of telling on him, anyway, and wanted to silence me. Maybe even take the money back."

Brock drew in a long breath through his nose. "Selena, thank you for telling us everything. I can't imagine how hard this has been." He paused, his voice low, but steady. "But because of what you've told us, I'm going to have to place you under arrest."

Selena hung her head. "I understand," she said in a broken voice, one of a woman who had lost everything. And in an attempt to not lose everything, she'd forfeited even more.

Brock slowly rose to his feet. "We're going to keep you at the hospital for now, to finish out your treatment and make sure you're safe. But I have to read you your rights before we go any further."

Olivia exchanged a glance with Brock, wishing there was an easier way. As it were, she found herself concerned for Selena's safety. They'd have to keep her here at the hospital until she was well enough to be moved. The thought concerned Olivia. What if Victor heard of her recovery and somehow managed to find her, here? She was in danger, as it was.

As Brock read her rights to her, Olivia got to her feet. She noticed the tears trickling down Selena's face. Her fear was as palpable as her despair. When Brock was finished, she cautiously asked, "Selena, you have the right to remain silent, but can I ask you one other thing?"

Selena looked up at nodded. "Go ahead."

Olivia sighed through her nose, resigned. "Where is the Ashford Circle?"

CHAPTER
THIRTY-EIGHT

T RICK-OR-TREATERS LINED THE STREETS OF RICHMOND,
Virginia. Ghosts and princesses alike, along with a myriad
of characters that brought every child and teenager's
fandoms to life. What a perfect metaphor, Olivia thought. On
a night when everyone got a chance to pretend to be someone
else for a few hours, she and Brock were closing a case where
they had done exactly that. Two FBI agents posing as security
guards in a museum, now waiting in a car outside the cheapest
self-storage lot around.

Olivia couldn't imagine someone as sophisticated as Victor
hanging out in the ill-maintained parking lot with ugly storage
units, which made it a perfect hiding spot for him. Especially

since the back units were smothered in shadow, conveniently located under a burnt-out street lamp.

Olivia waited in the car beside Brock, who was wrapping up the last of a small bag of chips he'd secured from the local gas station. "Are you always eating? Even on stakeouts?" she asked him.

"It has the word *stake* in it, and I'm hungry." Brock grinned, tossing the bag into the back seat of the car.

Olivia sighed and rolled her eyes, teasingly. "It's not even spelled the same."

"I know it's not." Brock's grin never faded. "But my ears hear it as the same. The first thing I'm doing when we get back to Belle Grove is hitting the diner and ordering the biggest chicken-fried steak in the state of Virginia."

Olivia laughed and shook her head. "That stuff is probably more lab-created sludge than real beef, you know."

"Who cares, as long as it's close enough?" Brock shrugged.

Olivia chuckled and checked the clock. Her backup's ETA was in five minutes, giving her a little more time in the nice warm car before she had to waltz back into harm's way once again. "I guess I'm glad Selena agreed to a plea deal to tell us more about everything."

Brock's humor faded. "She seemed pretty broken."

"I would be, too. I wouldn't be surprised if she didn't last very long in prison." As Olivia hated to admit it, a woman as far down as Selena might give up mentally before they even sentenced her. "I can't believe that all this time, the real thief was right under our noses. Why couldn't we see it?"

"Sometimes the most obvious answers are hidden." Brock sighed. "I talked to Levi today. I guess he is stepping into the role of head curator of the Virginia Museum of Art History, so at least the museum's gonna make it. For now. The one good thing – not that any of it was good – about this whole thing was that there's nothing like a scandal to draw a crowd. They won't be there for the Pompeii exhibit, they'll be there because the curator of the museum pulled off a heist in her own museum."

"If we get back the Ratnashree, do you think they'll put it back on display?" Olivia knew she shouldn't care so much about what happened, but she couldn't help herself. "I wouldn't think they would do that."

"Levi said, if we find it, it would be better to send it back to India. I think they might be keeping the fake on display, though. Not showcasing it as real, but that's what the real Ratnashree looked like, so they can hold onto that exhibit through December. It was a representation of glory for the Gupta Empire and that lasted throughout Indian history. I think that Levi's hoping to close out the year with some kind of promise of glory for the coming days. He sounded so dejected, though. Like he couldn't believe that Selena would do such a thing. I didn't tell him about her trying to frame Ivy, though."

"He'll hear about it through the grapevine at some point." Olivia leaned back in her seat. "These things have a way of coming to the light. Especially if Nick has anything to do with that. I swear that boy has some kind of sixth sense and knows stuff that no one else would have any idea how to figure out."

"You're telling me." Brock chuckled.

She was ready for this. She and Brock had eyes on the place all day and had observed Victor going in to meet with thirteen others. Although it was going to be quite the showdown, once backup arrived. She glanced at the clock. They should be here any second, now.

A car pulled into the parking lot and the headlights immediately dimmed. As they did, Olivia's radio crackled. "Agents Tanner and Knight, backup Agents Cullen and Barnes arriving on site. Confirm visual?"

Brock answered on the radio in the car. "Copy, Command, backup confirmed on site. We're standing by for the go-ahead."

"Confirmed. SWAT is in place. Proceed."

Olivia opened her door at the same time Brock did and slipped out. A blast of frosty air hit her face, but the body armor she wore underneath dulled the edge of the cold and helped her focus. She moved quickly, keeping the car between her and the storage units. Brock met her on the passenger side. He spoke into the radio mic clipped to his shoulder. "Ready."

He raised a megaphone. "Victor Sterling! This is the FBI. We have you surrounded! Come out with your hands up!"

He paused, giving him a chance to respond. Olivia hated this the most. The unknown after a warning was called. It could end with a surrender or a fight. It usually was never the first option.

Brock raised the megaphone again. "Victor Sterling! This is the FBI. You are surrounded. Come out with your hands –"

A gunshot cracked through the air. Brock's car mirror splintered.

"Down!" He ducked down behind the car. Olivia hit the pavement with him. The windshield exploded above her. She clenched her jaw.

A shout from either Cullen or Barnes pierced the chaos, followed by a staccato burst of return fire. SWAT broke from their cover, sweeping into position.

Olivia hadn't forgotten what it was like to be in the middle of gunfire. Her adrenaline spiked with each bullet grazing overhead. She kept her gun steady.

"SWAT, moving into position."

Bang! A flashbang detonated near the door, drowning out the gunfire for a brief second. Then came another, bringing with it a wave of lights, noise, and chaos. Victor's gunfire ceased. Olivia popped up from behind the car, in time to see the SWAT team breach the door with practiced precision. Shouts erupted for Victor's men to get down.

As the gunfire ceased, Olivia waited until the all-clear came through on the mic.

"Clear! Suspects restrained!"

Another voice followed.

"All units, scene secure. Repeat, scene secure."

Brock exhaled. Olivia slowly rose, weapon still drawn until the SWAT officer near the door gave her a sharp nod.

"Moving in," Brock said into the mic. Olivia sprang out from behind her car. Cullen and Barnes raced in from their position, reaching the door at the same time. Brock stepped in ahead of Olivia, taking control of the situation. She shadowed him, counting the fourteen men she'd seen earlier. One of them lay near the door, clutching his arm as blood oozed from the wound. Victor was on his knees in the back, glaring hot anger at the team who had disrupted him.

"Everyone down!" Brock ordered. "Everyone get down on the ground, hands up!"

"Hands where I can see them!" Olivia shouted along with Brock.

"Get down! Stay down, stay down!" Cullen echoed.

Olivia worked her way toward Victor first, held at gunpoint between two team members. His face pressed into the ground, but she recognized him by the black ponytail woven underneath his fingers as he assumed the arrest position. Olivia cast a glance at Brock to ensure that he had her back and made her way to the back. Brock kept his weapon trained on Victor as Olivia holstered hers. She took out a pair of handcuffs and crouched down beside Victor. She grabbed one of his wrists. "Victor Sterling, you are under arrest for the—"

The word *arrest* triggered a violent reaction in Victor. He twisted. Strength pulsed through his arm, yanking it away from Olivia's grip. Before she could catch him, he aimed a fist at her face, colliding hard knuckles against her jawline. Olivia let out a cry, not expecting the sudden reaction from him. Another twist of his arm in a blink sent her stumbling back. Her shoulder slammed into a crate, stunning her for a moment.

Victor lunged. A stupid move on his part. Brock tackled him before he made another step. Barnes rushed in from the side, pinning Victor's legs.

"Hands! Hands!"

Olivia slowly got to her feet, her face stinging. Brock took over for her, wrestling Victor's hands behind him and slipping the cuffs on him faster than he could make another move. Anger burned in his gaze as he looked up at Olivia. "You good?"

Olivia nodded. "Yeah. Just get him down," she said through clenched teeth.

"Victor Sterling," Brock said in a voice like iron. He completed the line that Olivia had started before he went rabid on her.

The fight ebbed out of Victor. He spat in fury as they hauled him to his feet. "You'll never pin it on me."

"Oh." Olivia stepped forward. "We already have."

Victor snapped around to face her. When he saw who she was, the rage disappeared into a cocky smile. One that told her that he remembered her, and would use that to his advantage if he could. "Why, hello, Olivia Knight. Nice to see you again. Did you stop by to check on that mural I donated? I have the receipt from where I purchased it from an honest dealer in Italy."

"Quiet," Brock hissed.

Olivia smiled, showing him that even though he'd tried, he still couldn't shake her. "What about for the forgery we traced back to you?"

Victor's face darkened. "You're going to regret this."

"I don't think so."

Brock handed him off to Cullen, who stood closest to the door. "Get him out of here."

Cullen took his arm and led him away, but not before Victor sent a sneer in Olivia's direction. "See you in court, darling."

Olivia stiffened, not letting him get to her. As soon as Victor was gone, Brock moved in rapidly to check on her. "Are you okay?"

"I'm fine." Olivia gingerly touched her bruises. "Let's get the rest of these guys out of here."

Brock studied her for a moment before nodding. Without waiting for him to protest, Olivia moved in to help with the other arrests the agents were conducting. Luckily the other thirteen weren't nearly as rowdy as Victor.

As the storage unit emptied, Olivia took a moment to glance around. Boxes and totes were stacked on either side of a table while some metal file cabinets lined the back wall. "This isn't a very organized hideout."

"I think it's more than a hideout." Brock flipped the light switch on. Olivia moved forward, her breath catching in her throat. Behind a stack of totes lay rows and rows of framed paintings, murals, and other things. Vases stacked on file cabinets and other artifacts lay strewn around.

"Don't tell me this guy's keeping a collection of ancient history in a storage unit that costs fifty bucks a month!" Olivia said indignantly. She glanced at the pictures lined up between two file cabinets to keep them upright. "I'll bet the real painting of *Storm on the Sea of Galilee* is in here!"

"Hopefully a few other things as well." Brock walked up to the file cabinet and pulled. "Of course, it's locked."

Olivia looked around. Her eyes fell upon the poker table which looked suspiciously like a picture of an antique table she'd seen a while back that had been stolen from a museum downtown. She slid the drawer open, examining its contents. While the gun Victor was using had been confiscated by the team, there was enough ammunition packed in here to load the clip several times, along with a deck of cards and a ring of keys. "Here." She grabbed the keys and made her way back over to Brock. When she was close, Brock held up his hand. She tossed him the keys.

Brock caught them midair and slipped the smallest one into the file cabinet's lock. "Seriously, how are you doing? He assaulted you."

"I'm really okay." Olivia put her hand to the bruises that blossomed on her face. "I think I moved just in time and he grazed me. I should have been expecting it."

"It's not your fault." Brock shook his head, pulling on the drawer. He cringed at the metallic grind as it opened and looked up at her, concern flickering in his gaze.

Olivia breathed a laugh. "I'm fine. Really. It'll be gone in a week or two."

"I know," he said, softly. "But you shouldn't have gotten hurt at all."

"Well, you took him down for me." Olivia shot him what she hoped was a comforting smile. Her gaze descended to the contents of the drawer, her interest piqued at what was inside. "Would you look at that?"

Stacked against the very back of the drawer were stacks and stacks of smooth hundred-dollar bills, all lined up as if they'd come fresh from a bank. Using the number on the currency strap, she estimated there to be upward of fifty thousand dollars inside. Did he just keep this kind of cash lying around? The money was pushed against the back of the drawer by several burner cell phones, chargers, and some USB ports piled on top of an auction catalog. Probably for the black market, if she had to guess.

"Rare art collector, indeed." Brock pushed the door closed and opened the second one. "Hello."

Rather than a messy scramble of a starter kit for a crime ring leader, the glitter of a cluster of diamond necklaces against black backdrop displays glistened in the lights of the storage unit. Brock pulled the drawer open all the way, revealing a few modern-looking necklaces and bracelets, along with some that looked antique.

Olivia had brushed up on the Ashford Circle after Selena mentioned them, confirming what she said about the crime ring hitting smaller stores, along with places that carried valuable historical artifacts. "I wonder how many original owners are missing this stuff."

Brock started taking the pieces out, one by one. He handed them off to Olivia, who worked to log them and examine them. One diamond-studded blue necklace came after a bracelet with more emeralds than Ireland was named after. But even after Brock had emptied the drawer, Olivia's heart began to fall. Necklaces, rings, brooches, watches, bracelets... but nothing that stood out by itself. Certainly no pink diamond the size of her fist. "Where's the Ratnashree diamond?"

"Let's hope he hasn't sold it yet." Brock checked the drawer for anything hidden. After confirming it was empty, he slammed it closed and paused at the bottom drawer. He glanced up at Olivia, with the same hope in his eyes. "Here goes nothing."

"We're going to have to search this entire storage unit anyway," Olivia said. She nodded to the agents behind her. "We've got help, but it'll take a while. I'm not giving up hope yet."

"Me neither." Brock carefully slid the drawer open. When he spied its contents, he visibly relaxed. Olivia peered inside and sighed with relief. There, nestled on a black satin scarf was the hot topic of October. The Ratnashree diamond glittered back in the fluorescent lights. The pale pink reminded Olivia of the color of the sky as the sun set over the sea.

Remembering what Levi said, Olivia looked at the diamond's interior, noting that the diamond reflected transparent beams inside, not rainbows. The diamond sparkled like it had never been through a theft and radiated beautiful beams upward, its surface busy with the gleam.

"This is beautiful," Olivia said, breathlessly.

Brock reached in with the gentleness of handling a newborn baby. He slipped his hand underneath the satin and lifted the diamond out with both hands. "Looks like we have it, safe and sound."

"I'll let everyone know." Olivia smiled. Contentment spread through her, along with relief. It was always a victory when she and Brock were able to recover something of value. Whether it was something as small as a historically crucial diamond to India, or a few teens rescued from a trafficking ring, she was always delighted to say that she hadn't failed when it mattered most.

EPILOGUE

You've got ninety seconds…

OLIVIA SIPPED IN A BREATH THROUGH HER TEETH. Rather than counting the seconds in her head or paying attention to the sweat that threatened to break out on her hairline, she dropped to her knees in front of the panel. The training vault door that sealed her inside wasn't half as intimidating, since it didn't trap a bunch of dangerous gasses inside with her. No one was dying, no one was screaming. This should be easy. Almost too easy. Olivia reminded herself to stay in check. She didn't want to get too cocky.

She pulled out her phone and typed in the code she'd secured from the inside. The screen lit up, bright red.

Wrong code. Dang it. This isn't the Virginia Museum of Art History; this is the Richmond, Virginia training center at the FBI field office. She'd have to delete that old code from her memory.

She x-ed out of the code and typed in the real one, sending the screen from a warning red color to a green. She was in the system. She scrolled through the diagram, more familiar with the inward parts of the Vanguard Core system than she liked to be. But here she was.

She found the wire she needed and after typing one final code to let her into the system, she looked around the room. Rather than having the tools she needed, all she could spot was a manicure kit. It would have to do.

Eighty seconds...

Eh, who cared?

She got up and snatched the manicure kit, almost wondering if she should do her nails with it after she passed this test. Well, she had to pass it first without frying anything or short-circuiting the unit, scaring anyone, or nearly setting the vault of priceless historical artifacts on fire. No big deal.

Olivia smiled. Should she smile? Maybe she should take it seriously and not get too confident.

She pulled out a pair of fingernail clippers and a nail file. Hopefully, this would do the trick. She inserted the nail file into the screw and turned it, snapping the nail file in half. The metal pinged onto the floor and Olivia jumped. Clearly, she was still a little nervous, but she reminded herself that she had done this before.

She thought for a moment before using what was left of the nail file to loosen the bolt on the panel. It was less flexible near the handle, so she turned it. Turned it, turned it until the screw was loose enough for her to unwind by hand. Setting it aside, she did the same with the bottom screw and lifted the panel to showcase the wires.

Which one was it, again?

Olivia checked her screen, wondering if her time in the museum's vault counted as training, or if this test was just mandatory to look good on paper. She found the wire, remembering not to accidentally pull another one up along with it. She grabbed it, making sure it was isolated before she pulled it out. A motor hummed and she quickly turned to her app for the final step.

With a hiss, the door started to open. There, on the other side, stood Brock and the instructor, looking down at a stopwatch. "One minute and six seconds."

Well, she'd cut it close. But she lived.

"And you passed."

Olivia couldn't help but smile. Brock beamed down at her and sent her a wink.

"I told you that you would do it!" Brock beamed as Olivia plopped back down on the couch in their apartment.

Olivia settled into the comfortable cushions and pushed her hand up through her hair. "I can't tell you how easy it is to crack that thing when there aren't people dying and a museum being pumped full of gas. Or my fiancé helping himself to some CO_2 while trying to be a hero."

"I can imagine." Brock grinned and went into the kitchen. "For a pro like you, I'm surprised you didn't do it in less than a minute."

Olivia's laughter followed him into the kitchen. "Whatever. Hey, what are you doing, by the way?"

She heard him rustling around in the kitchen, before emerging back with a bottle of merlot and two wine glasses crisscrossed in his left hand. "You said you wanted to celebrate, remember? No instant coffee. You're finally stepping up in the world."

Olivia snorted a laugh and rolled her eyes. "You're so full of it." She softened and smiled back up at him. "Thank you."

Brock settled down beside her and poured her a glass. "I'm so proud of you."

"Thank you." Olivia took her glass and toasted his. He leaned around her to settle a kiss on her lips before drawing back. "I couldn't have done it without you."

"But you did. I wasn't in the vault." Brock sipped his wine. "I was outside, snacking on some popcorn."

"That's what I mean!" Olivia smacked him, lightly. "You believed in me. That's all I've ever needed."

Memories of their relationship flashed through her mind and softened both their gazes. Olivia remembered the time when she was nothing more than a confidence-shaken girl, trying her hand at solving cases and not believing she could. Then Brock had shown up and little by little, he tore down the walls of the timid girl she was and rebuilt her back up with confidence. Now here they were.

Olivia set her glass down on the coffee table beside her and pressed her head into his shoulder. "I can't wait to spend forever with you."

Brock cradled her with one arm, securely tucking her against him. "I'm looking forward to that. And looking forward to doing it in a house bigger than the cardboard box we live in now."

"It is not a cardboard box!" Olivia exclaimed, more delighted than mad. She loved bantering with him. Not only that, but the fact that she'd passed the test kicked her delight up into overdrive. "But it is a little cluttered. And you know what else I'm looking forward to?"

"Cancun, next month?" Brock grinned. "I know. Me too."

"Well, that too." Olivia's cell phone rang, cutting into their daydream. She sat back up again and dug it out of her pocket. "It's Calvin."

"Probably calling about your test today."

Olivia answered. "Agent Knight."

"Great work on the Vanguard Core test, Knight." Calvin congratulated her. She heard the smile in his tone even over the phone's speakers. "A-plus job. I knew you'd do it."

"Thank you, sir." Olivia reached for her wine and sipped a little bit.

"I also wanted to let you and Brock know. You remember Alasdair Crosby from that case you worked in South Carolina over the summer?"

Olivia paused, taking her time in setting her glass down. "Yes."

"He's ready to talk. He got with his lawyer and accepted a plea deal. He says he has more to tell you, so I'm sending you and Tanner down there tomorrow to talk with him."

Olivia caught her breath. "He wants to tell us more?"

"That's what he said."

Olivia's mind suddenly switched from playful banter with Brock to remembering a few cases back. When she and Brock had gone undercover as a newlywed couple to Cape Fremont, South Carolina, they'd uncovered a trafficking case led by Carl and Angela Schmidt. She and Brock had thought Alasdair was the mastermind behind it until they found out he was just a patsy. What more did he have to say? Maybe the exact location of all the young women he had forced into slavery in the Netherlands? Maybe the reason that the *Black Rose Syndicate* was still alive and well on the black market? "We'll be there. What time?"

She gathered the details routinely, eager to tell Brock what this was about. When she hung up, her stare had turned cold. "Alasdair's ready to talk."

"It's about time." Brock set his drink down. "I still think about all those kids taken from Cape Fremont. Maybe this will help us track down a few more."

Not that there was much hope of that, Olivia thought bitterly. Not when they'd been shipped overseas and only reappeared again on some website, being sold like common possessions. "That would be nice." Olivia had never forgotten Melissa, the red-haired thirteen-year-old girl with a smile and a necklace that tied the case together. "I also wonder if he knows where the headquarters of the *Black Rose* are."

"I'd thought we put that to bed." Brock ran his hands over his face. Olivia was in the same boat. She'd thought they'd put a stop to the trafficking ring since Carl and Angela were dead. That is until she found another member in the form of Claude McMillian, who murdered both women in his life. If it wasn't for Connie, however, Olivia and Brock would have never found the website linking them to the *Black Rose Syndicate,* clearly still active somewhere. Just how many people were involved in this thing?

Maybe tomorrow, they'd all find out.

Olivia didn't even feel tired from the long drive it took to get to Alasdair's holding place. The resolve to get to the bottom of a trafficking ring kept her going. She strode in beside Brock and flashed her credentials to the guard. "Special Agents Olivia Knight and Brock Tanner, we're here for a talk with Alasdair Crosby."

"Charlie Sims. We've been expecting you," the corrections officer said. "Give us just a minute, we're getting him and putting him in the interrogation room. We didn't want to move him until you guys got here. If you'll come with me, I'll escort you there."

Brock thanked Charlie as he scanned himself into the hallway leading to the interrogation room. "Right this way."

The air in the prison felt stuffy and hostile. Olivia was tempted to hold her breath until she was on the inside of the interrogation room. Charlie opened the door and stepped aside. "We should be bringing him here, shortly. He's been—"

A shout from somewhere inside cut his sentence in half. Olivia felt herself spring into high alert, sending a look up and down the hallway. Running footsteps brought another corrections officer running up to Charlie, who Olivia assumed was his supervisor.

His face was streaked with panic as if he'd lived through a bomb. "Sims! Inmate 838, we need you there, now!"

He disappeared back down the hall. Charlie glanced at Olivia and Brock, shocked. "That's your prisoner." He didn't miss a beat and shot off after the other officer. Olivia shot Brock a look, conveying her shock before Olivia sprang out the door after Charlie.

Alasdair? Olivia and Brock looked between them, before sprinting off after the guard. Several other guards joined in step as they ran down the aisle to the holding cell, and then passed it. The situation looked even more grim, as Olivia realized they weren't near the holding cells. Why hadn't Alasdair been brought to one yet? Olivia kept pace, her pulse thudding in her wrist until they came to the row of cells. An alarm raged overhead, flashing warning red colors into the scene below. Olivia rounded the corner, startled at what she saw.

Alasdair Crosby, the blond, charming man they'd arrested in South Carolina lay on his side. His hands were twisted behind him and fastened with something. He faced the front, eyes forever closed, but blood leaked from his temple onto his face. A large piece of duct tape sealed his mouth closed.

"Get the medics in here, get them now!" one of the guards shouted.

Brock looked up and down the hallway. "Who has access to his cell?" he demanded.

"Just us! He hasn't had a visitor since he got in!"

"Roll the logs! Who was on duty last night?" Brock took command, but Olivia stepped closer to the cell. Her ears roared with the shock of it all. All the sounds of the prison – the commencing lockdown, Brock barking orders and questions, all of it – faded as she studied Alasdair's unusual form. How did this happen? How did someone get inside his cell, kill him... tape him up? Alasdair's eyes were closed, but she wondered what he had seen before someone had killed him.

Her memory flashed back to her prior conversation with Calvin, how he'd mentioned Alasdair had agreed to tell them everything. Everything about what?

Melissa's image flooded her mind, along with all the other faces of the teenagers in the trafficking ring. Maybe this wasn't connected, but it struck Olivia as highly irregular that someone would break into a cell and kill a man who was about to talk to the FBI about what he'd been involved in. This was no coincidence.

Olivia stared at the tape sealing Alasdair's mouth, forever quiet. Brock came up beside her. "This isn't fear." Olivia nodded to Alasdair, murmuring to Brock. "This is a message."

AUTHOR'S NOTE

Thank you so much for reading THE GRAND HEIST! We're so glad to have you back with Olivia and Brock for another unforgettable ride. The inspiration for this story came after a visit to a museum exhibit featuring some absolutely stunning gemstones. There was something about seeing those priceless stones up close—how easily they could be admired behind glass, yet how quickly they could become the center of a high-stakes crime. That was all it took to ignite our creative spark. We started wondering: What if one vanished? What if the switch was seamless, the replica flawless, and no one noticed... until it was far too late? From these questions, THE GRAND HEIST was born.

As indie writers, we rely heavily on the support and feedback from readers like you. If you enjoyed this book, please consider leaving a review. Your words make a significant difference, helping us reach more readers without a big marketing budget or a massive following.

Next up, Olivia and Brock head to Cancun for a well-earned vacation... or so they think. But when a dead American politician turns up in their hotel room closet, the trip takes a sinister turn. As more bodies begin to surface and secrets unravel, they find themselves tangled in a web of crime, cartels, and buried betrayals. THE FATAL GETAWAY is shaping up to be an explosive case full of twists you won't see coming, and the truth may be more dangerous than anyone imagined.

Thank you for your continued support, and we can't wait to take you on more exceptional adventures!

By the way, if you find any typos, have suggestions, or just simply want to reach out to us, feel free to email us at egray@ellegraybooks.com

Your writer friends,

Elle Gray & K.S. Gray

CONNECT WITH ELLE GRAY

Loved the book? Don't miss out on future reads! Join my newsletter and receive updates on my latest releases, insider content, and exclusive promos. Plus, as a thank you for joining, you'll get a FREE copy of my book Deadly Pursuit!

Deadly Pursuit follows the story of Paxton Arrington, a police officer in Seattle who uncovers corruption within his own precinct. With his career and reputation on the line, he enlists the help of his FBI friend Blake Wilder to bring down the corrupt Strike Team. But the stakes are high, and Paxton must decide whether he's willing to risk everything to do the right thing.

Claiming your freebie is easy! Visit
https://dl.bookfunnel.com/513mluk159
and sign up with your email!

Want more ways to stay connected? Follow me on Facebook and Instagram or sign up for text notifications by texting "blake" to 844-552-1368. Thanks for your support and happy reading!

ALSO BY
ELLE GRAY

Blake Wilder FBI Mystery Thrillers

Book Twenty-Eight - *The Silent Hunt*
Book Twenty-Nine - *The Hunter's Game*

A Pax Arrington Mystery
Free Prequel - Deadly Pursuit
Book One - I See You
Book Two - Her Last Call
Book Three - Woman In The Water
Book Four- A Wife's Secret

Storyville FBI Mystery Thrillers
Book One - The Chosen Girl
Book Two - The Murder in the Mist
Book Three - Whispers of the Dead
Book Four - Secrets of the Unseen
Book Five - The Way Back Home

A Sweetwater Falls Mystery
Book One - New Girl in the Falls
Book Two - Missing in the Falls
Book Three - The Girls in the Falls
Book Four - Memories of the Falls
Book Five - Shadows of the Falls
Book Six - The Lies in the Falls
Book Seven - Forbidden in the Falls
Book Eight - Silenced in the Falls
Book Nine - Summer in the Falls
Book Ten - The Legend of the Falls
Book Eleven - Whispers in the Falls
Book Twelve- Sins of the Falls
Book Thirteen - Shades of the Falls
Book Fourteen - Revenge in the Falls

A Chesapeake Valley Mystery Series
Book One - The Girl in Town
Book Two - The Lost Children
Book Three - The Secrets We Bury
Book Four - The Secret Cabin

ALSO BY
ELLE GRAY | K.S. GRAY

Olivia Knight FBI Mystery Thrillers
Book One - New Girl in Town
Book Two - The Murders on Beacon Hill
Book Three - The Woman Behind the Door
Book Four - Love, Lies, and Suicide
Book Five - Murder on the Astoria
Book Six - The Locked Box
Book Seven - The Good Daughter
Book Eight - The Perfect Getaway
Book Nine - Behind Closed Doors
Book Ten - Fatal Games
Book Eleven - Into the Night
Book Twelve - The Housewife
Book Thirteen - Whispers at the Reunion
Book Fourteen - Fatal Lies
Book Fifteen - The Runaway Girls
Book Sixteen - The Woman Next Door
Book Seventeen - The Grand Heist

A Serenity Springs Mystery Series
Book One - The Girl in the Springs
Book Two - The Maid of Honor
Book Three- The Girl in the Cabin
Book Four- Fatal Obsession
Book Five - The Secret Packages
Book Six - The Hunting Ground

ALSO BY
ELLE GRAY | JAMES HOLT

The Florida Girl FBI Mystery Thrillers

Made in United States
Cleveland, OH
29 July 2025

18962331R00164